GAME ON

A Breaking into the Black Elite Novel

SHONETTE CHARLES

Seamare Press LLC

www.seamarepress.com

Seamare Press LLC
PO Box 99095
Raleigh, NC 27624
www.seamarepress.com

Publisher's Note: This is a work of fiction. Names, characters, places, organizations and incidents are a product of the author's imagination. Locales and public names are sometimes used for atmospheric purposes. Any resemblance to actual people, living or dead, or to businesses, organizations, events, institutions, or locales is completely coincidental.

Quantity sales. Special discounts are available on quantity purchases by corporations, associations, and others. For details, contact the address above.

GAME ON/ Shonette Charles. -- 1st ed.
ISBN 978-0-9964568-2-1
eBook ISBN: 978-0-9964568-3-8

Library of Congress Control Number: 2016908842

Published in the United States of America by Seamare Press, Raleigh, NC.

Acknowledgments

Thank you to God for his blessings and his lessons. He never ceases to amaze me! To my family, friends, and readers, thank you for all of the support and encouragement. The overwhelming response to my debut novel truly warmed my heart and inspired me to write the sequel. Thank you.

Lillie, I wish you were here to read this book. I know that you would love it! You are missed, Sands.

ONE

....

SAHARA

Trying to find a tiny bit of relief from the July heat, Sahara fanned herself with her hand, as Teri read her magazine, and Zora slathered sunscreen on her arms. Sahara could feel little beads of sweat popping up on her copper colored skin, and she was pretty sure that the heat had sucked all of the moisture out of her hair turning her shoulder-length twist-out into an afro. Even a tank top and Bermuda shorts were not enough to stop her from feeling the scorching effects of a North Carolina summer.

A black cat lay on the grass licking its paws with its green eyes fixated on the three women sitting on the park bench. Sahara stared back at the cat, giving it a taste of its own medicine, when something new came into view. Legs—long, dark legs—were all she saw as the young man strutted out of the woods like a proud filly.

With his white t-shirt knotted on the side and pink Daisy Duke shorts, he sashayed past the swings and around the monkey bars on his way to the parking lot. His pink high heels were not the norm in playground footwear but the mulch floor did not slow his gait or wipe the broad grin off his face. He didn't seem to notice or care about the wide-eyed stares from parents and children alike that he left in his wake.

Midtown was bohemian and trendy—but he was pushing the envelope. It was still the South. Restaurants and boutiques were adjacent to million dollar condos and urban parks. Yes, Midtown was chic and eclectic—and overwhelmingly heterosexual and white.

Sahara wasn't sure if the looks Mr. Daisy Dukes got were because of his flamboyance or his skin tone. To be honest, the response had been similar, not quite as open but still present, when she and her friends arrived with their children.

As he pranced past the park bench where Sahara was sitting with her girlfriends, Teri looked up from her magazine and shook her head as she followed him with her eyes. "Ain't no shame in his game! If I had those legs, I could get anything I want from my husband." Five foot nine, thick, and with a face that was always beat, Teri seemed to get whatever she wanted from her husband even without the legs, as evidenced by the three carat "just because" diamond ring on her finger.

"Those legs...will get somebody in trouble," said Zora matter-of-factly. With her cat-shaped glasses, black and white plaid shirt, and converse sneakers, Zora was the more reserved of their trio, even though she looked more like a hipster college student than a stay-at-home mom.

Sahara stood up to stretch her legs—they weren't as nice as Mr. Daisy Dukes, but she was sure that her husband, Noah, wouldn't complain—and scanned the playground. Everyone was braving the heat because her daughter, Clarissa, and Teri's daughter, Jayla, had insisted that they have a play date at the park that day. The mothers tried to convince the girls to go roller skating or to the movies, so that they could be inside enjoying the cool breeze of an air conditioner. However, the two little girls would not hear of it, so a play date at the park it was. Since misery loves company, Sahara had convinced Zora to join them with her one-year-old son, Darius.

However, Clarissa and Jayla weren't the only ones that didn't let the sweltering heat stop their fun. The playground was packed. Since Sahara and Zora lived on one side of town and Teri lived on the other, the three friends decided to meet in the middle at Honeycutt Park, which was very popular with the "young and well-off" crowd.

Children were everywhere—running, swinging, climbing, sliding, and even crying. Zora's son was having a toddler meltdown near the swings. The nanny was trying to calm him but was failing miserably. Zora must have seen him, because she stood up and made her way in his direction.

Sahara's eyes continued to move across the playground until she spotted her two year-old son, Trevor, building a castle with another little boy in the sandbox. After a few seconds, Clarissa came into view climbing on the monkey bars with Jayla and another little girl. They looked like they were having fun.

As she was about to sit down, Sahara saw some movement past the playground out the corner of her eye. She tapped Teri on the shoulder and pointed in the direction from where Mr. Daisy Dukes strolled moments earlier. Another man in a green polo shirt and khakis followed the same path, as he walked with his head down through the playground to the parking lot. As he passed their park bench, Sahara noticed the glint of a wedding ring on his finger.

Teri must have seen it, too, because she let out a quick "Scandalous!" under her breath.

"Basically," said Sahara. She sat down as Zora walked back to the bench with a crying Darius in tow and the nanny trailing behind them. The nanny was a gift from Zora's mother-in-law, but Zora seemed reluctant to rely on the nanny's expertise.

Teri put her magazine down. "Well, I know that I am from Mississippi and relatively new to Fairchester and all...but, were they behind those trees over there? I thought Midtown was more respectable than that." She and Sahara giggled as Zora plopped down on the bench.

"I think he's cranky because he got too much sun," said Zora as she rocked Darius back and forth trying to settle him down. "I don't want him to get too dark. When I was growing up, Daddy always made sure that we stayed out of the sun, especially me. He said that I was already dark enough."

Sahara opened her mouth to say something but thought better of it. Since Zora's complexion was close to ebony, many people thought Zora's white husband explained Darius' light skin color and blue eyes. But, Sahara knew that Zora's mother and sister had the same features.

Zora looked over at her friends. "What did I miss?"

"Girl, you missed the walk of shame from the bushes!" said Teri laughing. "The guy with the to-die-for legs walked out proud as a peacock. After you left, another man came out of the woods, pulled his baseball cap down really low, and practically ran to his car. And, get this. He had a wedding band on his finger." Teri said as she crossed her arms.

"What? He was married?" asked Zora, still rocking her wiggling toddler. "Oh, Darius, please close those beautiful blue eyes and go to sleep."

Teri rolled her eyes but continued, "Yes, girl! I feel for his wife. You never know what men are doing in these streets." She paused. "I saw on Facebook that one of my college classmates found out that her husband was leading a double life. He owns a large staffing agency in Memphis and was a pillar of the community. He's a Rho and in The Shield and The Coalition. She is a

Darling and in the Gazelles.

"Apparently, he had two illegitimate kids with his mistress. His wife found out when the mistress got mad and posted all the photos she had on Instagram with him and their children." Teri shook her head. "Talk about embarrassing."

Sahara shifted in her seat.

"Wow," said Zora.

"Yes, honey. You never know what is going on behind closed doors," said Teri.

A woman walked up to the park bench with the little blonde girl that Clarissa and Jayla had been playing with on the monkey bars. "Hi, are those little girls yours?" She pointed past the playground to the blacktop where Clarissa and Jayla were now jumping rope.

"Yes, they are," Sahara and Teri said in unison. Sahara could hear a little tension in their voices as she sat up straight. Since Clarissa, Jayla, and Trevor were the only black children playing, it was pretty obvious that the girls belonged to them.

"They are so well-behaved," said the woman, as Sahara and Teri glanced at each other. "Emily had such a great time playing with them. I want to get your contact information so that we can get them together again for a play date, if that's okay." She flashed her pearly whites with her best "you can't say no to me" smile and tossed her blonde hair over her shoulder as the final pièce de résistance.

"Oh, that would be nice. Here let me give you my card," said Sahara, as Teri sat there in silence. Out the corner of her eye, Sahara could see the look of disdain creeping up on Teri's face. Sahara looked in her purse and pulled out one of her mom cards and handed it to the woman.

"Oh, how cute! I love the drawings of the children...and..." She paused as if she was going to say something else but decided against it. "It has their names on it. How clever!"

Sahara guessed that "the cleverness" was that the children pictured were an accurate depiction of her children, with brown faces and kinky curly hair.

"I'm Hannah, by the way. I see from the card that you are Sahara, Clarissa and Trevor's mom." Hannah turned to Teri but something about Teri's expression must have dissuaded her. She turned back to Sahara. "I'll be in touch!" And, she and Emily walked away.

Once they were out of earshot, Teri broke her silence. "They are so well-behaved," she said imitating Hannah's shrill voice. "That just grates my nerves whenever I hear someone say that!"

"Girl, I know." replied Sahara. "Like it's a surprise that there are well-behaved black children in the world."

"Anyway, that reminds me that I wanted to talk to you about something. Have you ever heard of Belles & Beaus?" asked Teri.

Sahara groaned.

Teri laughed. "Really? It's like that?"

Where was Teri going with this? Belle & Beaus was a social club for black children from well-to-do families. When they moved to Fairchester, Sahara had quickly learned the social scene in Fairchester revolved around black organizations, specifically black women's organizations—like The Sphinx, Darlings, Marigolds, Gazelles, and Belles & Beaus. Thanks to her neighbor, Meranda, who was a member of most of these groups, Sahara had attended many of the city's galas, luncheons, and parties.

At one point, Noah was really pushing for her to join this exclusive black social circle. But, he had been busy at work (he was a senior vice president at First Southern Regional Bank) and had relaxed some about pushing her to join this powerful network. She didn't need Teri to pick up where he left off.

Sahara tried to laugh off her first response. "No, you just caught me by surprise. The question came out of the blue."

"Well...I was thinking that we should try to become members." Teri put up her hand. "Now, hear me out." She must have seen the look of protest already on Sahara's face. "A bunch of my friends in Mississippi just became members of the chapter there, and they love it."

"Well, I think it is a great idea!" said Zora nodding her head rigorously.

Teri clapped her hands with glee, while Sahara

looked at Zora with surprise. Zora always expressed reluctance in getting involved in the black elite scene in Fairchester, even though she was from one of the area's most prominent black families and lived in the super exclusive Walnut Forest neighborhood with her husband. She was still a "ball and gala gal," but she usually attended red carpet events with her husband's family and had only recently started going to some of the black events in town. Hell must have frozen over if Zora thought it was a good idea to join Belles & Beaus.

"I...I was in Belles & Beaus for a little while," stuttered Zora.

Teri's eyes lit up. "Oh, so you're a legacy."

"Well, I wasn't in it for long." Zora looked down at her sleeping son. "But, maybe things can be different for Darius."

"Well, I definitely want to get Jayla involved. Hearing all the things that the organization does—providing leadership training, offering civic and educational opportunities, and serving the community—I want that for Jayla." Teri sounded like Noah. "Sahara, your last name is Allymer, right? The cluster coordinator's last name is Allymer-Tate. Are you related?"

Sahara could see the look of hope in Teri's eyes. She was not about to go down that road. Not wanting to sound like Debbie Downer, Sahara said, "Well, I think it's a terrific organization. It exposes children in the chapter and the community to wonderful opportunities." She had witnessed firsthand the children in the local Belles & Beaus chapter performing community service at the MLK Day unity project. "One of my college roommates was in it, and she loved it. But, you know, Clarissa and Trevor are so young. Clarissa is starting preschool next month, and I'm sure that she will make plenty of friends. I just don't think we really need it right now."

All of a sudden, Zora nudged Sahara—hard—in the ribs.

"Ouch! What's go—" Sahara was about to ask Zora if she had lost her mind when she saw what had prompted her friend's aggression.

A short, light-skinned woman with hooded eyes and thick lips was coming towards them. It was Rozlyn Wormly—actually a new and improved Rozlyn Wormly. The old Rozlyn looked okay but this Rozlyn was fly, no doubt about it. She was wearing an emerald green sleeveless romper with a Louis Vuitton purse on her arm, and her short hair was laid. Suddenly, Sahara felt underdressed in her tank top, Bermuda shorts, and flip flops styled by Old Navy.

As Rozlyn approached the three friends sitting on the bench, a sly grin crept up on her lips. She slowed her stride and pulled her Prada sunglasses down a bit on her nose. As she passed the park bench, Rozlyn looked down at Sahara and curled her lips in icy contempt. Then, she rolled her eyes, pushed the sunglasses back into place, and walked away with her nose in the air.

Sahara squirmed a little in her seat. If looks could kill.

"WHO was that?" Teri asked once Rozlyn was safely sitting on a bench on the other side of the playground.

Sahara was shell shocked. She hadn't seen Rozlyn since the Gamma Boat Ride in May but didn't expect that reception.

Thankfully, Zora answered for her. "That's Rozlyn. She's nobody."

Teri raised her eyebrow and gave them the side-eye. "Nobody, huh. Not the way that she looked at Sahara. Give up the tea." Teri leaned in eager to hear the history between Sahara and Rozlyn.

Having regained her composure, Sahara tried to keep the backbiting to a minimum. "There's really no tea to give. Rozlyn was one of the first people that I met in Fairchester, and we became friends. Let me clarify that. I thought we were friends, and apparently we weren't. End of story."

Sahara leaned back. She wanted to be perceived as unbothered. "And, I haven't seen Rozlyn in months. I'm not sure what all that was about. Just because we aren't friends doesn't mean we can't be cordial." Based on the look that Rozlyn gave her, civility apparently was not on the menu. Whatever.

Teri looked at Sahara. "Well, you know what they

say. When your friends display the same behavior as your enemies, you got somebody in the wrong category."

"Mommy! Mommy!"

Sahara looked up and saw Clarissa looking wild-eyed and running towards them with Jayla a few steps behind her. Clarissa collapsed in Sahara's arms and burst into tears.

"What's wrong, ladybug?" asked Sahara. By this time, Jayla had reached Teri. Her actions mimicked Clarissa's, except with a thirty second delay.

"Jayla isn't being fair! There's only one jump rope, and we were supposed to take turns using it. Now, she won't let me have my turn! I don't want to be her friend anymore! Waaaaahhhh!" Clarissa lowered her head into Sahara's lap, as Sahara rubbed her daughter's back and caught the tail-end of Jayla's version of the story.

"She didn't even want to jump rope! I was the one who wanted to jump! Mommy it's not fair! I don't want to be her friend anymore either!"

Sahara and Teri looked over their crying daughters at each other and shook their heads. So much drama.

Teri held Jayla's head up and touched Clarissa's arm to get her attention. "Look, you two are not just friends, but good friends, and good friends are hard to find. A jump rope is not worth losing your friendship. You need to work it out."

Clarissa and Jayla shyly looked at each other with

tears in their eyes. By the look on the girls' faces, the few minutes of not being friends had taken its toll. A couple of seconds later, their mouths turned up with the tiniest of grins as an olive branch of peace. Truce declared, they were free to resume their fun and ran to the playground.

The jump rope, the reason for the disagreement, lay on the ground beside the bench completely forgotten. Oh, to be a child again. Sahara looked across the playground to where Rozlyn was sitting. Adult friendships were not that easy.

"Move, cat! Move!" Zora stomped her foot on the ground trying not to wake Darius who was asleep in her arms. The black cat slowly walked towards to them, but Zora's stomping episode was enough to make it stop advancing but not retreat. It circled the oak tree beside them and lazily lay down on the ground, ears up, green eyes back on them.

Zora rose to her feet. "Alright, ladies, I think that I'm going to head out." She put Darius in his stroller and then shot an awkward glance at the nanny who was standing behind them. "I'll talk to you later." Zora gave Sahara and Teri air kisses and walked to the parking lot pushing Darius' stroller with the nanny ten steps behind them.

Teri waved at Zora and then slid down the bench closer to Sahara. "Okay, so what happened with you and old girl?" She nodded her head in Rozlyn's direction.

Sahara really didn't feel like getting into it. And, if she learned anything from her friendship with Rozlyn, it was to be more cautious of what she said to "new friends."

Sahara and Teri met last year when Teri was a vendor at a Lambda Upsilon Alpha Sorority conference in Hampton. Teri had the cutest pink and green "Future LUA" t-shirts that Sahara wanted to get for Clarissa. While talking, Sahara found out that Teri and her family were also recent transplants to Fairchester, and she had a daughter only a year older than Clarissa. They soon became fast friends.

Sure, Teri seemed nice, and Sahara enjoyed hanging out with her. But, they hadn't known each other for long. Sahara didn't want to make the same mistake twice.

"Nothing worth spending any time on. We just aren't friends anymore." Sahara paused for a second. "So, is Jayla ready for kindergarten?" Sahara was sure that Teri realized that she was trying to change the subject, but Teri played along.

"You shouldn't ask 'Is Jayla ready for kindergarten?' but 'Is kindergarten ready for Jayla?'" They laughed.

Teri talked about all the things she had to do before Jayla's first day of school—buy school supplies, set up a lunch account, and shop for clothes. Sahara tried to pay attention...Clarissa would be starting preschool next month...but her mind couldn't help but wander to the other side of the playground.

Rozlyn was still sitting on the bench by herself. Why was she here? It was the middle of the afternoon on a workday. Rozlyn worked at the same bank that Noah did but in the IT department. She wasn't talking to anyone. She didn't have her son with her. It was weird.

Teri laughed so Sahara laughed, even though she didn't know what was funny. After half listening a little while longer, Sahara felt that enough time had passed that she could leave without causing any further Rozlyn-related questions.

"I'm going to head out, Teri. I have to get the house in some sort of order before Noah gets home." Sahara stood up and shouted towards the playground, "Clarissa! It's time to go!"

Clarissa ran to her mother but reluctantly this time. After saying goodbye to Teri and Jayla, Sahara and Clarissa walked toward the parking lot. The black cat sat under the tree watching their every move.

Clarissa skipped beside her mother replaying how much fun she had and reiterating that Jayla was her very best friend. The fight over the jump rope was now a distant memory.

A smile came across Sahara's face as she listened. Clarissa already had friends and with her starting preschool, Sahara was sure that there would be many more friends and plenty of exposure to new and exciting things. If Teri brought up Belles & Beaus again, she would let her know—

That's when Sahara saw her, and everything clicked. Five foot two inches tall, she had thick, jet black hair that was cut in a shoulder-length blunt bob that moved flawlessly like she was filming a shampoo commercial. Her caramel skin, angular face, and high cheekbones hinted at her half black, half Korean heritage. As usual, she was dressed to perfection in her striped blue and white Peter Pilotto romper and nude Sophia Webster sandals. Walking from the parking lot hand-in-hand with her daughter was Emery Edmonds.

That's why Rozlyn was at the park. She was meeting Emery.

The two mother-daughter pairs mirrored each other. Sahara and Clarissa were walking from the park to the parking lot, and Emery and her daughter were walking from the parking lot to the park. And, the sidewalk was only so big. Sahara or Emery would have to move to avoid colliding into each other.

However, by the looks of it, that wasn't going to be Emery. Emery's eyes were hidden behind her Gucci sunglasses so Sahara couldn't see where she was looking. But, her head and her shoulders were steeled straight as if guiding a ship to port.

Sahara could hear Clarissa chatting away recounting today's fun in the background, but she was focused on the unspoken battle before her. Why should she move? She hadn't done anything to Emery, or Rozlyn for that matter. Why should she back down?

You know what? She wouldn't.

Holding Clarissa's hand, Sahara walked straight ahead and braced herself for impact. Then, at the last minute, she shifted an inch, but only an inch, to the left. She saw Emery do the same.

Those two inches were just enough to prevent them from slamming into each other but not enough from touching. Their shoulders brushed, and they were so close to each other that Sahara could smell Emery's perfume—Jimmy Choo.

However, they both kept walking, without saying a word to each other. No hello. No excuse me. Nothing.

Sahara and Clarissa continued to the parking lot. She didn't dare look behind her. Sahara unlocked the door to her Lexus, and Clarissa climbed into her car seat. In the distance, Sahara could see Teri standing and looking in her direction. By the look on her face, she had seen the whole thing.

TWO

....

SAHARA

"Who's daddy's favorite girl?" Noah asked Clarissa as he held her in his arms and twirled her around the family room.

"I am, Daddy! I am!" Like watching someone on a merry-go-round, Sahara could see the look of pure joy on Clarissa's face every time the rotation of their father-daughter dance brought Clarissa's face into view.

"And, who is going to have a great first day at pre-school?"

"I am!" Clarissa held out her arms and tilted her head back to the warmth flooding the room, soaking in the moment along with the sun. Noah gave Clarissa one last twirl and put her down on the floor.

Dressed in a pink polka dot sundress and sporting a ladybug backpack and afro puffs, Clarissa was beaming. She looked like one of the little girls in the Macy's back-to-school advertisement in the newspaper.

Sahara looked at the clock on the microwave. It was almost eight thirty. Ordinarily, Noah would be at work by now, but it was August seventeenth. The date had been circled on their family calendar for months. Today was Clarissa's first day of preschool.

Sahara took a sip of her coffee and looked out the kitchen window. It was hard to believe that Clarissa was already starting preschool. It seemed like she was just born yesterday. Sahara remembered how hard it had been to leave Clarissa at daycare when she returned to work. After crying every day for a week, she and Noah figured out that they could live on his salary alone. She quit her job the next day and had been a stay-at-home mom since then.

Clarissa's first smile. Her first word. Her first steps. Sahara was able to be there for all the big moments, and the small ones, too. She had watched Clarissa grow so much in the year that they'd been in North Carolina, and now her baby was going to preschool.

She got up from the stool where she was perched and put her coffee mug in the sink. They'd better get moving, if they were going to get there on time. Just as she was about to call for Clarissa, she remembered. She wasn't taking Clarissa to school. Noah was.

When he said that he wanted to take her to school, Sahara was hesitant to not be there to see Clarissa off, but she later changed her mind. She would be the one to pick up Clarissa because Noah would be at work. It was okay to let him take Clarissa to school on her first day so he could have some alone time with his baby girl—not many fathers would take the time.

Noah was a good man. A good father.

Sahara felt her body perk up when Noah walked into the kitchen wearing a charcoal gray Canali plaid suit along with his signature square metal Tom Ford glasses and picked up his keys from the kitchen counter. Six foot one with chestnut brown skin, Noah was shaped like a boxer with the holy grail of male shapes—the "v" shaped body, a broad back with a slim waist. He caught her looking at him and smiled showing his perfectly white teeth and cleft chin. Yes, he was a good man. And after seven years of marriage, he was still fine, too.

Noah walked over and kissed Sahara on the cheek. "Are you ready to go, ladybug?" he asked Clarissa, who was giving Trevor instructions on how to survive the morning without her.

"I have to tell Mommy goodbye before we go!" Arms outstretched, Clarissa ran to Sahara, who gathered Clarissa into her arms and hugged her tightly.

Clarissa wasn't a baby anymore. Her little girl was growing up. She let Clarissa go and felt tears well up in her eyes, as she watched Noah and Clarissa walk into the garage.

Sahara stood there for a moment, staring at the closed door. It wasn't until she heard the car drive away that she forced herself to move. She had to face it. They were gone.

Armed with his morning survival instructions, Trevor sat on the floor "reading" his books to Lamby, his favorite stuffed animal. Noah won the small white sheep for Trevor at a carnival a few months ago. Since then, the two of them had been inseparable.

Sahara walked into the family room and sat on the floor. She pulled Trevor onto her lap and pulled him close, as if doing that would slow down time.

She didn't know how long she'd been sitting there when she heard her cell phone chime. It was a text message from Zora. *Will be over in fifteen minutes.*

Tissues and Mimosas. Sahara had been so wrapped up in the emotions of Clarissa going to preschool that she'd forgotten about Tissues and Mimosas.

Today was the first day of school for all the schools. To celebrate the end of summer and the children's return to school, the moms in the neighborhood marked the occasion with what else—tissues and mimosas.

Since this would be Sahara's first time attending, she asked Zora to come with her as backup. Zora didn't live in Sugarberry Grove, but in nearby Walnut Forest. Both gated communities were adjacent to Jordan Lake, highly sought after, and had similar sized homes. The major difference between the two neighborhoods was that Walnut Forest was white and Sugarberry Grove was black.

"Mommy will be back in five minutes, and then we will go outside to visit some of our neighbors," said Sahara.

Instead of giving her the "Yes, Mommy" face that she

was expecting, Trevor looked like he had a question. But, then he picked up Lamby and toddled away.

Sahara walked upstairs to change her outfit. She was dressed in her mommy uniform of a tunic and leggings but knew that she should wear something nicer. There was "hanging around the house" casual, and there was "I look like I stepped out of a magazine" casual. She was pretty sure that this was a stepped out of a magazine type of event—even if it would be held on someone's front lawn.

Sahara knew most of her neighbors in passing. However, she was closest to Meranda Barrett, who lived in the colonial across the street. Meranda and her husband, North Carolina State Senator Tyrone Barrett, were older than Sahara and Noah, but they became friends shortly after The Kyles moved to North Carolina. Noah had worked on Senator Barrett's reelection campaign last November, and Meranda had introduced Sahara to many people in her social circle in Fairchester.

Both Sahara and Meranda were members of Lambda Upsilon Alpha Sorority, Incorporated, but Meranda was also a member of The Sphinx, Darlings, and Gazelles. Without a doubt, Senator Barrett and Meranda were movers and shakers in Fairchester, but Meranda was out-of-town so Sahara had to call in reinforcements.

Ding, ding, dong.

There was Sahara's backup now.

GAME ON

....

The buffet table on the Gipson's lawn was overflowing with trays piled high with pastries, quiches, and fruit. Champagne and wine bottles stood at attention awaiting the opportunity to replenish the glasses of the mothers milling around outside. As the gentle breeze floated in from down the street, the white linen table cloth flapped in the wind threatening the feast that it was supposed to protect.

The little boy on the tricycle picked up speed as he got closer to the table. Beads of sweat slid down his forehead as his legs peddled faster and faster. In one quick swoop, he grabbed a strawberry from the tray, knocking down a bottle of chardonnay in his haste. He turned around quickly as if he expected to be chastised. Nothing. He smiled and rode past Zora and Sahara as he enjoyed his bounty, while wine dripped down the table onto the lawn.

Sahara, dressed in a cobalt blue chiffon top and turquoise shorts, and Zora, in her embroidered tunic and cut-off denim shorts, examined the smorgasbord at the table and the fashion show on the sidewalk in front of the Gipson's house. As Sahara expected, there were designer sunglasses, statement necklaces, and luxury handbags galore at this informal morning gathering. Even the few young children that were there were dressed to impress.

Sahara looked down at Trevor in his hand-me-down stroller and was glad that she decided to dress him in the white Ralph Lauren polo shirt and red and white gingham shorts her mother bought from Neiman Marcus. Trevor and Darius both looked content to check out the scenery and new faces. Sahara figured they had about thirty minutes before one of them got fussy.

Zora walked over to say hello to someone that she knew so Sahara scooped up a champagne flute and a cheese danish and joined the conversation of the ladies that were nearest to her.

"Sahara, I didn't know you were here. How have you been, dear?" said Soror Benetta Jackson, who was in Sahara's LUA chapter and the chair of the Strengthening the Black Family committee, of which Sahara was a member. She was a former member of Belles & Beaus and also had invited Sahara to the chapter's Black Santa Breakfast last year.

"We've been doing okay, Soror. Today's Clarissa's first day of preschool. I came because I thought that I would need the tissue, but I think that I will dry my tears with a mimosa instead," said Sahara. They laughed.

Mrs. Gipson, the owner of the charcoal gray brick house they were standing in front of said, "Enjoy it. The time goes quickly. I can't believe that Essence is a senior in high school."

"It does. Before you know it, you'll be an empty nester like Meranda and me." Soror Benetta turned and looked over her shoulder. "By the way, where is she? She normally comes to Tissues and Mimosas, if only to say a quick hello and have a mimosa."

"Or three," added Mrs. Gipson with a smirk, before lifting her champagne flute to her lips.

"I believe she went to Washington to visit Dara," said Sahara. Dara was Senator Barrett and Meranda's youngest daughter.

"She did?" Soror Benetta furrowed her brows but then quickly changed her expression and the subject. "Dorothy, has Essence decided where she wants to attend college?"

Mrs. Gipson shook her head as she took another sip from her champagne. "She seems to have her heart set on attending North Carolina Union. You know that I went to Hampton so I hoped that she would go to the 'Home by the Sea,' but she's a daddy's girl. You know what they say...a father has the power to instill in his child a lifetime of lessons or a world of hurt. And apparently, an unbreakable love for his alma mater."

Sahara took a bite of her danish. NCU was also Noah's alma mater. He and Sahara met when they were in business school at Ross School of Business at the University of Michigan, but he went to NCU as an undergraduate.

"And, sports teams...don't forget about sports teams. But, you know it is hard to resist the allure of NCU when you are from North Carolina," said Soror Benetta.

Mrs. Gipson groaned. "It is. Now, how is Jerome doing at Harvard?"

"He loves it. He wasn't sure how he would like Massachusetts but so far so good. Sahara, you went to college near Boston, right? Did you enjoy your time in New England?"

"Yes, I went to Wellesley. It's about forty-five minutes from Cambridge."

"Did you ever get a chance to visit Harvard?"

Sahara gulped down some champagne before answering. "Yes...yes, I did." Her voice was almost a whisper. "I got accepted to Harvard and visited for Pre-Frosh Weekend."

Soror Benetta perked up. "Oh...why didn't you want to go to Harvard?" Mrs. Gipson and Soror Benetta's eyes were fixed on Sahara as they waited for an answer.

Why had she chosen Wellesley? Harvard had been her first choice, and she had a great time at Harvard's PreFrosh Weekend. The classes, the students, the parties. Then, she received the phone call—

Zora walked up and interrupted Sahara's thoughts.

"Oh my goodness! Zora! What are you doing here?" asked Soror Benetta. Both she and Mrs. Gipson hugged Zora. "I just saw your aunt at the Sphinx meeting. Is this the baby? He is getting so big."

"Yes, it's nice to see you, too!" added Mrs. Gipson, as she smiled at Darius in his stroller.

While Soror Benetta and Mrs. Gipson made a fuss

over Zora, Sahara took advantage of the distraction and quickly slipped away. She moved over to a group of ladies that lived a couple of streets over from her. Paula Donovan's husband was the son of the first black obstetrician in Fairchester, and she and Emery were friends. Crystal White's husband was a dentist. However, the other ladies only looked vaguely familiar.

As Sahara stood in the circle making small talk, she rolled Trevor's stroller back and forth. He was getting fussy from sitting too long. The little boy that rode past them on the tricycle when she and Zora arrived had his arms wrapped around Crystal's legs. He was eating a blueberry muffin and eyeing Trevor. Sahara was trying her best to pay attention to what everyone was saying while she kept one eye on the little boy.

"Look who decided to make a grand entrance." Everyone turned to see to whom Paula was referring.

Meranda's metallic blue Mercedes slowly rolled up the street. As the car got closer to their group, Sahara saw that it wasn't Meranda driving but Senator Barrett. Meranda was in the passenger seat, and there was another person in the backseat. Whoever it was had on a hood so Sahara couldn't see the face. The car didn't stop but continued its slow drive to the Barrett's house, up the driveway, and into the garage.

With the spectacle over, the chatter commenced.

"Who was that?"

"Did you hear...?"

"Some people say...."

Suddenly, Trevor started screaming. The ladies in the group stopped talking and shot Sahara and Trevor dirty looks before resuming their conversations. Sahara leaned down and saw that Trevor's face was covered with blueberry muffin. Her eyes immediately moved to Crystal's little boy, who was still holding his mother's leg— minus the muffin he had been eating. He stared back at Sahara with an impish grin on his face.

Sahara glared at him while she wiped the muffin from Trevor's face and calmed him down. The ladies kept talking, and Paula shifted her weight so that Sahara was no longer inside their little circle.

Sahara rolled her eyes. It was time to go.

As she walked through the crowd looking for Zora, she heard whispers and murmurs as everyone talked about the mystery person in the back of the Barrett's car. However, the only thing on her mind at that moment was how to get the blueberry stains out of Trevor's white shirt before they picked Clarissa up from preschool.

....

WELCOME!!

The large block letters written on the smiling cardboard lamb greeted Sahara and Trevor when they stepped inside the main hallway of North Fairchester Preschool Academy. The hubbub and excitement from the continuous stream of parents and children that flowed by them was almost palpable.

"Did you eat all of your lunch?"

"Mommy, Jack is in my class!"

"The teacher said that you had to go to timeout."

"Our class has a turtle!"

Sahara couldn't wait to hear about Clarissa's day. As they meandered around the parents and children on their way to her classroom, Sahara kept a firm grip on Trevor's hand as he walked beside her holding his stuffed animal to his chest. With the hallways packed with so many little people, she didn't want Trevor to get lost in the crowd. He seemed to feel the same way about Lamby.

However, Sahara noted that it wouldn't be too hard to find Trevor if they were separated from each other. They hadn't passed any black people in the hallway. She had seen one Chinese girl with whom Sahara assumed was her adopted mother. But, that was it. Everyone else was white.

At the end of the hallway, Miss Waller, Clarissa's teacher, stood at the classroom door. Sahara met her during orientation last week. The preschool scheduled one-on-one time between each student and the teacher so that they could get some time to get to know each other without the distraction of the other students. Clarissa had such a good time that she couldn't wait to start school.

When Sahara and Trevor reached the classroom, a little girl walked out with her mother. "Goodbye, Kristen! I'll see you and those beautiful blue eyes tomorrow!" said Miss Waller, as she flashed her megawatt smile at the little girl and waved. Kristen was beaming. "Hello, Mrs. Kyle! Clarissa is inside."

"Thank you!" Sahara noticed that Miss Waller's eyes were also blue as she walked into the brightly lit classroom.

Many children had already left, but there were some children coloring at the table. Two little boys were on the mats playing with trucks—but no Clarissa. Then, Sahara saw two little afro puffs by a bookshelf in the corner. Clarissa's face was buried in a book.

"Clarissa, honey, it is time to go," said Sahara. She was surprised that Clarissa was sitting on the floor. She had picked out her pink polka dot sundress and told Sahara that she was going to be very careful to not get it dirty.

Clarissa looked up and slowly got to her feet. The usual happiness that Sahara saw in her daughter's eyes was not there. Clarissa picked up the backpack and lunch box beside her and didn't say goodbye to the remaining children in the room. She just took Sahara's hand and walked to the door.

"Bye Molly! I'll see you and those curly, blonde curls tomorrow," said Miss Waller to the little girl in front of them. "Goodbye, Clarissa! I'll see you tomorrow." She smiled and waved.

Clarissa didn't say much as they walked to the car or during the ride home. "How was school?" Sahara asked.

"Okay," replied Clarissa as she looked out the window.

"Did you make any new friends?"

"No."

"What did you do today?"

"Nothing."

Sahara looked in the rearview mirror at her daughter sitting in the backseat. This was not the mother-daughter moment that she had envisioned.

....

When Sahara heard the garage door go up that evening, she was glad that Noah was home. They had read books and played that afternoon, but Sahara could tell there was something on Clarissa's mind. And, she still said very little about her day at preschool. Maybe Noah could get to the bottom of it.

Noah walked into the kitchen and put down his briefcase. He gave Trevor a big hug and a kiss and sat down at the kitchen table. "Where's my favorite girl? I want to hear about your first day," said Noah as he pulled Trevor onto his lap and started tickling him.

Any other day, Clarissa would have come running at top speed as soon as she heard Noah's voice. Today, she peeked around the corner and slowly dragged her feet to her father. She whispered, "Hi, Daddy," as she stood fidgeting before him with her head down.

Not used to this subdued greeting, Noah knew something was wrong. While balancing Trevor on one leg, he kissed Clarissa on the forehead and rubbed her back. "What's wrong, Clarissa?"

Either the fact that it was her father or something about the exchange included the magic words to get Clarissa to open up. "Oh, Daddy!" was all that Sahara heard before Clarissa burst into tears and buried her head in her father's chest.

Noah looked at Sahara for answers. Unfortunately, she didn't have any. Even Trevor seemed to feel sorry for Clarissa and wiggled off his father's lap and gave her a hug.

"What's wrong?" Noah asked again as he continued to pat Clarissa's back.

"I don't want to go to preschool again! I hate it!" she said in between sobs.

Noah looked over at Sahara again, and she shrugged her shoulders. That was the most Clarissa said about preschool since Sahara picked her up this afternoon. Sahara walked over to the kitchen table and sat down beside Noah and Clarissa.

"What happened today?" asked Noah. Clarissa raised her head, and Noah wiped away her tears.

"Well...I...was...I...was...playing...." Clarissa was choking back her tears. "...and Molly asked...."

Molly? Sahara's mind flashed back to this afternoon when she had picked up Clarissa. *I'll see you tomorrow with those beautiful blonde curls.* Molly was the little girl that had been walking in front of them.

"And, Molly asked me why my hair looked like this." Clarissa pointed at her afro puff. "I...I...I told her that my Mommy...." Clarissa looked over at Sahara. "I told her that my Mommy did my hair. Then, she said that my hair was weird, and that hair was supposed to be straight and go down, not be poufy and go up." Tears welled up in Clarissa's eyes again. "Then, Molly laughed and everyone else started laughing, too." Clarissa paused as tears came down her cheeks.

Noah looked over at Sahara. His face was not happy.

Clarissa continued, "Then, I told her that I had hair like my Mommy." Clarissa looked over at Sahara again. "Then, Molly said that Mommy must have weird hair too!" Clarissa broke down into another round of sobs.

Sahara looked at Clarissa crying on Noah's lap and was completely heartbroken. She had wanted her little girl's first school experience to be wonderful. Instead, it was tainted by a seemingly innocent comment rooted in racial ignorance and insensitivity.

Should Sahara have seen this coming? Even though Sugarberry Grove was a black neighborhood, North Fairchester was still considered the "white" part of town. Most black people in the city lived on the west side.

Logistically, a preschool close to their house made sense. And, since Clarissa would go to kindergarten next year, it offered the potential to meet future class-mates. Sure, Sahara had noticed the brochure and the website included only smiling, white children. But, she assumed there would be other black children at the school. When she visited the school in the spring, there were a few other Black families on the tour. They must have decided to not enroll their children.

Zora told Sahara that her mother-in-law wanted Zora to put Darius in the same preschool because of its strong academic curriculum. That's what Sahara had been focused on—the curriculum. Maybe she should have paid attention to some other things.

Clarissa had calmed down so Noah asked, "Have you been holding this in all day? Why didn't you talk to Mommy?"

Clarissa rubbed her eyes and looked at Sahara. "Be-cause I didn't want to hurt her feelings."

Sahara held her arms out for Clarissa and pulled her in close. She only wanted the best for her daughter. Had she made the wrong decision?

She looked at Clarissa. "Sweetie, you can talk to me about anything—even if you think it will hurt my feel-ings, even if you think that I will be mad. And, yes, you do have hair like your mommy, and it is beautiful on both of us," said Sahara.

Clarissa looked up at Sahara and showed Sahara

something that she hadn't seen since she picked Clarissa up from school that afternoon. A smile.

....

"Okay, the little girl said what?" asked Teri. She had called to see how Clarissa's first day of preschool was. Sahara recounted the events of earlier in the day, concluding with Clarissa's breakdown when Noah came home. "Lord, please excuse my language, but...oh hell no! So, how is Clarissa now? What are you going to do?"

"Well, after getting everything off her chest—"

Beep.

Someone was calling on the other line, but Sahara didn't recognize the phone number so she didn't click over. It was probably a telemarketer.

"We are going to discuss it with the preschool director and teacher first thing in the morning," said Sahara.

"Okay, good. I'm telling you...This is the reason why you need to think about Belles & Beaus. Even if you decide to switch preschools, let's face it—all of the ones by you are going to have a couple of black kids, if any. What happened today could have happened at any one of them. But, being in Belles & Beaus will give Clarissa and Trevor the opportunity to spend time with children that look like them and be exposed to other families like yours."

Teri was like a dog with a bone when it came to this

Belles & Beaus thing, but she had a point. There would be limited diversity at any of the preschools close to their house. And, from hearing some of the conversations at Tissues and Mimosas today, diversity was an issue at all levels of education—both public and private—in North Fairchester. Clarissa's experience today was probably the first of many.

Sahara knew that was part of the reason that many of the black social clubs—including Belles & Beaus, The Shield, Darlings, Marigolds, The Sphinx, and The Coalition—were founded. To give upper class blacks a forum to network and to socialize. For people whose day-to-day lives were filled with faces unlike their own and culture different from theirs, these clubs were a safe haven and a needed respite.

On the other hand, membership in this circle was by invitation only, just like the black fraternities and sororities. Although most of these organizations were based on the tenets of sisterhood, networking, or service, they took exclusivity to a whole other level.

Sahara had friends that were members of some of these organizations, but before she moved to Fairchester she would have never seen herself mixing with this circle. Although she had managed to snag a coveted invitation to The Sphinx Masquerade Ball in May, attending galas and luncheons was one thing. Seeking membership was something else entirely.

And, then there was her father—although he didn't

really deserve the title because he had never really been a part of her life. This was his world. She wasn't sure she could—or should—be an official member.

The *beep* of the call waiting snapped Sahara out of her thoughts. It was the same number as before, but she still didn't recognize it. Maybe she should answer.

But, Teri was still going on about Belles & Beaus and Sahara didn't want to have another awkward ending like in the park—so she didn't click over. When Teri paused, Sahara said, "Well, I'll think about it. I appreciate your concern."

"You know that I just want what is best for her," said Teri.

Sahara knew that was a true statement, and she did appreciate it. "I know. So, how was Miss Jayla's first day of kindergarten?" Sahara was glad to hear that Jayla didn't have any of the drama that Clarissa did. But, then again, Teri lived on the black side of town.

Beep.

It was the same number. Whoever it was had called three times. It couldn't be a telemarketer.

"Teri, someone keeps calling. Let me get it, in case it is an emergency."

After a quick goodbye, Sahara clicked over, but it was too late. The person had already hung up. Oh well.

The children were in bed, and Noah was in the office working. Sahara got up from the couch to get a glass of wine. She needed something to help her unwind. It had been a long day, and she needed to collect her thoughts for tomorrow's meeting with the preschool director and Clarissa's teacher.

She was glad that she wouldn't have to go by herself. Noah would be there, too. He was such a good father.

There was a notification on her cell phone. The unknown caller must have left a message. Sahara took a sip of her wine and listened.

"Sahara…." Although the caller's voice sounded shaky and it had been years since she'd heard it, she recognized the voice immediately. "This is your father."

She was going to need another glass of wine.

THREE

....

EMERY: CONTROL THE CENTER

*In chess, controlling the center squares allows you to better manage
your pieces and hinder your opponent's development.*

The large silver mirror shook when Reynard pushed
Emery against the bedroom wall. He quickly un-
buttoned her navy blue blouse and hiked up her
sand-colored skirt. Being six foot four, it was easy for
him to lift Emery's petite frame up in the air, and she
quickly wrapped her legs around his waist.

No words were exchanged. More than enough had
been shouted this morning. Right now, they were letting their desire do all the talking.

Reynard entered Emery, and she let out a soft moan.
Her mind wanted to resist the pleasure that her husband was giving her. She had all day to let her anger
from this morning's argument burn. But, with each
thrust, she was moving further from that goal and closer
to another.

Emery held her breath as the waves of ecstasy
washed over her. Reynard must have felt her body tense
up because a few seconds later, his eyes rolled back into
his head. As Reynard leaned over to put Emery on the
floor, she noticed red lipstick on his collar. She was

wearing fuchsia.

Reynard was a cheating bastard, plain and simple. Normal couples disagreed about money and household chores. They fought about his uncontrollable need to flirt, and do everything else, with any woman within a five mile radius. Maybe it was karma. Whatever it was, she needed to keep her eyes on the prize.

Emery picked her black lace panties off the floor and walked to the bathroom to take a quick shower. She didn't have time to think about Reynard right now. There was a North Carolina Union alumni meeting tonight, and she hadn't budgeted time for makeup sex. Moochi...she meant Rozlyn...was picking her up soon. She had to hurry up.

As the hot water hit Emery's skin, she rehearsed what she was going to say in her mind. The August meeting was the first since the summer hiatus and several alumni were being recognized at the dinner for achievements on behalf of the University and the Club. Emery wanted to make sure that she looked and sounded just right.

When she got out of the shower, Emery wrapped a towel around her naked body. What should she wear? She looked at the rows of clothes in her walk-in closet. The gold and cream Alberta Ferretti palace dress? Too fancy. The peach ruched dress with the jeweled Grecian collar? Too simple. The embroidered Marchesa Notte dress? Emery looked at the black above the knee dress with the embroidered pale green flowers and antique gold overlay. Perfect.

With its plunging neckline and fitted waist, it would provide the perfect silhouette to showcase the body that her sessions with the personal trainer at five o'clock in the morning provided. Plus, it would look nice with the gorgeous, green emerald necklace that Reynard had just brought home as a gift.

Emery slipped her dress on and stepped into her gold multi-strapped Giuseppe Zanotti high heeled sandals. When she walked back into the bedroom, Reynard was sitting on the bed and talking on his cell phone. He whispered something and quickly hung up. Emery acted like she didn't see him.

"Reynard, I think that I'm going to wear the necklace you bought me. Can you help me put it on?" said Emery as she stood in front of the silver mirror.

Reynard picked up the necklace from the bed and draped the apology gift around Emery's neck. He then took his time putting soft, delicate kisses up and down her neck as he cupped her breasts. Emery's body tingled at the touch of his lips against her skin, but her eyes focused on the reflection of the emerald necklace in the mirror. It was gorgeous.

Reynard was a dog, but he certainly knew what he was doing in the bedroom. Lord knows he had enough practice. But, more importantly, he showed his love with gifts and not his fists.

Emery heard the doorbell chimes ring. It was Moo—Rozlyn. She had to start calling Moochi by her real name and not her college nickname. Rozlyn was here. Emery stole one more glance at the necklace.

As she walked down the stairs, she looked through the two-story window at the McMansions lining the streets of the neighborhood and fingered the emerald necklace. When she and Reynard bought their house in Cabrini Estates, this area was supposed to be the west side version of Sugarberry Grove. But then, the housing bubble burst.

They thought that they were getting in early in a neighborhood that would be filled with estate homes. It turned out that they were underwater on a house that had neighbors that took advantage of short sales and foreclosures. She agreed to forgive Reynard's latest indiscretion in exchange for his compliance to build a bigger house in a more exclusive community. To seal the deal, he had given her the emerald necklace as a bonus.

....

"When did you get this?" Emery asked when she got into the black Cadillac Escalade.

Rozlyn was grinning from ear-to-ear. "Omar picked it up from the dealership last week."

Emery wasn't surprised. The Escalade still had the new car smell. "I saw this car turning into the neighborhood a couple of times. I had no idea that it was you."

"Yaaasss!" said Rozlyn, and they both laughed.

Rozlyn and her family lived a few streets down from the Edmonds in Cabrini Estates. The Wormleys bought a foreclosure a couple of years ago. Emery was glad that Reynard agreed to the new house.

"That black and red ombre dress looks nice on you," said Emery.

"Thank you so much for helping me. You were right. This is better than the green dress for tonight," said Rozlyn. "I wish I had your fashion sense."

"So, what's been going on? Besides styling and pro-filing in your new car, that is." Emery grinned at Rozlyn. She had to admit. This car was nice.

"I've been crazy busy. We just got a bunch of new furniture. I've been trying to spruce up our house some. Well...a lot. But, I've enjoyed it." Rozlyn lowered her voice. "This is really the first time that I've lived some-where that I can be proud of....that felt like a real home."

Emery didn't know much about how Rozlyn grew up. They'd met in college, where everyone called her "Moochi." Emery's friend, Karyn, had told her that someone gave Rozlyn that name because she was a moocher—always asking people for things—food, clothes, money. Emery didn't know anything about that. She had called her Moochi because everyone else did. But, over the past year, Rozlyn had been a good friend to her. The least she could do was call Rozlyn by her real name.

"Well, I can't wait to come over and see everything, Rozlyn. I know. You should throw a party! It'll be fun, and I'll help."

Rozlyn's eyes lit up. "Oh, it would be fun to have a party and show off all my new stuff!"

"Yes, it would be great for you to have something at *your* house."

Rozlyn had a birthday party in the spring for her husband, Omar. He was from West Fairchester and as Reynard would say, "looked like he worked on the corner." The party was at his mother's house—a lot of red Solo cups, weed, and scantily-clad women. Reynard wanted to stay, but Emery got them out of there quickly.

"Well, what have you been doing? I feel like I haven't seen you in a while. I missed you," said Rozlyn.

Emery liked Rozlyn. She was a little rough around the edges, but she was nice. Emery knew a lot of people, but she didn't have a lot of friends. Not real friends— ones that she could talk to when she really needed it.

And, she always had to be careful letting women into her life because of Reynard. He was attractive, successful, and had a wandering eye. She had learned all too quickly that some women didn't mind cozying up to her to get access to him. Women were a trip, but Rozlyn had shown that she was a true friend.

Emery and Rozlyn were still catching up when Rozlyn pulled up to the valet in front of the large white brick building. The alumni meeting was at the restaurant, Hush, on the outskirts of downtown.

"Teeeerrrrrrrwoooo!" The Xi Tau Delta sorority call pierced the evening air as Emery and Rozlyn got out of the car. Emery responded with a ""Teeeerrrrrrrwoooo!" to her sorority sister and glanced over at Rozlyn, who was looking straight ahead.

Rozlyn had expressed interest in becoming a member of Xi Tau Delta. However, Emery had seen many sorors make the mistake of thinking all of their friends should be their sorors. Emery knew better. Her alumnae chapter was doing an intake next fall. If Rozlyn got in, they would not only be friends but also sisters. That could be interesting.

Emery looked over at Rozlyn again. Maybe she would submit her name. Maybe.

"Rozlyn, I'm going to hurry inside to see if they need any help with setting up." Emery was on the NCU Alumni Club's fundraising committee so she wanted to make sure that everything ran smoothly tonight. She wanted everyone in a good mood so they could write big checks with lots of zeroes.

Plus, there would also be a lot of VIPs tonight so she wanted to have time to network. If the meeting ran too long or something was off, people would clear out of there so fast it would make your head spin. She definitely did not want that to happen because there was one person in particular she wanted to meet.

A piece of paper fell to the ground, and Rozlyn bent down to pick it up. "I'll come with you," she said looking up at Emery. "It always helps to have an extra hand."

Emery helped Rozlyn up and then linked her arm in Rozlyn's arm. "Sounds good to me, sis. Thank you," she said as they walked inside the restaurant.

The hostess at the entrance asked, "Are you here for the NCU alumni meeting?" Emery and Rozlyn nodded yes. "They are meeting on the rooftop. You can take the elevator or the stairs."

Rozlyn and Emery walked up the stairs to the second level. Before they could go any further, Delia Speight stopped them. "Emery dear, I'm glad that you are finally here," she said in a tone dripping with superiority and scorn. Although a slight woman, her heavy voice carried throughout the room—and with a lot of people.

The Speights were an old guard family that lived on family land on the south side of Fairchester. All of them—there were five remaining children from the long deceased parents that were pioneers in establishing the black upper class in Fairchester—were quick to let you know that they were Speights, and most were not worthy of their time.

However, Delia Speight was also a member of the Marigolds, so she had to deal with Emery on a regular basis. Just as Emery started to protest, Delia said "I need for you to babysit the VIPS in the private room over there." She pointed to a closed door on the other side of the room.

"Okay, Marigold Delia." Emery was always respectful but made sure to let her know that they were on the same level, as far as she was concerned. "Rozlyn is also willing to help."

Delia looked Rozlyn over from head to toe before speaking. "Please go up to the rooftop. You can help hand out the programs as people arrive."

Rozlyn had passed Delia's test. Emery knew that the green dress that fit like a second skin that Rozlyn originally planned to wear would not have. Rozlyn smiled. She seemed pleased with her assignment.

"See you later, Rozlyn," said Emery as she headed to the holding room on the restaurant's second floor.

The Club was honoring Congressman Charles Allymer, NCU Class of 1973, and Dr. Edward Atwood, NCU Class of 1965. Emery had offered to follow-up with the honorees about tonight's logistics. She'd encouraged the Congressman's assistant to have all of his family attend because it would present a picture perfect photo opportunity for his black constituents in North Carolina. Ties to NCU ran long and deep.

When Emery opened the door, she was surprised. Neither of them was in the holding room. The only person there was a light-skinned black woman wearing a white sleeveless dress with blue and gold flowers on it. She was reading a book but looked up and smiled when Emery came in. Emery recognized her immediately. It was Fallon Allymer-Tate, Congressman Allymer's daughter.

Emery knew that Fallon was already in most organizations—The Sphinx, Darlings, Marigolds, and Gazelles—in which her mother, Winnie Allymer, was a member. But more importantly, as far as Emery was concerned, Fallon was the cluster coordinator for Belles & Beaus.

Emery walked over and extended her hand. "Hello, Mrs. Allymer-Tate. I'm Emery Edmonds."

"Hello, Emery. It's nice to meet you. My father stepped out to take a phone call. I'm not sure to where my mother scattered off."

The door swung open and in walked Dr. Atwood, the other honoree that evening. Emery gave him a quick smile. She didn't want to seem impolite. Dr. Atwood looked like he didn't need anything, so she turned her focus back to Fallon.

Emery sat down across the table from Fallon. "Oh, that's okay. I'll wait." The elephant charm on Fallon's silver bracelet caught Emery's eye. "Are you a Xi?" She asked the question, but she already knew the answer. She had done her research.

Fallon perked up. "Yes, I am. Are you?"

"I am, soror." Emery walked over and gave Fallon a hug, but she didn't return to her seat. Instead, she slid into the chair beside Fallon. "Where did you pledge?"

"I pledged at Harvard. Spring '99."

"I crossed in Spring '99. We're sands!" Having made that sorority connection, Emery and Fallon talked about their experiences in Xi and realized that they met when they were undergraduates at the Greek Picnic in Philadelphia one year. They also were new members of the Marigolds, although Fallon was in the Raleigh Chapter, with her mother, and Emery was in the Fairchester chapter.

They were deep in conversation when Delia Speight opened the door. "Emery, Congressman Allymer is already in position. You can bring Dr. Atwood out to be seated," said Marigold Delia. She narrowed her eyes when she saw Emery chatting with Fallon, while Dr. Atwood sat in the corner alone.

Oops. Emery tried to make her best "I'm sorry" face, but it was met with a scowl.

Fallon chimed in, "Please forgive me for holding Emery hostage. She came in looking for my father, but I asked her to keep me company until he returned." Fallon's eyes narrowed as she smiled. Emery could see that her lips said, "Please forgive me," but her eyes said "Don't test me."

Delia Speight got the message. She gave a quick, "No problem," before sticking her head back out the door and closing it.

Emery knew that Marigold Delia would make her pay for the little slip-up later, but for now, she was Team Fallon. "Thank you," said Emery.

Even though they were all adults, there was still a hierarchy in this circle. And, in the NCU Alumni Club, the Speights were near the top. However, Fallon showed that even though she was not an alumna, her father's credentials gave her what Emery's father taught her was a promotion in chess. Fallon's pawn status was promoted to queen, just like her mother, Winnie Allymer.

....

Emery stepped on the roof and gave her eyes a few seconds to adjust. The white string lights that hung from the restaurant's glass-covered rooftop lit up the evening sky as candles flickered on the tables giving the area a magical feel. She waved and smiled at people she knew as she walked across the room.

As fundraising chair, Emery was kicking off this year's alumni giving campaign at the meeting. Since she was on the program, she and Rozlyn were seated at one of the tables near the podium. Congressman Charles Allymer, his wife Winnie, and Fallon were seated at the table front and center, along with Professor Atwood. When Emery sat down, Fallon looked behind her and smiled.

Attorney Daniel Strong, the president of the alumni chapter was at the podium. Although Congressman Allymer and Professor Atwood were being recognized, they still had to get through the agenda.

Emery discreetly scanned the room to see who was

there. Councilman Vernon Combs...Dr. Sean Lee...Judge Michael Bradley...Sportscaster Terrance Mooney...North Carolina Senator Tyrone Barrett...Vesta Cummings Brantley.

Emery waved at her. Vesta's mother, Landy, was in Emery's Marigold chapter. Vesta was also in Belles & Beaus.

President Strong made a joke and everyone laughed. But, someone was laughing a little too loudly. Another joke by the president. More excessive laughter from someone.

Out the side of her eye, Emery noticed others looking around trying to see who the perpetrator was. Emery stared straight ahead at President Strong. She didn't want to miss her cue.

The too loud, too often laughter continued. After a few minutes, Meranda Barrett stood up and helped the young woman that was sitting with her and Senator Barrett up from her seat. The woman continued to giggle as Meranda escorted her out. Emery didn't recognize her, but she'd heard that the Barrett's daughter, Dara, was staying with her parents. Something about her seemed a little odd.

Clap, clap, clap.

Emery turned her attention back to the podium. The president had finished his introduction, and Congressman Allymer walked to the podium to accept his award.

"Good evening, fellow Bears," said Congressman

Allymer with his booming voice. A tall, light skinned man with short wavy hair, he always reminded Emery of an older version of Reynard.

Emery glanced over at the table where the Congressman's wife and daughter were sitting. Winnie's back was to her, but she could see Fallon's profile. Fallon, with her fine, naturally curly hair like her father, was sitting tall in her chair and leaning forward slightly, as if she was literally hanging on to every word that her father said. She looked absolutely mesmerized.

The president returned to the podium after Congressman Allymer finished his remarks for one more photo op of the two of them together. President Strong then nodded in Emery's direction.

Emery rose out of her chair and walked confidently to the microphone. Most people were afraid of public speaking. She lived for it. So many people in the world feel that they are without a voice or unheard. She never wanted to be in that situation—voiceless.

"Let's give another round of applause to Congressman Allymer." The audience clapped. "Now, Bears, our HBCUs are in trouble, and North Carolina Union is no different. The North Carolina Legislature has cut the school's funding significantly in recent years and continues to try to erode the mission of HBCUs to educate our youth. It is only because of alumni donations and support that we've been able to keep some of the programs and amenities in place. Let's make sure that all the great opportunities and advantages that we had at North Carolina Union are available to today's students. Now, who is ready to join the Gold Circle?"

Emery looked around the room, but it really was a rhetorical question. She figured that no one would give such a large amount here. That level would take some coaxing and hand holding, but she hoped with a little networking and cajoling after the program was over, she could get....

"I'm ready! I want to join the Gold Circle!" shouted someone.

Emery turned and looked in the direction from where the voice came. It was Rozlyn. She was waving what looked like a check back and forth and smiling.

Emery squinted her eyes. Was she serious? Or, was Rozlyn pulling a prank? To be in the Gold Circle, you had to pledge ten thousand dollars. Sure Rozlyn had a new car and had redecorated her house, but could she just write a check for that large an amount?

The crowd began to fidget. Emery couldn't continue to just stand there staring at Rozlyn. She had to say something—but, she didn't know what. She wasn't prepared for someone to announce they would join now. She would have to wing it.

"Wonderful! Wonderful! We have someone who wants to join the Gold Circle! Please come up!" Emery waved her to the podium.

Rozlyn walked with check in hand up to the front.

She put the microphone close to her lips and said, "Hi, I'm Rozlyn Wormly." A screeching sound came from the speakers, and everyone winced. Rozlyn didn't seem to notice. Instead, she looked over at Emery so Emery smiled. "I'm the Class of 2001. I love my school and just want to support North Carolina Union and my best friend, Emery!"

Everyone clapped and Rozlyn returned to her seat. Emery was still blown away that Rozlyn gave ten thousand dollars. And, did she say, "her best friend, Emery?" If Rozlyn was writing checks for ten grand, Emery didn't have a problem with that. After giving her final comments, Emery returned to the table and gave Rozlyn a big hug—because that is what best friends do.

After President Strong gave his closing remarks and adjourned the meeting, people started mixing and mingling. Since things had gone her way that night, Emery decided to make amends for ignoring Dr. Atwood earlier. Plus, he was talking to Dr. Grant, a cardiologist at Fairchester Hospital. She had been trying to schedule an appointment with him for weeks to talk about a new medication that her company was rolling out. She thought it would be beneficial to his patients—and could make her a lot of money if he started prescribing it regularly.

"Dr. Atwood, it was a great honor to have you here tonight. Thank you for all that you do."

"I may be a Wolverine now, but I will always be a

Bear at heart." Dr. Atwood waved someone over. "Noah! I'm glad that you were able to make the meeting." Normally, this would have been Emery's cue to leave, but she really needed to setup an appointment with Dr. Grant.

Dr. Grant turned to Emery. "Now, I know who you are. You were a student in my class when I taught at NCU." He looked over at Noah. "It's so good to see a Bear marriage still going strong. I remember when you two got engaged."

Emery and Noah gave each other an awkward glance. "Noah and I aren't married," Emery said in a matter-of-fact way. She needed to salvage this situation if she wanted that appointment. "But, he is married to a wonderful woman that gets my stamp of approval."

"Yes, I met Sahara and Noah when they were both students at Ross. Intelligent, beautiful, a great mother, and a sincere and genuine person to boot, Noah is certainly lucky to have her," added Dr. Atwood.

Emery forced herself to smile, but she caught the shade that Dr. Atwood threw her way. Touché. "Now, Dr. Grant, I've been trying to get on your calendar. When do you think we will be able to get together to talk about some of my company's new offerings?" asked Emery.

Twenty minutes later, Emery had a lunch meeting scheduled with Dr. Grant and dinner scheduled with Dr. Atwood to talk about leveraging his Ross Business

School travel schedule for NCU alumni fundraising efforts. Not bad at all.

As she and Rozlyn were leaving, Emery saw Fallon talking to some recent graduates. "Hold on for a second, Rozlyn." She could feel Rozlyn's eyes boring a hole in her back as she walked the few feet over to Fallon.

"Excuse me." Emery smiled at the people with whom Fallon was speaking and turned to Fallon. "I just wanted to let you know that I'm leaving, but I'll see you next Friday."

"I'm so glad that we met! I'm looking forward to our lunch date."

Emery smiled. "Me, too!" As she waved goodbye, she could see Rozlyn glaring at them.

"Who is that?" asked Rozlyn as they walked down the stairs.

"Fallon Allymer-Tate. She's Congressman Allymer's daughter."

Rozlyn turned up her nose. "She seems a little stuck up."

Stuck up or not, Fallon was a good person for Emery to have in her corner if she wanted to get into Belles & Beaus.

....

FOUR

SAHARA

"Let's go! The birthday express is now ten minutes late!" Noah shouted.

As Sahara came down the stairs she heard her father-in-law say in a slow baritone, "Son, you know that you catch more flies with honey."

Noah put his hand on his father's shoulder. "I'm not trying to catch any flies, Pop. Just trying to make sure that the birthday girl isn't late for her own party."

"Noah, what is this?" Sahara asked when she walked into the kitchen and saw the pink and black balloons on the kitchen table. "These aren't the balloons that I ordered."

"Really? Well, that's what the cashier gave me when I went to Party Central this morning. Sorry."

Sahara frowned. She had ordered pink and purple balloons. Black didn't fit in with the theme of the party or the other decorations. White balloons would have even coordinated better than black.

"That's okay," she said trying to mean it. She looked at her watch. There was nothing she could do about it now. They should have left ten minutes ago. She'd have to call the shop when they returned. "Are you ready for the party, Pop?"

Noah's father slowly rose from the chair in the family room. "I am."

Sahara noticed that Pop was moving a little slower during this visit. He was a dishwasher at a restaurant in Charlotte, and the many years of manual labor seemed to be catching up with him. However, he insisted on coming up for Clarissa's birthday.

After they packed Noah's car with the gifts from the family, the birthday cake, and paper products, they realized that there were too many people and too many car seats for everyone to sit comfortably in one car. The boys climbed into Noah's red BMW, and Sahara, Clarissa, and the pink and black balloons jumped in Sahara's champagne Lexus.

The drive from North Fairchester to the outskirts of town was idyllic. The gated communities surrounding Jordan Lake soon gave way to multi-million dollar estates with manicured gardens. As they got closer to the Chatham County line, the views shifted from suburban to rural with cows and horses occasionally dotting the lush green landscape.

When the two-car caravan arrived at the horse farm on the outskirts of town, they drove past the wooden fence up the gravel path to the large red barn. The white sign at the barn entrance indicated that Clarissa's party was past the breezeway in the stables to the left and another party to the right. That party must have been booked this week. When Sahara gave the final count for Clarissa's party a week ago, the facility coordinator told her that Clarissa's party was the only event that afternoon.

They unloaded the cars in the parking lot by the barn and walked to the party area on the left. Sahara tied the pink and black balloons to one of the trees overlooking the picnic tables and looked at her watch. 1:40pm. The party officially started in twenty minutes.

Sahara looked in the distance and saw pink and white balloons swaying from a tree in the distance. That must be the other party. It looked like it was already in full swing.

1:50 pm. 1:55 pm. 2:00 pm. 2:04 pm. 2:10 pm.

Time seemed to pass slowly as they waited for the first of the party guests to arrive. Clarissa stared at the path like she was willing someone, anyone, to show up. Even Sahara was starting to worry.

She decided to have Clarissa's party at the horse farm, because a mother had mentioned that some of Clarissa's classmates took riding lessons there. Sahara thought having the party there would guarantee that most of the preschool children would come, but most of Clarissa's classmates responded that they couldn't make it. The few who were coming canceled this week for one reason or another.

There were only two children—Gwendolyn Brantley,

the only other little black girl in the school, and Connor Hawkins—from Clarissa's preschool that were still coming. But, Sahara knew that most of her friends were bringing their children.

They heard the crunch of gravel under someone's feet. It was Zora, Cass, Darius, Teri, Jayla, Milton and his daughters, and a couple of other guests arriving. Sahara quietly breathed a sigh of relief.

Jayla dropped Teri's hand and ran to Clarissa, who was already running towards her. "Happy birthday, Clarissa!" The two friends hugged, and all was right with the world.

"We accidently went over to the other party. Then, it seemed to take forever to walk over here from there," said Teri.

"Didn't you see the sign in front of the barn?" asked Sahara.

Teri looked confused. "Sign? There wasn't a sign." She turned to Zora. "Did you see a sign?"

Zora shook her head no, and Sahara shrugged her shoulders. "Well, it doesn't matter. You're here now." FINALLY.

More people arrived, and the children were laughing and playing. Clarissa smiled from ear-to-ear now that her friends were there.

The stable assistant distributed helmets to the children so they could walk the horses from the stable into the fenced pasture and start the lesson. Sahara saw

Gwendolyn Brantley and her mother walking up the path and hurried over to meet them.

"Hi, Gwendolyn! The children are starting the riding lesson. If you go see Miss Ann...." Sahara bent down and pointed in the stable assistant's direction. "... She will help you."

"Oh, she doesn't need help. Gwendolyn takes riding lessons," said her mother as Gwendolyn skipped away.

Sahara stood up. "Hi, I'm Sahara Kyle, Clarissa's mother."

"I'm Vesta. Vesta Cummings-Brantley," she said as she shook Sahara's hand. "I apologize for being a little late, but we just came from another party in Raleigh, at Congressman Allymer's estate for one of his grandchildren." Sahara clenched her jaw but Vesta didn't seem to notice. "Gwendolyn certainly is going to have her fill of horses today! They also had horses there...." Vesta looked around. "...but, you know, they were at their estate." Vesta pressed her lips together and gave Sahara a half smile.

Sahara tried to not seem annoyed. "Oh, that sounds nice." She noticed how paltry the grass looked, and there was some paper and other debris blowing around on the ground. She could tell that she and Vesta were not going to be friends.

"Did you go to the Marigold fundraiser this spring?" Vesta asked as they walked to where the other parents were sitting.

Ugh. Sahara wanted to put that memory behind her. "Yes, I did. Were you there?"

"No, we weren't able to make it. My husband received an award from the National African-American Insurance Association the same night in New Orleans so we didn't attend this year."

Whew.

"I thought your name sounded familiar. My mother is Landy Cummings." Vesta stated as they reached the others.

"Ohhhhh...," said Sahara.

This should be interesting. Landy Cummings and her husband were generous supporters of the Fairchester Urban League, and Sahara had met her at the Urban League's art auction. Landy and Meranda had history so that complicated Sahara's relationship with Landy, but they were still friendly.

Sahara introduced Vesta to the other parents and sat down at the picnic table next to Teri. Miss Ann, the stable assistant, was teaching the girls some basic riding skills and they looked like they were having a ball—even Gwendolyn.

"You have another guest," said Teri.

An older white man was walking up the gravel path with a little girl. He looked familiar.

"Is that Dwight?" asked Noah.

It sure looked like Dwight Corbett, Noah's executive vice president at the bank. Although Dwight Corbett had taken Noah under his wing and mentored him, Sahara had only seen Dwight a handful of times.

"Did you invite him?" asked Sahara.

"No. I mean...his children are grown. And, you know we don't really socialize outside the office."

"We better go over and say hello," said Sahara.

As Dwight got closer, his pace slowed. He probably was not expecting a party filled with black people.

Noah walked up and shook Dwight's hand. "Dwight! We didn't expect to see you here! You remember my wife, Sahara."

Dwight looked a little embarrassed as he surveyed the guests. "Of course. It is good to see you, Sahara. I apologize. It appears that we have stumbled accidently upon your party. Is it one of your children's birthday?" Sahara and Noah nodded their heads.

"We are looking for Molly Granger's party. My daughter gave me directions on how to get here, but I think I'm in the wrong place." Dwight kept looking around as if he searched long enough a face that he recognized would appear.

Something must have caught his eye because he stopped talking, and his eyes got wide. Sahara looked over her shoulder to where he was looking. She didn't see anything unusual, just Teri talking to Jayla.

"I'm sorry, Noah. It was good to see you again, Sahara." Dwight quickly gathered his granddaughter and scurried back down the gravel path.

Did he say Molly Granger? Molly Granger was the name of the little girl that talked about Clarissa's hair on the first day of school. Was she having a party, also?

But, that didn't make sense. The teacher had mentioned that Clarissa was the only birthday in the class for the next two months. Maybe it was someone else. There was only one way to find out.

"Who was that?" asked Teri causing Sahara to jump. She hadn't seen Teri walk up.

"Noah's boss, Dwight Corbett."

"Dwight Corbett? He looks exactly like my grandfather...."

"You know Dwight is white, right?" asked Sahara.

"Right...but he does look like Grandpa and ...."

Sahara didn't know what point Teri was trying to make, but she needed to get to the bottom of this Molly Granger situation. "Teri, can you hold that thought? I have to tell Noah something." Sahara walked away before Teri could answer.

Noah was shooting the breeze with his father and Milton when Sahara walked up. "Noah, I'll be back. I'm going to make sure that the sign is up so that people don't keep mixing the parties up." She felt a little guilty for not giving him the whole truth, but the sign did need to be checked.

"Are we expecting anyone else? I thought most of the children were already here."

"Tania is still bringing her son. And, Connor Hawkins, from Clarissa's class isn't here."

"Sure." He didn't look convinced—but she wasn't going to let that stop her.

Sahara walked up the gravel path. She could see Zora a few feet in front of her. "Zora, wait up." Having a companion would make her look less conspicuous.

Zora turned. "Is something wrong? Why are you leaving the party?"

Sahara jogged to catch up with her. "I'm going to fix the sign. Guests between the two parties keep getting mixed up."

"Been there, done that," said Zora, and they laughed. "Darius was getting fussy so Cass took him for a walk, but they've been gone for a while. I want to make sure everything is okay."

As soon as she said that, Sahara saw Cass and the stroller in the distance. He was standing and talking to a woman, who kept tossing her blonde hair over shoulder. It was only as they got closer, that she saw that it was Hannah, Emily's mom, from the park.

Since they met at the park, Sahara and Hannah got Clarissa and Emily together for a few play dates. Sahara had even invited Emily to Clarissa's party today, but Hannah said that they would be visiting family out-of-town. She couldn't believe this. Who else was at this Molly Granger's party?

Zora must have seen Cass, as well, because she picked up her pace. Cass heard their footsteps and a big smile spread across his face. Sahara wasn't sure if he would receive the reception from Zora that he was expecting.

"Look Darius! Here comes, Mommy!" He gave Zora a quick peck on the cheek when she stepped by his side.

Hannah's eyes opened wide. "This is your wife?"

"Yes, I am. Hi, I'm Zora." She and Hannah shook hands and quickly let their hands fall back to their sides.

"Hannah is an old family friend. We grew up together. We are practically brother and sister." Cass let out an awkward laugh.

Hannah smirked and touched Cass' arm. "Well, I certainly remember us doing things that I hope a brother wouldn't do to his sister." Cass' face turned beet red.

Sahara figured that she better change the subject. "Hannah, I didn't realize that you were back in town."

Hannah unwillingly took her eyes off of Zora. "Sahara! What are you doing here?" Hannah looked like she had been hit with a one-two punch.

What was she doing here? No, what was Hannah doing here? She was supposed to be out-of-town. "Clarissa's birthday party is today." Sahara smiled sweetly.

"Oh, oh. That's right. Yes...." Hannah paused for a second as if she was trying to collect her thoughts. "...Yes, we had a change in plans. But, I had already told you that Emily wouldn't be at the party so I didn't want to disturb you. And, Emily's friend, Molly decided this week to hold a big play date today so I figured that I would just bring Emily here." Hannah smiled and flipped her hair.

How convenient. "That's fine. Clarissa is still having a wonderful time." Sahara stopped short of saying—without her. "I walked down here to check the signs. Our guests keep getting mixed up."

"Well, I better head back to the party...I mean play date." Hannah put her lips close to Cass' ear. "It's been too long, Cass. Keep in touch." She then looked back at Zora and Sahara. "It was nice seeing you again."

That's right. Zora was with Teri and Sahara that day in the park. Hannah had seen Zora before. She just didn't realize that she was Cass' wife, his black wife to be exact.

Zora looked like she had steam coming out of her ears as Hannah walked away. "Let's head back to the party, Cass," she said through clenched teeth.

Even if she hadn't been on a mission, Sahara was pretty sure that she didn't want to be anywhere near that conversation. She had never seen Zora so angry. "I'm going to check the sign. You two, go ahead without me. I'll catch up."

"Okay," said Zora.

Sahara thought that she saw a little hesitancy in Cass' eyes. Sahara almost felt sorry for him. Almost.

When the trio was far enough in the distance, and Sahara could no longer hear Zora fussing at Cass, she crept to one of the trees on the party's perimeter. She thought it would serve as a good vantage point without being seen.

The party, well Dwight said it was a play date, was still going on. They must have bought the premium package because the party was in full swing before Clarissa's started, and that was almost two hours ago. There were so many children—running around the playground, riding horses, and playing games.

For a minute, Sahara felt a silly. She was a grown woman spying on a children's party. She was about to leave when she recognized a face. Then two. Then three. Children from Clarissa's class. Timmy Smith. Judy Carrington. Elysa Graham. Justin Finnigan. Half of the children there were from Clarissa's preschool class. These were the same children whose parents responded that they couldn't attend Clarissa's birthday party.

And, there was Connor Hawkins. His mother assured Sahara that he would be at Clarissa's party when she ran into her at the grocery store. Connor Hawkins was here, too.

Then, Sahara saw her. Molly Granger. There wasn't another one. It was the same Molly Granger from Clarissa's class. The same one that made her baby cry. And, apparently, most...no all...of the children from their preschool class had chosen to go to her play date, rather than Clarissa's birthday party.

What did Hannah say? Her mother had decided this week to host it. That was well after Sahara sent Clarissa's birthday invitations out. She couldn't believe that Molly's mom would have the audacity to host a competing party.

Sahara was fuming, but she had to get back to her daughter's party. She'd probably been gone too long already. Sahara hiked back to the other side of the farm.

As soon as she returned to the party, she saw some of the parents exchange awkward glances. "What took you so long? We're ready to cut the cake," said Noah.

"Well, I...." Sahara looked around. Everyone looked like they had been waiting on her. Tania, her children, and Donna had even come while she was gone. Sahara's cheeks felt warm as she muttered, "Sorry."

Miss Ann lit the candles on the birthday cake, and everyone gathered around the picnic tables to sing happy birthday. Clarissa looked so happy as she blew out the candles on the cake.

The children were finished riding the horses so some played Pin the Tail on the Horse while others painted horseshoes. Sahara walked over to Tania, whose Halle Berry cut was on point as always, and Donna. They were always together so people sometimes got them mixed up. Both of them were in her LUA chapter and had attended NCU with Noah.

"Hello, Ms. M-I-A. Where were you?" Tania asked while giving Sahara a hug.

Sahara was embarrassed that she'd been missing from her own daughter's birthday party for so long that it was noticeable. "Oh, I went to make sure the sign was still up so people knew where to go. There's another party going on near the other stables."

Tania raised her eyebrows. "Uh huh. That's what Noah said, but we didn't see you when we came in."

Busted. Sahara sighed and told them the whole story about Molly Granger's party and seeing most of the children from Clarissa's preschool class there.

Donna shook her head. "That's awful. It sounds like she purposely planned a party the same day as Clarissa's. But, why?"

Sahara explained what happened on Clarissa's first day of school. "I thought that after meeting with the preschool director and the teacher that everything was done. Clarissa has enjoyed school after that day." She shook her head. "But, maybe I was wrong. I mean none of the children from Clarissa's preschool came." Maybe the teacher or the preschool director said something to one of the other parents. "Well, one came...Gwendolyn, the other little black girl at the school, but she's in the transitional kindergarten program and not Clarissa's class."

"Gwendolyn Brantley?" asked Tania.

"Yes, do you know her?"

"Her mother is a member of my Belles & Beaus chapter. You know, Sahara, there is always Belles & Beaus."

Before Sahara could say anything, Donna said, "Speaking of Belles & Beaus...let's talk about my beau,

Alton."

They all laughed. Alton was a Gamma and Cass' college roommate. He and Donna met at the Gamma Boat Ride in April and had been dating hot and heavy since the beginning of the summer.

"He is truly a McDreamy," said Donna, as she blinked her hazel eyes a few times. "He's handsome, intelligent, romantic...he's perfect!" Donna was glowing at the thought of him. Then, her face became serious. "Well...almost perfect...." She looked over at Sahara. "Apparently, he is...or was...good friends with Emery."

Emery. That was a major mark against him. But, Sahara wanted her friend to be happy. "Well, everyone has a strike against them. It's a good thing you found out early."

After the children ran around on the playground for a while, people started to leave. When they got to the car, Sahara could see Molly's play date was also over because most of the cars in the parking lot were gone.

Clarissa was asleep as soon as Sahara buckled her into the car seat. Sahara smiled. Clarissa had a great time at her party. Sahara turned the key in the ignition, when she saw Molly and her mother strolling to their car. Molly's mother bent down and whispered in her daughter's ear.

As Sahara drove towards the front gate, Molly waved as the Lexus passed and shouted, "Bye, Clarissa!" Molly's mother stood there smirking as she waved.

Maybe she should give Belles & Beaus some consideration.

···

FIVE

SAHARA

It was a beautiful September afternoon to be at the park. Old school music and gales of laughter floated to the parking lot as Sahara, Noah, and the children got out of the car. Noah bent down to tie Trevor's shoe, before they walked down the hill to where the Belles & Beaus Welcome Back Picnic was being held.

Even from a distance, Sahara could see that picnic was an understatement. Carnival booths and rides encircled the large pink and blue striped tent that was in the middle of the park. It looked like a pink and blue carnival paradise.

When they got to the bottom of the hill, they could see children and parents were everywhere—walking, talking, eating, playing—enjoying all the festivities. The welcome sign with pink and blue balloons at the top showed games, face painting, bounce house, and popcorn were to the left and pony rides, photo booth, prizes, and cotton candy to the right. Directly, in front of them was the registration table.

"Hi, I'm Sahara Kyle," she said as she tugged at her peach and gray flowered sundress.

The woman behind the table looked like a carnival worker. She had on a pink and blue striped vest over a white t-shirt with a pink bowtie. A straw hat with a pink and blue band completed the look.

"Hello! I'm Yancey Vinson. Welcome to our Belles & Beaus Carnival!" she said after she checked Sahara's name off the list in front of her. "Here are you admission passes and tickets. We have games, pony rides, face painting, and a lot of other attractions. There are signs that can direct you to where you need to go." She turned and pointed to the big pink and blue tent to her left. "The food, drinks, and picnic tables are under the big tent. The deejay is also there so if you have any special requests, let him know. Enjoy the carnival!"

Sahara thanked her and handed out the admission passes—really name tags on lanyards—to Noah, Clarissa, and Trevor. She looked at hers.

Sahara Kyle, Prospective Member.

Prospective member. She wasn't sure that was accurate, but she put the lanyard around her neck.

After Clarissa's party, Sahara decided to accept Tania's invitation to attend the Belles & Beaus picnic. Luckily, Teri and Zora were also coming. Teri was so excited that she called Sahara last night to talk about what they should wear and pointers for the day. Sahara had laughed and told her that she was acting like they were attending sorority rush. Although she still wasn't sure she wanted to be a member, it couldn't hurt to find out more about the chapter.

Sahara thought about the voice mail from her father. He only stated that it was him—no message, no "how are you" or even a "call me back." Sahara wasn't sure how she would feel about talking to him, but she never got the chance. She'd kept the line open for days, not wanting to risk him getting a busy signal or not hearing the call waiting click, but he'd never called back. And, she knew better than to phone him. These black elite social clubs and organizations were a mainstay in her father's world—and, she wasn't sure that it was big enough for both of them.

"Noah, come get in on this game! We're heading to the basketball court," said Milton, Kia's husband, bouncing a basketball with a group of guys. Noah already knew a lot of the Belles & Beaus fathers because they all participated in a youth mentoring program together.

Noah turned to Sahara. "Can you manage the kids on your own?"

Sahara smirked. He looked like a kid asking if he could go out and play. "I think I'll be able to manage. Have a good time."

Noah jogged over to the other guys, and Sahara stared at the direction sign trying to figure out what to do. She looked at Clarissa in her pink and green short set and Trevor with his orange and white checkered shirt and khaki shorts. Maybe they should get their pictures taken at the photo booth first.

"Sahara, I thought that was you. I didn't expect to see you here." One of Sahara's Sugarberry Grove neighbors, Crystal White, walked up with her husband and son. "Do you know my husband...Dr. Henry White?"

Sahara shook his hand, "Yes, I believe that we've met. It's nice to see you again, Dr. White." She glanced at the Prospective Member lanyard around Crystal's neck before turning her attention to Crystal's little boy whose eyes were fixated on Trevor. The last time that they had seen Crystal and her son was at Tissues and Mimosas, where he stuffed a blueberry muffin into Trevor's face. Sahara tried to discreetly move Trevor behind her.

"Well, we are on our way to the photo booth. Where are you guys headed?" asked Crystal.

"We're going to the face painter," said Sahara quickly.

Sahara and Crystal said goodbye and went their separate ways. As Sahara and her children came around the bend, she could see the long line for the face painter. She smiled at the mothers and children they passed on their way to the back of the line. Hanging out with Tania and Kia, Sahara had met a few of the mothers in the chapter. She also attended last year's Black Santa Brunch and remembered a couple of faces from there.

Suddenly, Sahara stopped. Emery and her daughter were at the end of the line. She looked at Clarissa and Trevor. Maybe they should do another activity.

"Sahara! Over here!" Too late. Her friend, Kia, was in the line in front of Emery and had spotted them.

Sahara forced her lips to smile and walked over with the Clarissa and Trevor. "Hi, Kia!" Should she say hello to Emery? Maybe she could act like she didn't see her.

Kia hugged Sahara. "Sahara, this is Emery Edmonds and her daughter, Riley. Emery, this is Sahara Kyle, and her children, Trevor and Clarissa."

Emery dressed in a red sleeveless blouse and white jeans with aviator sunglasses on her head smiled. "Sahara and I know each other." Emery leaned in and gave Sahara two quick pats on the back before standing upright again. "We always bump into each other when we're out. You know, Fairchester is too small to keep a secret for long." Emery smiled but the contempt in her eyes told another story.

"That's the truth," said Kia before she and Emery went back to the discussion they were having before Sahara arrived.

Sahara just stood there with a fake smile plastered on her face, while Kia and Emery talked. Sahara would nod and laugh on cue but was sidelined for most of conversation as they mentioned people she didn't know and events she didn't attend. Every now and then, Sahara would see a twinkle of amusement in Emery's eyes.

Finally, Kia was at the front of the line. While Kia's daughters, Daryn and Beckett, got their faces painted, Emery stared straight ahead. When the girls were finished, Kia waved goodbye and Sahara and Emery waved back.

With Kia gone, Emery didn't feel the need to keep up any pretense. She and her daughter walked up to the face painter without saying another word. Whatever.

While they were waiting for their turn, Clarissa and Trevor studied their choices intently. Superhero or Tiger? Fairy or Zebra? After the face painter finished, Sahara took her Spider Man and Frozen's Elsa to ride the ponies.

On their way, they stopped at the snack stand. Sahara and Clarissa were laughing at Trevor devour his cotton candy, when Sahara saw Zora and her family standing in the middle of the path. They looked like they were trying to figure out which way to go.

"Are you guys headed to the pony rides? That's where we are going." Sahara said when they reached the Montgomerys.

"It's so good to see you!" Zora hugged Sahara liked they hadn't seen each other in years.

Sahara had been friends with Zora long enough to know that Zora got nervous in social situations—especially black ones. Sahara didn't understand it because Zora's parents socialized in these circles. Her aunt was the president of the Fairchester Sphinx chapter, and her father was a member of The Coalition.

"We'll head over there too," said Zora. Cass and Darius, who was in his stroller, looked like they literally were along for the ride.

The line to ride the ponies was longer than the face

painting line, but at least Sahara was with Zora, rather than Emery. As they were talking, a Belles & Beaus mom, dressed like the ladies at the registration table, walked up to them.

"Zora? Zora Wilkins? Is that you?"

Zora looked over at Cass, who gave her a reassuring nod. She smiled and said, "Hi, Violet. Yes, it's me."

"I haven't seen you in forever!" Violet leaned in and gave Zora a hug.

Zora returned her embrace, but she looked stiff and awkward. "This is my husband, Cass, and my son, Darius...and my friend, Sahara."

After shaking everyone's hands, Violet said. "I didn't know you were back in town. There are a few others that were in Belles & Beaus with us that are in the chapter now. Wait, there is Charlotte now. Charlotte!"

Violet waved over another Belles & Beaus mom. "Charlotte, look it's Zora!"

Charlotte looked at Sahara and then Zora, as if she wasn't sure which one of them she was supposed to remember. Violet put her hand on Zora's shoulder. "Charlotte, we are not that old! Remember Zora? She was in Belles & Beaus with us. Remember all of us were at the sleepover at Vivian Lemmon's house when her parents had that huge fight, and her mother stormed downstairs and started throwing the patio furniture in the swimming pool." There was still no look of recognition in Charlotte's eyes. "Remember, we all wanted to be like her sister, Nellie—"

The light bulb went on. "Zora! Oh my goodness! Now, I remember! How is your sister, Nellie?" said Charlotte.

Zora lowered her eyes and her voice. "Oh, she's fine. She lives in Greensboro."

Charlotte was grinning now. "I remember that all of us wanted to be just like her when we got older. We thought she was so sophisticated. Please tell her that I said hello," She looked at her watch. "I'm actually heading to the registration table for my shift, but it was great to see you again."

"Good to see you, too," Zora said softly.

"Zora, I know that you've mentioned that you were in Belles & Beaus. I guess it didn't register that you were in this chapter," said Sahara when Violet and Charlotte left.

"Yes, it was this chapter. But you know, like I said, I really wasn't involved. As you see, my sister, Nellie, was super active in the chapter. Daddy would say with her skin and those eyes, she was destined to be a star." Zora stared off in the distance.

"Well, guess who I met today."

"I don't know. Who?" asked Zora.

Sahara crossed her arms matter-of-factly. "Emery. Kia introduced me to her while we were standing in line for the face painter."

Zora burst out laughing. "Emery? Oh goodness. That

sounds interesting. How did that go?"

"Like you would expect two prospectives that don't like each other to behave in front of a member. We played the game and acted like things were cool between us."

Zora laughed. "I wonder if Kia bought it."

"Hey, I don't have any issues with Emery. She's the one that declared war on me."

"Hmmm, I don't know if that is what happened—"

"Step right up! Step right up! It's time to ride the ponies—but watch the horse pucky!" said the man wearing the cowboy hat. Some of the children laughed.

Sahara helped Clarissa on the pony and told her to hold on tight. Since Trevor was so young, the handlers let Sahara walk beside him on the pony. Zora did the same with Darius.

All the children squealed with delight as the ponies walked in a circle around the pole. Sahara looked at Zora, who was walking in front of her. What was she about to say before they were interrupted? Emery was definitely the one that had an issue with Sahara. If Sahara hadn't gotten the message at the Gamma Boat Ride, she definitely heard Emery loud and clear when they literally almost ran into each other at the park this summer. She may have everyone else fooled, but Sahara knew that whatever team Emery was on, she was on the other.

When the pony ride finished, Sahara took Clarissa

and Trevor to the hand washing station. She had just finished asking them if they wanted to get something to eat when she heard a voice behind her.

"Sahara, what are you doing here?" It was Vesta Brantley, Landy Cummings' daughter. She had on the same attire as the other Belles & Beaus mothers. By the look on her face, Vesta was surprised to see Sahara.

"Uh...uh...I was invited by Tania Hughes," Sahara stammered.

"Really?" asked Vesta. "I didn't know that you knew Tania."

Yes, we are in the same LUA chapter."

"Hmmmm."

Sahara didn't know how to take that. "Well, it looks like the girls are happy to see each other." Clarissa and Gwendolyn were laughing and talking in front of them.

Vesta smiled. "Well, it was nice to see you. Gwendolyn, let's go find your father, honey."

Sahara watched them walk away. Forget about her father. Between being forced to interact with Emery and the reception she just got from Vesta, the evidence was mounting that she was not prospective member material.

Sahara' looked down at her rumbling stomach. Whether she was going to seek membership or not, she needed to eat. She and the children walked back to main tent where the food was. It seemed like everyone had the same idea. The tent was jam packed with mothers and children.

There was so much food that they didn't know where to start. There were turkey legs, corn dogs, roasted corn, old fashioned onion rings, fried dill pickles, funnel cakes, caramel apples, and fried candy bars—all of the carnival favorites. Sahara and the children filled their plates and looked around for a place to sit. There were some seats next to a woman with a white shirt. She hurried Clarissa and Trevor along so they could grab them before anyone else got there.

"Are these seats taken?" asked Sahara.

The woman looked up and smiled. "No...no one is sitting here."

While Sahara was getting Clarissa and Trevor situated across from the woman's three boys, she noticed the straw hat with the pink and blue band in front of her. Great. She was a Belles & Beaus member. Sahara could take advantage of the opportunity to get to know someone else in the chapter.

"Hi, I'm Sahara Kyle."

"I'm Leslie Watts, and these are my sons—-Glenn, Gary, and Gavin."

Sahara looked at the three little boys that were dressed exactly alike. They looked like they were around two, four, and six. "They're cute. And, it's nice to meet you."

"Are you having a good time so far?"

"We are. I can't believe how much there is to do.

Clarissa and Trevor got their faces painted, rode the ponies, and played some of the games so far."

"Don't forget to take them over to the playground. That's a real circus!"

They both laughed and started talking about the challenge of raising children in Fairchester.

"Mommy, I'm tired of sitting here," said Leslie's oldest son. Sahara and Leslie got so wrapped up in their conversation that they didn't realize that the children had long finished eating and were just sitting and looking bored. They gobbled up the rest of their food and then walked the kids over to the playground.

Leslie was right. The playground was a madhouse. Everywhere Sahara looked children were running, swinging, climbing, and sliding. Some of the older boys were playing basketball, while the older girls strolled around the basketball court whispering and giggling amongst themselves. The scene looked exactly like the ones that she, Clarissa, and Trevor saw when they were at the park this summer—except all of these faces were brown.

"Hey, babe. Where were you?" Noah walked up to Sahara, a little sweatier than she would like, but she introduced him to Leslie, whose eyes widened. She probably couldn't believe that he looked so unkempt. "I'm starving. Have you eaten?" asked Noah.

Sahara grinned. "Yes, Noah. We've eaten, we've played games, rode the ponies—"

"I've been out there that long?" Noah glanced at his watch and then looked sheepishly back at Sahara. "Yea, I guess I have. Well, I'm going to get something to eat."

Sahara was about to say that they could come with him but stopped. She probably should continue talking to Leslie—at least for a little while longer. "Okay, we'll come get some funnel cakes in a minute."

Leslie and Sahara watched Noah walk to the tent and then continued to talk. After a while, Sahara felt her stomach rumble again. Maybe she had been doing too much talking and not enough eating earlier, because she was still hungry.

Trevor was running around with two of Leslie's sons, and Clarissa was playing hopscotch with a group of girls. Both of them looked like they were having the time of their lives. Since some of the Belles & Beaus mothers were chaperoning the children at the playground, Sahara told Leslie goodbye and returned to the main tent to get something to eat.

Noah wasn't the only father to take a break from playing basketball. The men swarmed like locust on the main tent just as Sahara got in line to make herself another small plate. As the line inched forward, someone bumped her from behind.

"I'm sorry. Pardon me."

The voice sounded familiar. Sahara turned around and said, "No problem." She was face-to-face with Reynard Edmonds, Emery's husband. "Hi, Reynard."

"Hi, Sahara. I didn't know that was you." Reynard barely looked up and didn't say anything else. He just continued to heap food on his plate.

Sahara was surprised that he didn't have more to say. Emery must have him on a short leash today. After fixing her plate, Sahara meandered through the tables to where Noah was sitting with Milton. As she ate her food, she could hear a group of mothers at a table behind her talking.

"I can't believe that she came. Who invited her again?"

"I don't know. Maybe Yancy."

"And, there he is walking around without a care in the world. Shameful."

"You know her husband left her...after he caught them together."

"I don't know her well. I thought that she was happy...at least she seemed like it."

"Well, he is fine. If I wasn't happily married...I would consider...." Then, they broke into a chorus of laughter.

"Well, you know that we can't have that drama in the chapter. There's no way that both of them can be in the chapter."

"I know. We CANNOT have that mess around our children and families."

"But, they both have so much to offer...."

"Well, there's no question in my mind, whom we should take. Look at all the work she has done in the community and money she has raised for the women's shelter and domestic violence."

Were they talking about...? Sahara leaned back so she could hear better.

"Right."

"Agreed."

"Agreed."

"Ssshhh! Here she comes now...."

Sahara nonchalantly craned her neck so that she could see who was coming. She was right. It was Emery.

Wow. Which part of the equation was Emery—the one being cheated on or the cheater? Knowing Reynard, it had to be the former. But, who was the other woman? Sahara looked around. It could be anyone. But, which woman were they saying they would take? Was it Emery or the other woman?

Sahara scanned the crowd, while she ate her macaroni and cheese, trying to figure out who the other woman could be. After a few minutes, Tania walked up and interrupted Sahara's analysis.

"Hey, Sahara! I thought that was you sitting over here. Where are the kids?" she asked.

"Clarissa and Trevor are on the playground. I was looking for you earlier."

"Come with me. I want to introduce you to a few of the mothers."

Sahara put her fork down and walked with Tania to the table behind her. She tried to hide her unease as she joined the ladies on whose conversation she had been eavesdropping.

"Rashida, Joy, Natalie, Sheree, and Lisa, I want you to meet Sahara."

"Hi, Sahara." They said in unison.

Natalie said, "You're friends with Teri, right?"

Sahara nodded her head. "Yes, I am."

Rashida asked, "Who is Teri?"

"You know, Teri. She's the secretary of the Black Chamber of Commerce, has the stylist business on the side," said Natalie.

"Ohhhh, Teri. I know her. Yea, she's a real worker."

Tania chimed in, "Sahara volunteers at the Urban League. She's the one that organized this year's art auction."

"Oh, I didn't go this year. But, that sounds nice," said Sheree.

Sahara felt like someone had let the winds out of her sails. "Yes, it was nice."

"Have you had an opportunity to meet some of the moms in the chapter?" asked Joy.

Sahara smiled. "Yes, I got a chance to talk to Leslie for a while. She's really nice."

The ladies exchanged awkward glances.

Tania stammered, "Leslie isn't a member of the chapter. She's a prospective."

More glances among the ladies.

Sahara shifted her feet. "Oh, I thought she was a

member," she mumbled.

"What made you think that?" asked Joy.

Sahara's eyes wandered over to the table where she had been sitting. The straw hat with the pink and blue band was still lying on the table. She thought the hat was Leslie's.

"Well...hmmm...I'm not sure...I guess I assumed...."

"You know what they say when you assume...," replied Joy sarcastically.

Sahara felt her face get warm. She still felt awkward as the conversation moved on and looked down at the admission pass around her neck. *Sahara Kyle, Prospective Member.* Like she initially thought, maybe she wasn't cut out for this. After a few minutes, she excused herself from the group.

"Sahara, wait!" Tania ran up behind her. She must have seen the look on Sahara's face. "Don't let Joy get to you. I love her, but she is kind of intense." Tania laughed. "But, she is one of the hardest working mothers in the chapter, and when she considers you family, she'll do anything for you."

Tania steered Sahara to a table near the deejay. "Here let me introduce you to my chapter president, Claudine Lockhart."

Sahara had a long discussion with Claudine, who attended the art auction and heard about Sahara's work in her LUA chapter. Claudine talked about how beneficial her membership in Belles & Beaus had been for her family and how her children loved it. Sahara also got a chance to talk to some other members of the chapter that were sitting at the table.

Everyone had such great things to say about the chapter and the organization. Great programming. A chance to network with other black families. Ability to help children in the community. Sisterhood. What really stood out to Sahara was the impact that everyone said that the organization had on their children.

"Who's ready for the Soul Train line?" shouted the deejay.

The first notes of Parliament's "Flashlight" came out the speakers, and people rushed to the dance floor. All the parents started moving and grooving like they were teenagers again.

The Roger Rabbit. The Humpty Dance. The Running Man. Everyone laughed as each couple delved deeper and deeper into their memory banks trying to dance better than the previous couple. Sahara and Noah did the Cabbage Patch down the line to Chris Brown's *Loyal*. A few couples later, Reynard and Emery did the Snake down the line. Sahara noticed Joy and Rashida exchange looks.

Then, some of the teenagers tried to get in on the fun. They came out on the dance floor with the Nae Nae, Whip, and the New Running Man and tried to prove they had the better dance moves. That started a whole new round of competition—old school versus new school. After pulling out the Wop, the parents declared themselves the winners.

The Welcome Back Carnival was winding down, and people started to leave. Sahara walked over to Noah, who was talking to some of the dads.

"Noah, are you ready to head out?"

He looked like he wasn't but said, "Sure. We can go." After saying goodbye, they headed to the playground to get the children. "Clarissa! Trevor! It's time to go!" yelled Noah.

After a few more calls, Trevor and Clarissa finally came running over to their parents. "Awww....is it time to go already?" asked Clarissa.

Noah laughed. "Already? We've been here for almost five hours."

"I don't want to go," added Trevor. Sahara and Noah looked at each other. Trevor was their flexible child that went along with the flow. For him to protest was unusual. Clarissa waved at a little girl with whom she had been playing that was also leaving.

"See. The carnival is pretty much over. Everyone is leaving," said Sahara.

Clarissa reluctantly took Sahara's hand, and Noah picked Trevor up and carried him. As the Kyles walked to the car, some of the other families that were walking up the hill back to the parking lot waved as they passed them.

"Bye, Sahara! It was nice meeting you."

"Bye, Clarissa!"

"Man, Noah, you know we overdid it with that basketball today. I'm going to pay for it tomorrow."

"Me, too!" replied Noah.

"Bye, Trevor!"

"Bye, Greg!"

Sahara looked up and saw Leslie walking behind them with her sons. She waved at Sahara so Sahara waved back. Leslie was nice. Sahara hoped that she got into the chapter, too.

"Mommy, this was the best day of my life!" said Clarissa.

"Really? The best day?" Sahara smiled. She was glad that Clarissa and Trevor had such a good time.

"Yes, the absolute best day! I can't wait for the next Belles & Beaus activity!"

Sahara looked down at the lanyard around her neck. She guessed that made it official. She was officially a prospective member of Belles & Beaus.

....

SIX

SAHARA: KNOW THE AREAS OF THE BOARD

*In checkers, if you know the board, you can strategize
and execute a systematic approach to your advantage.*

"Well, I don't think the issue is so black and white," said Glynda Clayton, the executive director of the Fairchester Urban League. "I think we should take a nuanced approach in the campaign and market to favorable demographics."

"Really?" said Mr. Johnson, the finance director. With his neck poked out and eyes bulging as he stared across the table at Glynda, Mr. Johnson looked like steam would come out of his ears at any moment. "I don't know how I could make it any clearer. We need to get these membership numbers up, or some of our corporate donors will walk. Plain and simple. We don't have the freedom to discriminate and tailor the marketing campaign to certain 'favorable socioeconomic demographics,' as you termed it." He sat back in his chair and swiveled it back and forth.

Glynda had asked Sahara if she would help with the Urban League's membership drive, after the success of the organization's art auction that Sahara coordinated. But, Sahara was having a hard time paying attention.

Although it was the beginning of October, the weather was unseasonably warm. They were meeting in Glynda's small, cramped office, and it felt like an oven. The fact that Glynda and Mr. Johnson were going back and forth like they were playing a tennis match didn't help.

Sahara looked at the picture of Glynda holding a big check from Game Masters Corp that was hanging on the wall. When Tania mentioned Sahara's work with the art auction at the Belles & Beaus picnic crossed Sahara's mind. What did Sheree say? "Well, that sounds nice." It wasn't what she said. It was the way she said it...like...whatever.

Clearly, Sahara had not won any points with that. But, they all seemed to be impressed with Emery's work—and Teri's. She just....Sahara realized that Glynda and Mr. Johnson were looking at her.

"What do you think, Sahara?" asked Glynda.

What were they talking about again? The membership drive. "You both have valid points. I really think we need to weigh our options and reconvene in a day or so," said Sahara.

Glynda raised one eyebrow but conceded. "Okay, let's mull everything over for a few days and make a decision then."

Whew. Sahara quickly gathered her things. Glynda

looked to her for marketing expertise, compliments of Ross School of Business. Unfortunately, what she got today was the Art of BS 101.

For whatever reason, it was hard for her to focus on this membership drive today, and she was supposed to meet Teri at the trendy boutique, The Price is Right, in Raleigh in an hour. She needed to get out of here anyway if she was going to be on time.

When she was at the Belles & Beaus picnic she noticed the designers—Duro Olowu, Versace, Tracy Reese, Marc Jacobs, b Michael, Prada—that many of the members wore. It reminded Sahara of the legions of fur coats that she saw during the winter months at her sorority meetings and the luncheons she attended. Meranda always said, "It is expensive to run in these circles. You have to show that money will not be an issue."

NAIL IT was an acronym that Meranda and her friend, Naomi, came up with when they were trying to get into these exclusive social clubs many years ago. A was for accessories—your car, your clothes, where you vacationed, the schools your children attended, et cetera.

Meranda had told her that accessories showed that you belonged and were well versed in the finer things of life. Sahara had traded in her Toyota Camry last year and bought the champagne Lexus, but she could see that wasn't going to be enough.

She looked at her reflection in the window. A gray cardigan over a blue shirt with black pants. No, the car was not going to be enough to make an impact. It was time to step up her clothing game.

NAIL IT had worked for Meranda. Maybe it could work for her, too. Sahara had thought about calling Meranda, but they hadn't talked in a while. Since Dara came to town, Meranda had been missing in action.

At first, Sahara thought that Dara was just visiting. However, that was a couple of months ago, and she was still here. Didn't she have to work? Sahara knew that she was an attorney for Kirk & Lesly, a prestigious law firm in Washington, D.C., but she had been visiting her parents for a long time. Noah mentioned that he saw Dara with Senator Barrett and Meranda at the NCU alumni meeting a few months ago and that Dara was acting strange. Later, Sahara had casually asked Meranda if everything was alright, but she clammed up. Maybe Dara was on some sort of sabbatical.

Sahara didn't ask anything else about the meeting. NCU was where Noah had met Emery. Just the thought of her, made a chill go up Sahara's spine.

But, she had to admit, like it or not, Emery certainly was NAILing IT. She was already in the Marigolds. From what she overheard at the Welcome Back Carnival, she would probably get into Belles & Beaus, too.

Parking was always horrible at Triangle Hills Shopping Center. Sahara kept circling to find a parking space, and when she did find one, it felt like it was a mile away from the boutique—uphill. When she finally reached The Price is Right, she saw Teri's black Maserati parked in the handicapped spot in front of the store entrance.

Sahara shook her head and laughed. That girl. With her stylist business on the side, Teri certainly had the accessories part down, but Sahara would have to give her some lessons on the other aspects of NAIL IT so that she could help her friend out.

When Sahara opened the door, the lavender scented air wafted gently over to her. She could hear the *click, click, click* of her shoes on the cold, white tile as she walked to the back of the boutique. Sahara sank into the plush purple loveseat next to her friend. Teri smiled and rolled her eyes at the cell phone that she was holding next to her ear.

"Thank you, Bruce, for being so patient. I will get those documents over to you as soon as the IT guy figures out what is going on with my computer. Thank you. Bye." Teri took the phone away from her ear and dropped it into her Chanel purse.

"Ma'am, here is your white zinfandel." The sales lady handed Teri a glass of wine and turned to Sahara. "Can I get you something?"

"I'll take a chardonnay," said Sahara.

"Now, that is not sweet enough for me. You know I love some moscato...." Teri closed her eyes and pursed her lips like she was reminiscing about the taste at that moment. "But, they didn't have any so this white zinfandel will have to do." Teri raised her eyebrows and took a sip of her consolation prize.

When the sales lady was out of earshot in the back, Sahara asked, "So, what's up with parking in the handicapped spot out front?"

Teri laughed and sat back on the couch. "Well, we all go through life with handicaps, don't we? Some are just more obvious than others." She took another sip of her wine and whispered. "It's my grandmother's pass. Ssshh! Don't tell."

The sales lady reemerged from behind the purple drapes hanging in the back of the store and handed Sahara her glass of chardonnay. Teri held her wine glass up in the air. "Let's toast. To us and our amazing friendship. And that when this is all over, we will be sisters— Belles & Beaus sisters to be exact."

"To us!" Sahara clinked her glass against Teri's.

"Okay...so don't get mad...but I found out the names of all the Belles & Beaus prospective members," said Teri.

"What? When? How?" asked Sahara.

"Well...." Teri was grinning so wide she looked like a Cheshire cat. "...when I was helping to clean up after the picnic, it was just lying there on the registration table." She looked around like she wanted to make sure that no one was listening. "So, I took a picture of the list with my phone."

Sahara's eyes opened wide. "You did what?" Sahara

scooted closer to Teri as she pulled her cell phone out. "I want to see."

Emery Edmonds. She would be listed first. *Raven Cole. Bethany Foster. Mia Johnson. Teri Katz. Sahara Kyle. Faith Lloyd. Zora Montgomery. Ronelle Richards. Eva Ross. Leslie Watts. Crystal White.*

"Fairchester is so small. I didn't realize that so many people were trying to get into the chapter," said Sahara.

"Don't worry about that." Teri's face became serious. "Let's talk about strategy." She rifled through the briefcase at her feet, pulled out some papers and a binder, and handed them to Sahara.

"What's this?" Sahara asked as she opened the binder. Inside were write-ups with headshots of different women.

Teri crossed her legs. "I'm calling it my Belles & Beaus profile book."

"Your Belles & Beaus profile book?"

"Yes, it has all of my research on the organization— and the chapter."

Sahara thumbed through the binder. "Who are these people?"

"Those are the biographies of the mothers in the chapter."

Sahara looked at the pages more closely. Yancey. Violet. Claudette. Joy. She turned the page. Staring back at her was a picture of Tania.

Name – Tania Hughes. Husband – Maxwell Hughes. Chil-

dren – 2; Pierre (10 yo) and Jennifer (6 yo). College-North Caro-
lina Union. Employment – Game Masters Corp

The page listed Tania's hobbies, other affiliations, even the name of her church. If nothing else, Teri was definitely thorough.

"See, whenever I talk to someone, I write down any new information that I learn." Teri pointed at one of the handwritten notes in the margin.

Sponsoring Sahara.

Sahara looked at the note next to it. "Wait. Are you having lunch with Tania?"

"Yes, next Thursday." Teri flipped to another section in the binder. "I write down phone calls or meetings that I have on this calendar."

Sahara's eyes opened wide. The calendar was filled with markings. *Lunch with Sara. Call Lynne. Coffee with Patrice. Call KiKi. Talk to Chandra at Black Chamber of Commerce meeting.* Apparently, Teri had been calling and meeting with members of Belles & Beaus since last month's picnic.

"Don't worry. You know that I didn't forget about my girl." Teri pulled another binder out of her briefcase and handed it to Sahara. "This one is for you."

Sahara took another sip of her wine and opened the new binder. It was identical to Teri's Belles & Beaus profile book, minus the handwritten notes.

"Thank you," said Sahara softly.

It wasn't that she didn't appreciate the information.

She did. But, really? Was all this necessary? Profiles. Phone calls. Meetings. What next...big sister gifts?

This reminded Sahara of when she wanted to pledge LUA as an undergraduate. Calling and meeting with the women who were in the chapter. Finding out their interests so that she could arrange "chance" meetings—all in an effort to communicate her desire to be part of their organization. To show that she was like them and worthy of being a soror, a sister.

But, they weren't undergraduates. Was she really expected to do this? "Well...uh...I wasn't planning to do all of this...actually any of it." Sahara pointed at the binder. "Meranda told me that when she and Naomi were trying to get in...." Even before she said the words, Sahara knew that she sounded outdated. "...they had this strategy called NAIL IT...it's like neighborhood, accessories...," Sahara pointed at the bags with their recently purchased goodies.

"Sahara, that may have worked for Mrs. Barrett thirty years ago...." Teri put her binder back in her briefcase. "But, today...." She picked up her wine glass and finished the last of its contents. "It's GAME ON."

....

The weight of Sahara's shopping bags made the walk to the car seem that much longer. But, at least she was walking downhill.

Game on. Game On. GAME ON.

That was Teri's strategy to get into Belles & Beaus. She had the profile book, her notes, and meetings already set up. Sahara had to admit, she was impressed. Teri's dedication and organization were truly something to be marveled. But, it seemed...so over the top.

And, Sahara had been overwhelmed when Meranda first told her about NAIL IT. Based on face value, NAIL IT had nothing on GAME ON.

Maybe she should talk to Meranda about it. Get her advice. Teri said that Meranda's strategy may have worked thirty years ago...first of all, it was only twenty years ago...but it was a successful strategy. Meranda was a member of almost all the exclusive black social clubs.

Yes. That is what she would do. Give Meranda a call later today.

Sahara was almost at the bottom of the hill. Her shopping bags must have known that she was getting close to the car because they were getting more difficult to manage with each step. She had to navigate the sidewalk like an obstacle course in order to avoid hitting someone with a La Perla or Jimmy Choo shopping bag. Even though it was the middle of the day, there were a lot of people milling around—talking, shopping, and eating.

And, apparently, Meranda was one of them.

Sahara spotted her Mercedes, with its LUA and Sphinx front license plate, parked in front of a jewelry store as she did another adjustment to her shopping bags to balance them. Maybe she wouldn't have to wait until later to talk to Meranda, after all. Maybe she could spare a few minutes and chat now.

Was Meranda in the store where her car was parked? Sahara tried to casually look through the shop's window while scurrying to her car. No Meranda.

Now, Sahara could see her own car. Thank goodness, she was almost there. Her arms felt like lead. The bags were getting too heavy.

Then, it happened. The Tods bag hit La Perla, which hit Tom Ford. Then, everything came crashing down, literally, in front of the café—two parking spaces down from Sahara's Lexus.

Sahara bent down to pick up her shopping bags. Once she got everything situated, she stood upright to finish her walk to the car. Facing the café window, she almost laughed at the sight of her reflection with all these bags.

A – Accessories.

Given all the shopping that she had been doing lately, she may have to keep these purchases hidden from Noah. Well, except for the La Perla. Noah would appreciate that one. Maybe she would surprise him with the little black negligee tonight.

As she turned to walk the last few steps to her car, a flash in the café's window caught Sahara's eye. There was Meranda. Sahara recognized her by her signature bun, even from the back.

But, it was Meranda's lunch date that caused the flash of light. The rock that was on her wedding finger was enormous. Even the rays of the sun could not resist dancing across the symbol of love and fidelity while blinding anyone that dared to look directly at it. Meranda was having lunch with Winnie Allymer.

Sahara stood outside the window with her arms filled with bags with the latest and greatest designer accessories. As she looked inside the café at her friend talking and laughing with a woman that had once called her a mistake not worthy of her time, Sahara felt like an imposter. And, at that moment, Winnie glanced in Sahara's direction and smirked.

....

Noah walked into the playroom. "Sahara, did you charge a bunch of stuff on the credit card at Tods?" He had been working in the office on their bills.

"Yes, I was there today," she said innocently. She had opted to leave the bags in her trunk until tomorrow, when she could put everything away without Noah seeing. Oh well. She guessed the jig was up.

Noah raised his eyebrows. "It couldn't have been today. It looks like the charges came through earlier in the month."

Oops. "I was there a couple of weeks ago, too. You know money is only good for one thing...paying the shopping bills." Sahara laughed. She had seen the inside of most of the upscale stores and exclusive boutiques between Fairchester and Raleigh since the Belles & Beaus picnic—and she had the receipts to prove it.

"You know I like nice things, too, but we've got to cut back on our spending," Noah said sternly.

This was a change. Of the two of them, Noah was the dresser--and the spender. Until recently, most of the expensive items in her closet were things he bought or persuaded her to get.

"Is everything okay, Noah? Are we okay? I mean...financially."

She stopped working not that long after Clarissa was born and not once had Noah tried to rein in her spending. She'd even wanted to go back to work when they first moved to North Carolina, but he threw a fit.

Noah rubbed his neck. "Yes, everything is okay. I just think we need to be a little more conservative with our spending. That's all."

"Okay." Starting tomorrow. Today's purchases were before the agreement.

Noah walked out of the room and Sahara went back to cleaning up the playroom. It seemed like for every toy that she put away on the shelf, Trevor, who was "helping" with Lamby, would take a different toy down. Consequently, the task was taking twice as long as it should have, and Sahara being distracted didn't help. She kept thinking about seeing Meranda with Winnie Allymer this afternoon.

Of course, they knew each other. They were in many of the same organizations and social clubs—except Winnie was in the Raleigh chapters and Meranda in the Fairchester ones. Their association was painfully clear the time that Meranda tried to introduce Sahara to Winnie at the Darlings luncheon. Sahara figured at the time that Winnie had not told Meranda about their connection—if for no other reason than self-preservation—but now she was not so sure.

She had assumed that Meranda was busy with what-ever was going on with Dara and that was why they hadn't connected lately. But, maybe Meranda had been avoiding her. She clearly had time to have lunch with Winnie.

And, then there was the phone call out of the blue a few months ago from her father. He never called back again. When Sahara finally got the courage to call the number back, the call went to the switchboard, not his direct line, so she just hung up. Maybe—

"Mommy! I need help with my family tree." Clarissa said as she ran into the playroom.

"I'm sorry, ladybug. What did you say?

"I need help with my family tree. We have to do it for homework."

Sahara had been tickled the first time Clarissa re-ceived homework in preschool, but now she got it con-sistently. Sahara guessed Teri was right. Things were not as they used to be—not even preschool.

"Well, let's take a look." Sahara and Clarissa sat down on the couch. Trevor seemed intrigued that the cleaning had stopped so he and Lamby joined them. Sahara pulled him onto her lap and looked at the paper that Clarissa was holding.

"Okay, you have a picture of Noah Kyle. Yes, he is the father." Clarissa giggled. Sahara knew that Clarissa didn't get the Maury Povich reference, but she couldn't resist.

"And, there's Pop Pop." Clarissa pointed at the picture of Noah's dad dressed in fishing gear from head to toe this summer.

Sahara smiled. Noah's dad was a simple but proud man. He didn't understand Noah's attraction to what he called "flashy clothes and cars," but he made sure that Noah stuck with some of the traditions they had when he was growing up. One was their annual camping trip. Sahara had asked what they talked about in the woods without any distractions since Pops was a man of few words. Noah had laughed and said, "Basically about all the things that I am doing wrong."

Sahara didn't know about that, but she did know that Noah looked forward to the trips. And, he always seemed a little gentler, more attentive after them. Pops insisted that when Trevor turned three that he would be old enough to join them on their Kyle Crew Camping Trip, as he called it. Sahara knew that Trevor would enjoy being an official member of the club with all the privileges.

"And, there's Grandma." Only one grandmother was okay with being called "Grandma," and that woman had not given birth to Sahara. "There's you. Now, here is where the questions come in." Clarissa's face got serious.

Sahara looked at the picture that Clarissa had of Sahara's mother. Her mother had on a black and white silk blouse with pearls and was seated in a robin egg's blue chair. It looked like a formal portrait taken in a high-end venue for that express purpose, but Sahara knew that wasn't true. The photo had been on a regular Saturday afternoon at her mother's house.

"Okay, so Nona's name is Janice Robinson. But, I thought that your last name before you and Daddy got married was Allymer. Shouldn't you have the same last name?" Clarissa looked up at her mother.

"Well...sometimes...parents...." Sahara was trying to figure out what to say, but Clarissa wasn't finished.

"And, you don't have any pictures of your daddy. I asked Daddy to help me, but even he couldn't find one. Not even when you were a baby. Connor Hawkins said that his dad's father died when his dad was a baby in a war, but even he has a picture of his grandfather. " Clarissa stared at Sahara. She was waiting for an answer.

"Well...um...my father...." Sahara's mind was racing, but she didn't know why. She had told the sanitized version of her paternal background a million times, even Noah only knew this version. Why was she having a hard time telling it now?

Sahara looked at Clarissa, sweet and innocent...and so trusting. Sahara and Noah worked hard to support their children—financially, physically, and emotionally. Sahara wanted to protect them as long as she could from the hurt the world inflicts on people. She knew all too well that sometimes those weapons come in the form of friends, and even family. She looked at Clarissa's family tree and sighed.

"My father and mother were engaged to be married when my father found out that the army was sending him to another country to help prevent a war. He'd already left when my mother found out that I was in her stomach. Unfortunately, like Connor's grandfather, my father was killed while he was over there. But, since he was killed before he knew about me or before he and my mother were married, there are no pictures of us together."

"Mommy, that's sad." Clarissa hugged her mother. Picking up on the emotions of the situation, Trevor also shoved Lamby into Sahara's face as if the white sheep would comfort her.

Sahara smiled weakly at her children. Unbeknownst to them, Clarissa and Trevor had just become pawns in a game of deception that had been going on for decades.

As Sahara looked at Lamby lying in her arms, she

saw a black smudge from her mascara on it. She attempted to clean it off, but instead the black smear spread and clung to the white wool. There was no way that she would be able to get rid of that stain.

SEVEN

....

EMERY: GET THE KING CASTLED TO SAFETY

In chess, move your prized piece, the King, to a safer place while positioning your Rook to be more active.

The light was not her friend. Emery sat in her Jaguar with her head on the steering wheel and her eyes squeezed shut. She'd been up for most of the night with a cluster migraine, and her head was killing her. But, she had to go for it.

Emery groped around the passenger seat for her Tory Burch handbag without opening her eyes. Water bottle. Note pad. Purse. She felt blindly inside for the little bottle that she prayed would provide some relief.

Peeking through one eye, she confirmed she had her migraine medication, opened the bottle, and slowly brought her cupped hand to her mouth. Every movement she made seemed to intensify the stabbing pain in her head and neck. After gulping down the tablets with water, she resumed the position. Head down. Eyes shut. Breathe.

She knew that she should be at home with the curtains closed and a blanket thrown over her head instead of sitting in her car in the parking lot of Honeycutt Park. She peeked at the clock in her car. 7:42 *am*. She was supposed to meet Fallon for the Sphinx Mental Health Awareness Walk downtown, but she had to pull over to get herself together first.

Her head felt like she was slamming it into a brick wall, but she couldn't back out of meeting with Fallon. With the Belles & Beaus membership process heating up, she needed the face time. More importantly, she needed to be seen with Fallon publicly in order to send a message.

Come on, medicine. Kick in. Kick in. Finally, the throbbing in her head subsided a little.

Emery sat up slowly and opened her eyes. The pain was like a tiger sitting in the trees patiently waiting to pounce on its prey—but for now it was subdued. Emery popped two more tablets in her mouth and took a swig of water. She needed to make sure that her migraine was tamed for at least a few hours.

As she reached for the key to start the car, Emery saw the windows fogging up in the black car a few spaces down from her. The car had been the only one in the parking lot when she pulled in, but she had been in so much pain that she hadn't really paid attention to it. She was too busy trying to get to her medication.

While backing her Jaguar out of its space, Emery noticed two heads pop up in the parked car. One head immediately dropped back down but not before Emery realized that it was two guys in there. She chuckled and shook her head. 7:53 *am*. Too early to be doing who knows what in a car in the park, but too late to get her to registration by eight o'clock to meet Fallon.

Shit. She did not want to be late. She should've parked at the event site instead of stopping at the park. On second thought, she made the right decision. That's all she needed was for someone to see her with her head on the steering wheel or popping a bunch of pills. No, late or not, it was better that she pulled herself together away from wagging tongues.

It only took two minutes for Emery to spot signs for the Walk, but it took ten minutes to find a parking space. As she jogged towards the registration table, she looked at the time on her Fitbit. 8:09 *am*. Emery could see Fallon in the distance.

"Sorry that I'm late," said Emery when she reached the registration area.

"No problem. Go ahead and check in. I'm going to sit down and rest a bit."

Emery walked over to the registration table. There were a lot of people milling around, waiting for the race to start, and the crowd was pretty diverse. This was only the Sphinx chapter's third year sponsoring the Walk, but they had a great turnout. These types of things always attracted the die-hard organization supporters and members of the Fairchester elite social circle. But, since the course was certified, Emery also recognized some of the runners from other races in which she'd participated. Maybe she should look into organizing a 5K to benefit the women's shelter.

"Hello! Ready to pick up your registration packet?"

Emery had been so busy looking around that she didn't realize that the line had disappeared and she was next. She turned and saw Meranda Barrett wearing a white Oxford shirt under a green embroidered Sphinx sweater with pearls seated behind the table. A green mental health awareness ribbon was pinned to her sweater.

Emery stepped forward and smiled. "Good morning, Mrs. Barrett. It looks like you have a wonderful turnout for the Walk today."

"Yes, we do! You know October in North Carolina is perfect—not too hot and not too cool. With the leaves changing colors, it's a great day for the Walk." Meranda paused. "Remind me of your name again, dear?"

"Emery...Emery Edmonds," she said with a nice, big smile on her face and her voice dripping with honey.

"Yes, of course...Emery Edmonds." Meranda returned Emery's smile with one of her own and then looked through the registration packets on the table. "Here it is." Meranda handed the packet to Emery. "Enjoy the race, and thank you for supporting The Sphinx."

"It's my pleasure." Emery turned on her heels and walked back towards Fallon. She never knew how to read Meranda Barrett. Being the wife of North Carolina

Senator Tyrone Barrett, she was in most of the black elite social clubs, so Emery always saw Meranda at galas and luncheons. And, Senator Barrett had ties to NCU so they were at VIP events at homecoming, even though they were both Howard University grads.

But, Meranda was an LUA, not a Xi, so Emery didn't get the opportunity to interact with her from a sorority standpoint. Emery was in the Marigolds, but that was the only social club that Meranda was not a member. By no means did she expect for Meranda to hug and kiss her like they were BFFs, but she always seemed a little...aloof.

The Barretts lived in Sugarberry Grove, across the street from Noah and Sahara. Just the thought of Sahara made Emery roll her eyes. Had Sahara spread her lies to Mrs. Barrett? Emery couldn't believe that Mrs. Barrett would believe any gossip or foolishness that Sahara would bother saying. She was too old for that.

However, she didn't know Meranda—so it was possible. What she did know was that Meranda Barrett was a Sphinx, a Darling, a Gazelle, and a former member of the Fairchester Chapter of Belles & Beaus. There was no need in making an enemy of her.

"Why is your bib a different color than mine?" asked Fallon when Emery got back from the registration table.

Emery looked down at the white bib on her chest. Fallon's bib was gray. "That's weird. I didn't even notice. You are registered for the 5K, right?" Emery said while touching her toes to get a quick stretch in before the race started.

Fallon looked to the side. "I forgot to tell you. I registered for the one mile walk."

Emery was confused. One of the first things that she and Fallon bonded about was their love of running. Fallon could do a 5K in her sleep. Why would she register for the one mile walk?

She looked at Fallon. Of course. Why hadn't she seen it before? She needed to rest. The skin, the eyes...She had the pregnancy glow.

"Oh my, God! Are you...?" Emery lowered her voice. "Are you pregnant?" The way Fallon's face lit up and she started grinning from ear-to-ear, Emery didn't need to wait for an answer.

"We just started telling people, but I wanted you to be one of the first to know." Fallon chuckled. "I really have preggo brain. I wasn't thinking when I registered for the race. Of course, you would think that I was doing the 5K."

Emery hugged Fallon. "I'm so happy for you!"

It was like a sixth sense. Emery could always tell when someone was pregnant. She saw that glow in her mother, but each time the glow was gone after a night of hitting and screaming behind her parents' closed bedroom door.

For a long time, Emery felt like she had seen too much cruelty at the hands of people who were supposed to love you to want to bring a child into the world. She had been careless and irresponsible a couple of times when she was young and got pregnant. But, she had taken care of it.

Before she was young. Earlier this year, she was just stupid. She thought that Reynard had changed and was really trying to make sure that they were a family—a real one. Then, she found out about Kesha Ferguson and Leslie Watts.

If only Ernest Watts had put them all out of their misery and killed Reynard when he found him in bed with his wife after coming home early from a weekend fishing trip with his sons. The scandal would have been almost unbearable, but Emery would have survived and re-emerged stronger than ever, like a phoenix.

Unfortunately, Ernest Watts had simply cried like a baby while Reynard was inside his wife. He then packed his bags and left her and his three boys. Ernest Watts let Reynard take him from loving and caring father to deadbeat dad in fifteen minutes.

But, Reynard had to pay. If Ernest Watts didn't have the balls to do it, then it was up to her. She knew Reynard loved being a father, and she knew that she couldn't bring another child into their mess of a marriage. It was bad enough that their daughter, Riley, had to deal with it.

But, Riley had been conceived in love. That was the one time that Emery had been pregnant and knew that she had to keep the baby.

Emery forced herself to focus. The runners and the walkers for the 5K started a while ago. Now, they were waiting for the start of the one mile fun run. Fallon was talking about how she hadn't been running since finding out about the baby and had been nervous about registering for the one mile walk, even though her doctor said it was fine.

"On your mark. Get set. GO!" The gun went off and they were on their way.

After asking the standard questions, "Are you excited? How are you feeling? Are you going to find out the gender?" Emery's voice became serious. "So will you still be the Belles & Beaus cluster coordinator?"

"Yes, my pregnancy will not be an issue with that. Plus, that's the last thing that I would give up." Fallon leaned over and whispered, "Cluster Coordinator is the first step. I want to be the national president of Belles & Beaus one day."

Wow. Emery had not known that. Her friendship with Fallon could prove to be more beneficial than she imagined.

Fallon continued, "But, that's down the road." She linked arms with Emery. "What I can't wait for right now...is for you to get into Belles & Beaus! We'll have so much fun. We can go to clusters and conferences together. This little one...." Fallon looked down at her stomach. "...has pretty much guaranteed that I will be in

Belles & Beaus forever!"

Emery couldn't wait for that either. "That will be great—if I get in. The competition is pretty stiff. There were a lot of prospectives at the Welcome Back Carnival."

"I heard. Do you know any of them? "

"A few."

First, there was that slut, Leslie. When Emery saw Leslie at the picnic, she'd almost fainted. She couldn't believe that Leslie had the nerve to show her face, let alone attend an event that was focused on families. For goodness sake, she was a home wrecker—and that included her own. There was no way they were going to take her. And, she was not even going to bother mentioning her name to Fallon. This little small-time Fairchester mess wasn't even worth Fallon's time.

Emery continued, "There's Mia Johnson. She's a KNuSig"

"Yes, but she has been interested for a while, and both her children are in high school. I think if she was going to get an invitation she would have received it by now."

"I didn't know that this wasn't her first time seeking membership." Emery moved on. "Eva Ross."

Fallon rolled her eyes. "Don't worry about her. It's really her husband that wants her in all these groups. I heard she goes through the motions for a while to appease him and then will inform the group that she has decided that this isn't the best time for her to seek membership."

"Ronelle Richards."

"Too much drama. She's had one too many clashes with people in the chapter."

"Sahara Kyle."

"Sahara Kyle?" Fallon's forehead crinkled. "Sahara Kyle?" Emery hoped the next words that came out meant Sahara's chances were doomed. "I don't think I know her."

That may actually be a fate worse than the others. Emery accidentally let out a small grin.

"I'm sure you know everyone in the chapter, but who is sponsoring you?" asked Fallon.

"Violet Lowe." She and Emery worked at BioPharm, but they weren't particularly close. Paula said that she thought Violet was trying to increase her standing in the chapter or wanted Emery to help her become a Marigold. Well, whatever the reason, despite all the people that Emery knew in the chapter, Violet had been the only one to offer to sponsor her.

"I don't really know her since she isn't a chapter president or an officer. It may be better if your sponsor had a higher profile."

"I think it will be okay. Violet seems to be well liked in the chapter, and she's a legacy."

"Well, that's a plus." Fallon paused. "I don't think you have anything to worry about, Emery. You'll see. Anyway, I got your back." Fallon winked at her.

Emery hoped so. No matter what, she had to keep her eyes on the prize.

As they passed the houses along the route, people rang bells and played music to cheer the walkers on and to show their support for the cause. At one house, there was a huge green sign hanging over the porch that read, "*Mental Health Awareness - Do you know the signs?*" The lawn was filled with green lawn signs shaped like ribbons, and there was a symptom on each ribbon. *Withdrawal. Suspiciousness of others. Dramatic sleep changes. Loss of appetite. Feeling disconnected.* The signs covered the entire lawn.

Emery thought about the women and children at the shelter. After years of abuse, many of the women suffered from depression. The children, who often witnessed the abuse even if they weren't the recipients, were also scarred. Emery was glad that there were skilled professionals that worked and volunteered their time at the shelter to help them.

"Mommy! Come get some water!" Riley in her purple and gold "*My father is Gamma Man*" t-shirt yelled from behind the Gamma water station at the halfway point. Emery and Fallon walked over and grabbed cups.

"Thank you, sweet pea! Are you having a good time?" Emery asked her daughter.

"Yes, I am. Hi, Ms. Fallon." Riley smiled showing her two missing front teeth.

Reynard walked over to them. "Babe, your pace is off. I expected to see you a lot sooner."

"Well, that's because of me...." Fallon patted her stomach. "...and the bun. Emery was sweet enough to abandon the 5K and walk the one-mile with me. Squad goals." Fallon laughed and extended her hand. "By the way, I'm Fallon Allymer-Tate. You must be Emery's husband, Reynard. I've heard a lot about you."

Emery raised an eyebrow. Because of his antics, Emery never talked about Reynard. She didn't know if Fallon was just being polite, or she had heard something about him elsewhere.

"My mother always says that a father has the power to instill in his child a lifetime of lessons or a world of hurt." Fallon smiled at Riley handing out water to passing walkers. "It looks like you are teaching this one right. She's lucky to have you as a dad." Reynard grinned.

"Are you ready, Fallon?" asked Emery.

"I'm ready when you are."

"Bye, sweet pea. Be good." Emery leaned over the table and kissed her daughter on the forehead. "Bye, honey." She waved at her husband and then narrowed her eyes. "Be good."

"Always." Reynard answered.

Fallon said to Reynard, "It was nice meeting you. My husband is going to be jealous. He is a huge Tarheel fan. He knows all of your basketball stats."

Reynard's face lit up. "Yes, those were my glory days."

Emery rolled her eyes.

"So, how did you and Reynard meet?" Fallon asked as they walked away from the water station.

Emery stared straight ahead. "We met freshman year. He was on the basketball team...mad because he was riding the bench...and I was a marketing major at NCU on an academic scholarship. I was focused on my studies and my goal of becoming a CEO when I graduated." Emery threw her head back and laughed.

Some of her NCU girlfriends would go to Duke, UNC-Chapel Hill, and NC State hoping to catch the eye of a promising college athlete destined to go pro, but Emery didn't have time for that foolishness. Getting an education was the only way she could guarantee that she didn't return home. But, the one time her friends forced her to go with them, she met Reynard.

Reynard was on the basketball team, tall, and handsome, but her friends weren't impressed with him. He was sitting out with an injury, and no one knew if he would play again. Also, Reynard came from money. They felt like he didn't have enough "thug" in him.

"I thought he was nice—but not my type. At the time, I preferred dark-skinned guys. Like they say, 'the darker the berry, the sweeter the juice.' But, Reynard was persistent so we stayed in touch."

"One of my cousins was a big football star at Georgia

State. It was ridiculous how girls threw themselves at him," said Fallon.

"I'm sure. Reynard and I were just friends at first, but yes, there were definitely some girls hanging around, so to speak."

Fallon looked off in the distance. "There always are."

By the end of her senior year of college, the picture was different. Vivian was married to a football player from East Carolina University that played in the Canadian Football League after college. Christina got pregnant and had a baby with a basketball player at Duke that got drafted into the NBA. DeShaun transferred and was engaged to a football player from NC State that didn't go pro but received a high paying job thanks to a football booster.

Her crew—Vivian, Christina, and DeShaun—all of them were at NCU. Each was running from something back home. They had made a pact freshman year that they would make it big. Live large. Want for nothing. And, they were doing it—and none of them had finished college.

And, by that time, Emery and Noah were engaged, and Reynard was an NBA prospect. Now, all the girls were throwing themselves at him. With doubts about her relationship with Noah, Emery joined the crowd. At one point, the "other" lipstick on Reynard's collar had been hers.

She was in so much pain then, she had to numb it

with something. Emery closed her eyes and took a deep breath. She had to bury those memories.

"Yes, there always are," repeated Emery.

Before long, the finish line came into view and Emery could see people cheering the final walkers with whoops and yells along with bells and whistles. The competitive spirit in Emery couldn't resist running the final yards. She high-fived the hands of the cheerleaders as she crossed the finish line.

"Congratulations!" said an older woman in a bedazzled Sphinx shirt as she put a participant medal on Emery's neck.

"Thank you," said Emery.

She watched the steady stream of runners and walkers cross the finish line as she waited for her pregnant friend among the hoopla. She hadn't realized that she left Fallon so far behind. Emery walked back over to the Sphinx that was handing out the medals.

"Can I give my friend her medal when she crosses the finish line? She's pregnant, and it would be really special to her."

"Of course, honey. That's nice of you," the woman said handing Emery a medal.

Emery thanked her and took the medal. Fallon was almost to the finish line.

"Congratulations, my friend!" Emery said as she put the medal over Fallon's head when she finished the race.

"Thank you, Emery! I was wondering why you ran

ahead. You are so sweet." Fallon hugged her. "I'm glad we did this together."

Out of nowhere came an awful shrieking sound from one of the speakers, and everyone covered their ears. "Hello. Hello. Testing, one, two, testing." More feedback from the speakers.

"Looks like they are going to say a few words," said Fallon. "Let's head over."

Emery and Fallon walked to the stage area where people had congregated. Emery waved to one of the Marigolds that was in the crowd. The other organizations were also represented. XTD. LUA. KNuSig. Marigolds. Darlings. Gazelles.

But, without a doubt, there were women with Sphinx t-shirts, hats, and water bottles everywhere. There was no way that all these women were in the Fairchester chapter. Sphinx from Raleigh, Durham, and other cities had to be here supporting the event.

A woman in a Sphinx jacket stepped on the stage. It was Marigold Ida. She was a member of Emery's Marigold chapter, and she was president of The Sphinx.

"Good morning, everyone! I am Ida Wilkins Marsh, president of the Fairchester Chapter of The Sphinx, Incorporated. I want to thank you for coming out and supporting our Third Annual Mental Health Awareness Run/Walk. It is because of your support and the support of our sponsors that we are not only able to promote awareness of mental health but also provide much needed support to programs that help those suffering from mental illness." The crowd clapped so Marigold Ida paused. "I would like for you to welcome our city manager, Mr. Jonathan Katz, as he gives greetings on behalf of the mayor."

Emery watched as Jonathan Katz walked up to the stage. She remembered all the excitement last year about the city hiring its first black city manager. She hadn't met him before, but his face looked familiar.

As the crowd applauded his arrival and he stood there soaking up the admiration before beginning his remarks, it came to her. She saw him at the Belles & Beaus Welcome Back Carnival. His wife must be a prospective.

She agreed with Fallon. She wasn't worried about the prospectives that she had mentioned. But, the city manager's wife was in the running. Getting an invitation could be a little more challenging than she first anticipated.

After Jonathan Katz left the stage, a tall white man walked up to the microphone. "Depression. Loneliness. Disturbed. Unhappy. Desperation. Problems. Worry. Shame. Stigma. These are the words that we associate with mental illness.

"But, with your help...Understanding. Illness. Recovery. Medication. Help. Hope. Acceptance. These can be the words that everyone focuses on when talking about mental health. Thank you for accepting mental illness as a disease. Thank you for watching for the signs and helping loved ones and friends seek help. Thank you for raising funds for an issue that is too often swept under the rug or hidden in the closet. Thank you for being here today. Thank you." Everyone clapped.

Marigold Ida returned to the microphone. "Thank you to Dr. Hopkins from the National Association on Mental Health." A couple of other Sphinx members came to the stage and presented awards to event sponsors and various teams.

"Mommy! Mommy!" Emery turned to see Riley and Reynard walking through the crowd.

Reynard kissed Emery on the cheek. "Some of the brothers are going out for lunch, but Riley doesn't want to go."

Riley looked up at Emery. "Mommy, I'm tired of being with the boys. I want to be with you and Ms. Fallon."

Emery laughed. "Okay, mini-me. You can go with me."

Reynard poked out his lip and put on his best sad face. "Okay, I will try to not take it personally. But, you will still be my date to the basketball game tonight." Reynard pinched Riley's nose.

"Okay, daddy. I promise that I will," said Riley.

Reynard leaned over and kissed her forehead. "Love you, peanut."

Riley giggled. "Love you, too."

When all the speakers were finished, Emery, Riley, and Fallon left the stage area and walked to the tables where vendors and mental health agencies were set up. Fallon excused herself for another bathroom break, so Emery quickly walked over to the NAMH table and looked at one of the brochures.

Depression is....

She picked one up and quickly stuck it in her pocket. She had to remember to call her brother when she was leaving—just to check on him. Emery moved to a table where they were selling Greek paraphernalia when she saw Fallon on her way back.

"These pregnant feet are tired. I think I'm going to head home," Fallon said when she reached the table.

They were walking away from the vendors when they walked right into Tania and Donna, with Sahara. Great. This wasn't the group that she was worried about seeing her with Fallon.

"Hi, Cluster Coordinator Fallon. Hi, Emery. CC Fallon, I want to introduce Sahara Kyle to you. She is one of our prospective members." said Tania.

Even though Donna and Tania were a couple of years older than her, Emery knew them from NCU. She couldn't remember a time that she had seen one without the other, even in college. However, Sahara was a new addition to the crew.

Fallon extended her hand and smiled. "What a coincidence! Emery and I were just talking about you during the walk."

Sahara's eyes opened wide, as she stammered, "It's nice meeting you."

Emery held back a smirk. Sahara seemed nervous. After making small talk for a few minutes, Fallon and Emery turned to go when someone yelled, "Donna, wait up!"

Everyone turned to see a fine specimen of a man jogging with flowers in his hand in their direction. Tall and bald...he kind of looked like Tyrese Gibson.

Emery blinked a few times. Were her eyes deceiving her? It couldn't be.

The guy ran up to Donna and kissed her on the lips, and Donna's face radiated love. "Alton, what are you doing here?"

"Can't a man surprise his girlfriend and take her out to lunch?" He handed the flowers to Donna. "These are for you, my lady."

Donna giggled and turned to Tania. "Is that why you've been stalling?" Tania answered with a laugh.

"How sweet!" Fallon exclaimed.

It was only then that Alton seemed to notice that other people were present. He turned and looked at Sahara, then Fallon. When his eyes focused on Emery, she thought that she saw a glimmer of something, but she wasn't sure what. Then he honed in on Riley, who was standing by her side, and his eyes opened wide.

Emery tried her best to hide the emotion that overcame her. But, she knew that she couldn't hide it for long. "Hi, Alton. Fallon, I have to go. I have an appointment." She leaned over and gave Fallon air kisses. "I'll give you a call later."

"Okay, I'll talk to you later." Fallon had a quizzical look on her face, but Emery didn't have time to explain. She had to get to the safety of her car.

"Bye, everybody!" Emery waved over her shoulder as she grabbed Riley's hand and high-tailed it out of there.

She tried to walk away leisurely, but she had to hurry up and get to the car. Her mind was racing. Put one foot in front of the other. Her head was pounding. If she had arrived at the race sooner, she would be parked closer.

"Riley, let's hurry. Mommy has to go to the bathroom." Emery was doing a quick trot now...trying not to jog. She could feel the tears welling up in her eyes. Finally, she saw her car at the other end of the block. Fuck it. "I'll race you!" she shouted to her daughter.

Emery broke into a full run. She could barely see through the tears in her eyes and almost tripped over a cat sleeping on the sidewalk. When she reached the car, she pulled her cell phone out of her pocket. She could hear Riley's little footsteps getting closer. She couldn't gather her thoughts...couldn't think straight. What was her brother's number? 945...no...845...she couldn't get her mind to focus. She pulled up the contacts as she pulled her keys out of her purse.

"Hey, Emery."

She heard her brother's voice as she fell into the car. Her head dropped to the steering wheel as she felt her heart in her throat, and the tears that she held back tumbled out.

"Jason! He's here! He's here!"

"What's wrong? Who's there?"

"Alton! He's back." Emery tried her best to stop the sobs that overcame her as she heard Riley open the car door, but she couldn't.

....

EIGHT

SAHARA: GRAB THE CORNERS

*In checkers, grabbing the corners positions
a regular piece to be crowned easily.*

"Daddy always says you got to have some skin in the game, but I didn't know that I needed that much," said Zora as she laughed. Since she was on the phone she couldn't see Sahara roll her eyes. "But, no, I haven't scheduled meetings with anyone. I didn't realize that we needed to do that."

Sahara quickly veered to the right to exit the parkway. She was meeting Vesta Brantley in Fairchester's swanky, European village-themed shopping center for dinner, and she was running late. "Are you going to the Thanksgiving service at St. Joseph's Episcopal Church later this month? It's open to prospectives," she asked.

Zora laughed again. "Isn't church open to everyone?"

"You know what I mean," snapped Sahara.

"I doubt it. Cass' mother prefers for us to go to church with her."

Sahara sighed. They were back to that again. She didn't understand Zora. When Teri approached them with the idea of trying to get into Belles & Beaus, Zora was all for it. Sahara had been the reluctant one.

Now, Zora was back to her old ways—spending all of her time with Cass' family. She hadn't been to any of the open Belles & Beaus events since the Welcome Back Carnival. And, from the sound of it, she hadn't been in contact with any of the members. Sahara wasn't sure what Zora's strategy was for getting an invitation to join Belles & Beaus.

As she pulled into an empty parking space right in front of the restaurant, Sahara couldn't believe her luck. "Alright, I'm parking. I'll give you a call later, and let you know how everything goes."

"Good luck! I'm sure you will do great." Zora sounded like Sahara was going to an audition. Well, in a way, maybe she was.

Sahara had been so busy talking to Zora that she forgot to check how she looked before getting out of the car. Using the restaurant's window as a mirror, she touched the pearl necklace around her neck and smoothed her hair bun. She was ready.

As Sahara opened the restaurant door, she looked at her watch. She was also five minutes late. Vesta was sitting on the couch in the waiting area when Sahara stepped into the restaurant. Vesta gave her a strained smile and then looked at her watch.

"Hi, Vesta—" Sahara leaned in to give her a hug but was met with Vesta's extended hand.

"Hi, Sahara. I love your outfit."

Wearing a black and white checkered sweater over a white button-down shirt with black pants, Sahara tried to go for nice without being too boring, trendy without being too flashy. Just the type of person Vesta would want in her Belles & Beaus chapter.

"Thank you. I'm sorry that I'm a few minutes late. Traffic was congested on Rand Road."

"Really? It was pretty clear when I drove up. I was starting to worry until I looked up and saw you checking yourself out in the window."

"I...uh...." Sahara stammered as the hostess walked up.

"Ladies, your table is ready."

"Thank you," said Vesta as she picked up her Prada handbag and followed the hostess.

Sahara took a deep breath and exhaled slowly. They were off to a great start.

After being seated and giving the waiter their orders, Vesta dispensed with small talk and got straight to the point. "So, what do you know about Belles & Beaus?"

Good. A question that she had anticipated. Sahara opened her mouth to answer, but before she could, she felt a tap on her shoulder.

"Hi, Sahara! We thought that was you. You remember, Alton," said her friend, Donna.

Sahara smiled. Donna was absolutely glowing. Anyone with eyes could see that she was in love. Sahara loved seeing her friend so happy—just not right now.

"Of course, I do. Hi, Alton. It's great to see you, again." Sahara turned and looked at Vesta. "Donna, Alton, this is....this is...."

What should she call Vesta? Should she introduce her as a Belles & Beaus member? When Sahara was trying to get on line in college, it was a huge no-no to let anyone outside the circle know that you were trying to pledge. She didn't want another strike against her for breaking protocol.

Should she introduce Vesta as a friend? That wasn't entirely true, and Vesta seemed like she didn't like for people to step out of their lanes. Maybe—

"Hello, I'm Vesta Brantley," she said before Sahara had figured out what to say.

Donna looked at Sahara funny before shaking Vesta's hand. "Nice to meet you. Well, we didn't mean to interrupt you ladies. I just wanted to say hello." Donna whispered to Sahara before leaving, "What's wrong? I'll give you a call later."

Sahara knew she had to explain. "Vesta, I know your name. I just didn't know the proper way to introduce you. When I was pledging in college, it wasn't proper to—"

"This isn't undergrad, and you aren't pledging a sorority." Vesta took a sip of her water.

Sahara felt her face turning red. "I just meant..."

But, Sahara was interrupted by the waiter bringing their food. They sat in silence while they ate.

Think of something. Think of something. "How's your lobster?" asked Sahara.

"It tastes wonderful. How's your steak?" replied Vesta.

"It's pretty good."

Back to silence. Sahara watched the shadow of the flame from the candle dance across the table as she tried to think of a way to get the conversation going again. Suddenly, Sahara felt someone standing over her. She turned expecting to see the waiter. Instead, she was looking at a black Chanel bag. It was Meranda.

"I thought that was you!" Meranda bent down, with the faint smell of alcohol on her breath, and gave Sahara air kisses on her cheek. "I was just telling Tyrone this morning that I've been so busy that I haven't talked to you. We have to get together...soon." Meranda squeezed Sahara's shoulder.

It was only then that she seemed to realize that Sahara was not sitting there alone. "Oh, hello." Meranda smiled at Vesta and then teetered away without waiting for an introduction.

"Well, you sure are the popular one," said Vesta.

"Not really. Meranda lives across the street from me."

"It sounds like you two are really good friends." Vesta's lips were pursed like she had eaten a lemon.

Sahara remembered how Meranda felt that Vesta's mother blackballed her from the Marigolds. By the looks of it, that feud didn't end with the mothers.

Sahara lied. "We know each other—but, we aren't that close."

"Mmmm," was all Vesta said.

They went back to eating in silence. Feeling guilty, Sahara quickly glanced over at Meranda, who was dining with someone that Sahara didn't know. It looked like the waitress was bringing her a glass of wine.

Sahara looked at her half eaten steak. She couldn't let the rest of the evening continue like this. "So, how long have you been in Belles & Beaus?"

"About five years," replied Vesta.

"Do your children enjoy it?"

"Yes, they do."

"What do they like about it?"

"Everything."

Sahara still wasn't getting anywhere, so they went back to eating in silence. After a couple of minutes, Vesta put her fork down. "Sahara, why do you want to be a member of Belles & Beaus?"

Okay, she was prepared for this part of the evening. "Vesta, I want to be a member of Belles & Beaus because I think the organization has a lot to offer my children and does a lot to help children in the community." Sahara smiled.

Vesta didn't. "Okay, now tell me why you really want to be in Belles & Beaus—not just your canned response."

Sahara opened her mouth to protest but closed it.

She blinked a few times as she sat up straight in her chair. "You know, Vesta. I think Clarissa starting pre-school was a wake-up call. There are only a few minori-ties at the school, and as you know, Gwendolyn and Clarissa are the only black children there. In talking to some of the neighbors with older children, the schools in the neighborhood have a little more diversity, but not much. I just want Clarissa and Trevor to grow up with other black children and get exposed to some amazing things. I think Belles & Beaus will do that. That's why I want to be a member."

Vesta smiled. "That's an honest answer. I appreciate that." She took a sip of her wine. "I know that a few of your friends are trying to get in, as well."

Sahara relaxed a little. "Yes, a couple of my friends are also trying to become members. I think it will be great for our children to share this experience."

"But, you can't guarantee that will happen."

"Yes...I mean...I know there is no guarantee that Teri, Zora, and I will get in this year...I mean next year...but I can hope!" Sahara laughed nervously and took a sip of water.

Vesta raised an eyebrow. "You know there is only one invitation being extended, right? The chapter is pretty much at capacity, and there is only one mother who is transitioning to alumnae status."

Sahara's water went down the wrong way. She start-ed coughing and couldn't stop.

Vesta sat forward in her chair. "Are you okay?" She turned around and looked for someone to help.

Sahara nodded her head yes, but her body was saying no. Her airways were screaming for more air. She started to wheeze.

Some of the other patrons in the restaurant glanced in her direction. Breathe, Sahara. Breathe. She closed her eyes and tried to relax. After what seemed like an eternity, Sahara was able to catch her breath. When she opened her eyes, the waiter was standing at her side. "Are you okay, ma'am?"

Sahara's hand shook as she took another sip of water. "Yes, I am." She was a little embarrassed at her uncontrollable coughing and tried to act like everything was normal.

"Vesta, did you say there will only be one invitation extended for membership?" Hearing herself say the words, Sahara wasn't completely sure if it was the water or the news that had caused the coughing.

Based on Vesta's expression, she wasn't sure either. "Yes, there is one invitation...excluding legacies. There are a couple legacies, including Zora, so they automatically get in. Aside from them, there will only be one invitation extended."

Sahara was having a hard time understanding. "Did you say that Zora automatically becomes a member?"

"Yes. Since she was a Belle growing up, a vote isn't required."

"But, I thought she stopped attending."

"Well, I don't know anything about that. I wasn't in the chapter. But, her parents must have retained the membership, because she is classified as a legacy."

Did Zora know that she didn't have to be voted on and was a shoo-in? Maybe that was why she was so detached lately about the membership process. She knew that she didn't have to worry.

"Look, I know that this year is an extremely competitive year. Don't get stressed out. If it doesn't happen this year, there's always the next membership intake."

But, who knows when that will happen? And, what if it's the same as this year with only one invitation being extended? The longer they went without an intake the greater the demand to get in the chapter would be.

Vesta continued, "But, I would make sure that you let members see the real you and know the reason you want to be a member. I know Emery Edmonds also is seeking membership. She knows a lot of people and has a reputation for working hard and raising a lot of money. And, she is a friend of the cluster coordinator...."

And, she is a Marigold. Don't forget about that. Sahara sank a little in her chair. If there was only one invitation to be extended, it would probably go to Emery.

The waiter came to the table. "Are you ready for the checks?"

Sahara looked up. "Yes, just one please. You can put it on this." Sahara handed her credit card to the waiter.

"You don't have to do that," said Vesta.

"No, thank you for coming. Are there any other tips you can give me?"

Vesta looked up at the ceiling for a second. "I'm sure this doesn't even need to be said, but I'll say it anyway. You don't have any skeletons in your closet, do you?"

"Skeletons?"

Vesta laughed. "I only asked because CC Fallon told a story during a membership workshop about a prospective member, who was leading a double life and was the mayor's mistress. The story was exposed. It was a big scandal, and so on and so forth. So don't have any skeletons—or huge ones at least—in your closet."

Sahara let out a high pitched laugh. "No skeletons over here."

Or, at least not any that CC Fallon would retell at a membership workshop. But, she didn't know who Sahara was. Sahara thought back to the glare that Winnie gave her through the window when she was having lunch with Meranda. Fallon didn't know who she was—but Winnie certainly did.

Sahara quickly signed the receipt that the waiter placed on the table, and she and Vesta said their goodbyes. The entire drive home, Sahara thought about the dinner with Vesta.

Only one prospective member would receive membership! Did Teri know that? She couldn't. She was the first one to really want to be a member of Belles &

Beaus—and she had the profile book. There was no way that she would have twisted Sahara's arm about trying to get in if she knew that there was only one slot. Who wanted to compete against her friends?

Should she drop out, and let Teri get the invitation? But, there was no guarantee that Teri would get it. And, Clarissa already loved Belles & Beaus. She was always asking when they were going to another Belles & Beaus event.

No, she had to at least try to get the invitation. Plus, if she or Teri got in, whoever received the invitation could help bring the other in during the next membership intake. And, Zora could help since she was automatically going to be a member. Without any effort.

Ugh. She forgot about Emery. Even Vesta seemed to indicate that Emery was pretty much a guarantee. If she was the one that got the invitation, Sahara would never become a member, even if Teri eventually got into the chapter. If Sahara wanted to get Clarissa and Trevor in Belles & Beaus, she had to get that invitation this year. There was no other way.

Sahara pulled into the garage and went inside the house. She was exhausted.

As soon as she got upstairs, Noah came out of nowhere. "Sahara, did you charge a bunch of stuff at..." He looked down at a piece of paper. "The Price is Right Boutique?"

When was she at The Price is Right? The day that

she met Teri at lunchtime—when she left the bags in the car. Lately, it seemed like Noah quizzed her about her spending every day.

"I did, but I'm tired. Can we discuss this later?" Sahara walked into the bedroom and put her purse on the dresser.

Noah looked at her. "I think we need to tighten the reins a bit on our spending. I thought that we were on the same page. Then, I get this credit card statement...." He waved the paper in his hand in the air.

Sahara kicked off her shoes and sat on the bed rubbing her feet. "I hear you, Noah. I bought the items at the boutique before we talked. Anyway, you are the one that wanted to get Clarissa and Trevor involved in Belles & Beaus. This is what it takes to socialize in these circles. A – Accessories."

"Is The Price is Right a children's boutique?"

"Well, no, but I can't go around looking like a pauper while I'm trying to get into the organization. That's not going to work." She yawned and lay down on the bed. "You know...it's like Meranda said, you have to show that you have the money to play in this sandbox...or something like that." She felt her eyelids getting heavy. "I just think—"

When Sahara woke up thirty minutes later, Noah was nowhere in sight, and she was still in her dress. She rolled over and felt something poking her. Her keys.

Sahara slowly got up from the bed. If she didn't put

the keys up now, she would be hunting all over the house for them in the morning when it was time to take Clarissa to school. She walked over to the dresser and opened her purse. The receipt from her dinner with Vesta was lying on top. Sahara opened her eyes wide and then rubbed them. Was that right?

She was still in a state of shock about the fact that only one invitation for membership in Belles & Beaus would be extended that she really hadn't looked at the bill. Two hundred eighteen dollars.

Money was only good for one thing...paying the bills. A couple more dinner meetings at that price and she wouldn't have to worry about getting an invitation. All bets would be off, and Noah would pull the plug on the whole thing.

....

NINE

SAHARA: REDIRECT THE ENEMY

*In checkers, sometimes it is necessary to redirect
the enemy so that you can penetrate its camp.*

It was only eight o'clock in the morning, but the kitchen was already humming like a well oiled machine. The smells of collard greens and homemade cranberry sauce cooking on the stove mingled with the rosemary and sage spiced turkey cooking to perfection in the oven. Cornbread dressing, baked macaroni and cheese, candied yams, and corn pudding lined the kitchen counters ready to make their dinner debut, while apple pie, peach cobbler, and sweet potato cake waited in the wings.

Noah walked into the kitchen and gave Sahara, who was cooking French toast and bacon, a quick kiss on the forehead before moving on to his mother, who was rolling dough for biscuits at the center island. He kissed her on the cheek and said, "It sure smells good in here. Today is going to be a great day!"

"Good morning, my darling," said Noah's mother as she touched the side of his face.

Noah put his arm around his mother. "Good morning, mom. I'm so glad that you and Pop were able to visit us for Thanksgiving. It's nice to wake up to you cooking breakfast for me. It's like old times."

Sahara rolled her eyes. Things had been tense between Noah and her. He still was nagging her about her spending, and she had been resisting. Sahara was on a mission to do whatever it took to get Clarissa and Trevor into Belles & Beaus.

Meranda told her that it was expensive to run in these circles, and she had to show that money was not an issue. It was like the saying "You have to spend money to make money." Well, she had to spend money to get into Belles & Beaus.

Unfortunately, their arguments about money now spilled over into other areas, and the fact that Noah had been working late all the time didn't help. If they weren't arguing, they were barely speaking to each other. You could cut the tension with a knife. However, Noah's parents were here for Thanksgiving and Sahara's mother would arrive later that day—so they had to be on best behavior.

After putting eggs, biscuits, and bacon on a plate for Noah, his mother asked, "What time does church start?"

"At noon," said Sahara, as she cut up the French toast on Clarissa and Trevor's plates.

"I thought the service started sooner, but it will be good to see Reverend Pinn again," said Noah's mother.

"We aren't going to our church today," said Noah before diving into his plate of food.

Noah's mother turned and looked at him. "We aren't? Where are we going?"

Here we go.

"The Belles & Beaus chapter is visiting St. Joseph Episcopal Church today so we are going there," said Noah in between bites.

"Belles & Beaus?"

"Yes, it is an organization for children."

"Oh!" Noah's mother turned to Sahara. "I didn't know my grandchildren were in organizations already! What do they do?"

Sahara shifted the weight on her feet. "Well...they're not. The mother holds the membership."

"So you're a member?"

"No....No, I'm not a member either."

Noah's mother looked up towards the ceiling. "Okay, so this is a children's organization but the children aren't members. The mothers hold the membership, but you aren't a member." She looked at Sahara. "Then, why are we going?"

"Well, I'm trying to become a member. It will be good for Clarissa and Trevor." Noah's mother raised an eyebrow.

Noah stopped stuffing his face for a minute and jumped in. "Remember Aunt Gloria was a member. I used to attend some of the activities with Donald when I visited them."

"Donald...Oh, okay." Noah's mother turned around and continued cleaning the frying pan without saying another word.

....

Sahara took one last look at herself in the mirror. She smoothed the tan and black Navajo print knit skirt that she had paired with the burgundy sweater and black statement necklace. Since it was cold today, the tan jacket and black suede boots were stylish but also would keep her warm. They would also make the transition from church to Thanksgiving dinner seamless. Yes, her mother would approve.

She picked up her purse and glanced at her watch as she walked down the hallway. They needed to leave now to get to the church on time.

Sahara poked her head into the playroom. "Let's go, kiddo. It's time for church." Trevor scrambled to his feet and grabbed his mother's hand. As they came down the stairs, Sahara caught the tail-end of Noah's conversation.

"I don't know what to do, Pop. It just seemed to come out of nowhere."

"Son, I wouldn't spend any time on trying to figure out why he is acting this way. You never know what issues people have that cause them to act the way that they do. Sometimes, it is just part of the game. You can only control what you say and do. But, I know that you have to be honest with Sahara."

What did Noah need to be honest with her about? Before she could ask, Clarissa ran up to her.

"Mommy! Look at my pretty dress. Grandma bought it for me!" Clarissa twirled around showing off the pretty yellow and white sundress that she was wearing.

"Oh, it's beautiful!" said Sahara. It would be perfect to wear to church...if it were the middle of summer. She couldn't let Clarissa wear that dress in front of the Belles & Beaus mothers today. "Let's get you a sweater and some tights...." Noah's mother looked up from her Bible at them. "...so you won't get cold in church." Noah's mother lowered her eyes and returned to reading her Bible.

After Sahara put a sweater and tights on Clarissa, she walked into the kitchen and checked the collard greens simmering on the stove one more time and covered the finished pies with foil. Her mother's flight from Washington D.C. arrived at three o'clock. Sahara offered to pick her up from the airport, but she insisted that she would reserve a car service. They wouldn't eat dinner until she arrived, but Sahara wanted to make sure that everything was pretty much done so that she could relax when they arrived home from church.

Now that everyone was accounted for, the men piled into one car and the ladies in the other. The weather had been perfect all week, but today fog clung to the sky making the day dreary and gray.

"Those are cute boots, Sahara. Are they new?" asked Noah's mother when they pulled out of the garage onto the street.

Sahara gave her mother-in-law a sideways glance. She hoped that Noah hadn't discussed her spending with his mother. "Thank you. No, I've had these for a while." And, by a while, she meant since last week.

"They're nice. They look expensive." Noah's mother looked out the window. "What time does your mother get in?"

"Her flight arrives at three, but then we have to wait for her to get from the airport to the house."

Noah's mother turned and looked at Sahara. "You aren't going to pick her up?"

"I offered, but she said that she would reserve a car service."

"Oh. Well, I know that Noah can't wait for Thanksgiving dinner so he can eat my baked macaroni and cheese and collard greens. He seems a lot thinner than the last time that I saw him."

Sahara gripped the steering wheel a little tighter, as Clarissa started singing from the back seat.

Father Abraham had many sons,
Many sons had Father Abraham,
I am one of them and so are you,
So, let's all praise the Lord. Right arm!

Noah's mother just looked out the window moving her head back and forth to the melody.

As they got closer to the church, you could definitely tell something big was going on at St. Joseph's. Cars lined the neighborhood streets up to the church from a quarter mile away.

"Mom, I can drop you off at the front so you don't have to walk," said Sahara.

"Don't worry about me. I'll be okay. We can walk with you," replied Noah's mother.

Sahara drove around the neighborhood looking for a parking space. Every luxury car—BMWs, Mercedes Benzes, Range Rovers, Maseratis, Porsches—that you could think of was parked along the curbs in front of the small houses in the declining neighborhood.

After seeing Noah, his dad, and Trevor walking towards the church, Sahara finally found a place to park. She got out of the car and put on her black fur jacket. As she helped Clarissa out the back seat, Sahara noticed how worn and frayed the gray peacoat that Noah's mother was wearing looked. She had to tell Noah to buy her a new one for Christmas.

Sahara, Noah's mother, and Clarissa joined the legions of fur coats making their way from their parked cars to the ivy covered, red brick church at the corner. There was even a limousine parked in the front of the church.

"Look, Mommy!" said Clarissa pointing at the stretch

limo. "There must be someone famous here. I want to meet them!"

"Yes, I guess there is a VIP here," said Sahara.

"What's a VIP?" asked Clarissa.

"VIP means very important person."

Noah's mother looked at Clarissa. "There's always a VIP at church, and that is Jesus." She gave Sahara a tight-lipped smile.

Sahara hurried Clarissa up the church steps. "Yes, we are here for church. Let's not worry about whose limo that is." The ladies joined Noah, his dad, and Trevor in the church lobby.

"Good morning! Welcome to St. Joseph," said the elderly gentleman holding the doors of the sanctuary open. "Are you here with the Belles & Beaus group?"

"Good morning," replied Noah. "Yes, we are."

Sahara stood on her toes to look over the greeter's shoulder. Since the service was about to start, the sanctuary was quieting down. People who were up talking were making their way to their seats. The older gentleman whispered something to the usher, and she whispered something back. Then, he whispered something again, and she walked away.

He turned to Noah. "It looks like the Belles & Beaus section is already full. The usher is going to ask the coordinator where she would like for the overflow to sit."

Noah nodded as they watched the usher traipse up the center aisle of the church to the front. She leaned over and spoke to a woman in a pink hat, who then got up and moved. The usher walked back to where the greeter and the Kyles were waiting.

"You're in luck. The chapter president's family is attending their home church today since it is their pastor's anniversary. They made room for her on the front pew so your family can sit on the second row." With a serious look on her face, she turned to lead the group to their pew in the sanctuary.

"Thank you," said Noah as he followed her up the center aisle.

Sahara, the children, and Noah's parents fell into line. As they walked up the aisle, Sahara waved at Teri and Kia. A few rows in front of them, she saw Emery, Reynard, and their daughter. She had to admit that Emery had on a fierce black and white hat. Sahara smiled at Tania and Vesta as she passed the pews where they were seated. Maybe sitting so far in the front was not the best thing.

"Mommy, go to bathroom," said Trevor.

Sahara leaned down. "Do you have to go right now?"

"Yes." Trevor replied looking up at Sahara.

She had seen that face before, and she certainly could not afford for him to have an accident right there in the middle of church. "Okay, let's go." She might as well take him now and get it out of the way.

She and Trevor dropped out of line and returned to the back of the church. Sahara asked the greeter where the restrooms were and tried to hurry Trevor along so that they wouldn't be too late for the start of the service. When they returned to the sanctuary, people were pulling out the hymns books on the back of the pews and getting a jumpstart on writing their checks for the offering. The service was about to begin.

As Sahara and Trevor proceeded down the church's center aisle for the second time, she felt self-conscious. She held her head down and tried to not make eye contact with anyone as she hurried to the row where her family was sitting. When Noah's father saw Sahara and Trevor coming, he slid to the left on the pew, creating a domino effect. Noah's mother slid down, then Noah, and then Clarissa. There was just enough room for Trevor and Sahara to slide into their seats as the musical prelude began.

Sahara stared straight ahead. There was something about the man in front of her that seemed familiar.

"Mommy, look." Clarissa said leaning over Trevor.

Sahara turned towards the back of the church. The clergy were standing in the back with their long liturgical robes and holding a large wooden cross. The congregation stood up.

As Sahara rose to her feet, she saw Claudine Lockhart, the Belles & Beaus chapter president, sitting in front of Noah. It was nice of her to let them sit in her pew. Sahara's eyes moved down the row, past the little girl to the woman beside her. It was Fallon. She was sitting right in front of Trevor and next to the older gentleman in front of Sahara on the front row.

Sahara's eyes moved to the back of the man's head. Sitting high above the top of the pew, you could tell that the man was tall. Although his hair was closely cut, you could easily make out the wavy texture that some still liked to call "good hair."

It couldn't be.

The clergy were proceeding down the center aisle with the cross leading the way.

Sahara grabbed the back of the pew. The man on the front row stood up and turned so Sahara could see his profile clearly. The fair complexion. The straight nose.

It was her father.

Sahara felt lightheaded. Her heart was pounding, and her hands felt sweaty. As the rest of the congregants said the Open Acclamation and then sang the next hymn, she didn't utter a word. She just looked from person-to-person, face-to-face trying to find something that would indicate that this was a dream. As the officiant prayed over the congregation, Sahara bowed her head and prayed that she would make it through the service.

The rest of the congregants sat down to listen to the reading of the scripture, but Sahara was still standing. She was frozen. Her body wouldn't move. Noah leaned forward and looked at her with raised eyebrows. Clarissa pulled on her sleeve. "Sit down, Mommy."

Her body, on autopilot, sat down. Fallon turned and looked over shoulder and smiled at Sahara. Sahara didn't acknowledge her. She continued to stare straight ahead at the back of her father's head.

Stand for the hymn. Sit for the sermon. The Creed. Prayers. Confession. Sahara just stared straight ahead and didn't say a word.

"Before we move on to part of the service where we greet our neighbors, there is a special guest with us today so I would like to invite him up to say a few words." The priest smiled down to the congregation and then extended his right hand. "Congressman Allymer, please join me."

Charles Allymer stood up and walked to the pulpit. Dressed in a black suit with a pink and blue tie, he turned to address the congregation.

"Giving all glory and honor to God, I would like to thank Reverend Charles Kirk for inviting me to say a few words. But, I am not here today as a Congressman representing the great state of North Carolina. No, today, I am here as a proud father." He smiled down at Fallon, who was sitting straight as a board in the pew. "My son-in-law is out of town on business so I am accompanying my only daughter, Fallon Allymer-Tate, who is the Cluster Coordinator for Belles & Beaus, today.

"Belles & Beaus is an organization that was founded in 1941 to develop children into leaders. My own daughter grew up in the organization as a child. Now, she is a leader in the organization helping to take Belles & Beaus to a higher level for my grandchildren, my granddaughter who is here today and the baby boy that will be born in a few months. Thank you to the parents that continue to strive to do what's right for our black children. Thank you to the apple of my eye, my dear Fallon, for inviting me here today. My wife is fond of saying that fathers have the power to instill in a child a lifetime of lessons or a world of hurt. I am blessed to be your father, Fallon, and you'll always be daddy's little girl."

The congregation clapped, and there were a few "awwws." Sahara thought that she was going to be sick.

When her father took his seat, Fallon leaned over and gave him a hug. After he kissed Fallon on the forehead, she looked over her shoulder. "Sahara? I thought that was you," Fallon whispered as she extended her hand. Sahara felt like a robot shaking her hand. "Is this your little boy? He is so cute! I'm having a boy. We're so excited." She was beaming. "Have you met my father?" She turned. "Daddy, there's someone that I want you to meet."

For so many years, Sahara had played this game of pretending that she didn't have a living, breathing father, pretending that his name was not Charles Allymer. However, this was a first—to play the game face-to-face with him. He didn't know her, and she didn't know him.

Fallon turned back to Sahara. "Daddy, this is Sahara...." Her face scrunched up. "I have pregnancy brain. What's your last name again?"

"Kyle. Sahara Kyle."

Fallon continued, "Yes, yes. Sahara Kyle. Daddy, I would like for you to meet Sahara Kyle."

Fallon's father—Sahara's father—turned around. Sahara looked at the silver low-cut hair, mustache, and beard. She always thought of him with salt and pepper hair, but it was definitely all silver now. Everyone said that she looked exactly like her mother, but she could see that she had her father's nose...and his jaw.

All the secret thoughts, tucked deep down inside, that he bragged about her to his friends, that he kept tabs on her from afar, that he wanted to know her—her likes and dislikes, her favorite color, her favorite movie—bubbled to the surface. She searched his face for a sign, any sign, that all these things were true.

Charles Allymer's eyes quickly danced over Clarissa and Trevor and settled on Sahara. He didn't flinch or hesitate as he extended his hand. "Hello, Sahara. It is nice to meet you."

There was no hint of recognition in his eyes. No small smile that secretly said that he was glad to see her. Instead, he simply shook her hand and turned back around to face the pulpit.

Sahara could feel the tears welling up in her eyes, but she quickly blinked them away. She wanted to get out of there as fast as she could, but she knew that she had to stay. For her to leave in the middle of the service would draw too many questions from the Belles & Beaus members, not to speak about Noah and his parents. Sahara did what she had been taught to do when it came to her father—not react. Continue to play the game.

As soon as the service came to a close and the final "amens" were said, Charles Allymer ushered Fallon out of the sanctuary and into the waiting limo. Sahara didn't know how much longer she could hold everything in so she said something to Noah about needing to finish dinner to speed him out of the church, as well. Thankfully, since it was Thanksgiving, the usual after church talking and fellowshipping was minimal. Everyone wanted to get back home to eat.

As they walked down the street, Sahara fought back her tears. Noah, his dad, and Trevor peeled away from the group to go to Noah's car. The ladies were at the end of the block. Four cars away. Three cars away. Two cars away.

"Look, Mommy! There's the limo! There's the limo!" shouted Clarissa.

Sahara turned in time to see the long black stretch limo drive slowly down the narrow street. Clarissa was jumping up and down and waving at the VIPs hidden behind the black tinted windows. The hypocrisy of the whole encounter overcame Sahara, and she vomited in the street.

"Mommy, are you okay?"

Sahara pulled a tissue out of her pocket and wiped her mouth. She gave Clarissa a small smile, while she fought back tears.

They drove back to the house in silence. As soon as they got inside, Sahara ran upstairs to the bathroom. She couldn't hide her disgust at the whole situation any longer. She was going to be sick again.

When she came out of the bathroom, Noah guided her to the bed. By this time, she was shaking. "What's wrong, Sahara?"

Her head was pounding. Her heart was racing. Sahara was afraid that if she opened her mouth the teeniest bit, everything would spill out—so she kept her mouth closed. She curled into a fetal position on the bed as tears rolled down her cheeks.

She was vaguely aware of people opening and closing the bedroom door as she drifted in and out of sleep. Noah. Then Clarissa. Noah's mother. Finally, Noah's father. At one point, Sahara opened her eyes, and Trevor lay in the bed beside her asleep. She opened her eyes again and Trevor was gone, but Lamby was her new companion.

As she lay in the dark room, Sahara pulled the white lamb into her arms. She tried to will herself out of the bed, but she couldn't. She could hear the clink of forks downstairs but no talking or laughter. She had ruined Thanksgiving, not just for Noah and his parents, but

Clarissa and Trevor, too.

There was a soft knock and then the door opened a little. The light from the hallway came flooding into the bedroom.

"Sahara?"

Used to the darkness, Sahara shielded her eyes from the bright lights. However, she didn't have to open her eyes to know who it was. It was her mother.

Was it after three o'clock already? Sahara hadn't realized that she had been in the room that long. What had Noah told her mother when she arrived? That she went crazy?

"Sahara, what's wrong?" Her mother sat on the bed and stroked her hair.

Sahara wanted to be strong. To prove that her father had no bearing on her life. To show that she could rise above. But, instead, she sat up and put her head on her mother's shoulder and cried like a baby. Her body heaved with each sob, and the tears flowed like a dam broke.

"He was there." Sahara finally said after crying for what seemed like an eternity. "At church."

"Who was at church?"

"My...my...my father." Sahara felt her mother's body tense.

"And, what happened? Did he say something to you? Did he hurt you?"

"No...yes...." Sahara knew that she wasn't making

sense. "He...he...he was there with Fallon. He went on and on about how she was the apple of his eye, and how he loved spending time with his grandchildren. And...and...and...the whole time we were sitting in the pew behind him, and he acted like he didn't know who I was. HIS OWN DAUGHTER! He didn't say anything to Clarissa or Trevor. He looked at us as if we were noth-ing. Nothing." Sahara broke down crying again.

"Oh, Sahara." Her mother's voice was shaking. She was crying, too. "I never meant for this to happen. You are still trapped in a web of lies that your father and I started long ago, and you've been forced to play this charade for far too long. You were the one that was in-nocent, yet you have suffered the most. I'm so sorry."

Sahara lifted her head and looked at her mother. "What should I do?"

"You have to live your life in your truth. You can't continue to live a lie with the people that you love." She put Sahara's face in her hands. "There's only one thing you can do. You have to tell Noah."

TEN

....

SAHARA: GAME OVER

K nock, knock.
"Come in," said Sahara as she turned off the television.

Noah poked his head in the door. "How are you feeling?"

"A little better." Sahara put another spoonful of chicken noodle soup in her mouth.

"You had me worried there for a minute." Noah sat down on the bed. "I've never seen you so sick, and it seemed to come out of nowhere. You seemed fine when we left for church this morning."

"I was fine when we left this morning...." Sahara didn't know how to even begin to unravel the web of deceit. "Please tell your mother that I said thank you for making the soup for me. It helped a lot."

Noah raised his eyebrows but played along. "You should tell her yourself. She'll appreciate hearing it from you a lot more than me." Sahara took another sip of the soup and then moved the tray to the nightstand.

"I know the soup must be good, but you missed a great Thanksgiving dinner. My mom really put her foot in that macaroni and cheese."

Sahara laughed. "I bet that was all that Trevor wanted to eat."

"You know it. That...and the cranberry sauce. You should have seen Clarissa. She was so proud to have made it."

"I know she was! She tried to eat some last night after it was finished. I had to tell her a million times that it needed to cool first."

"It was pretty good. You would have liked it." Noah rubbed her arm. "So, what's going on, Sahara? Your mother said that you wanted to talk to me."

She sighed. She knew that Noah loved her, and in return, she had lied to him—been lying to him—since she met him. What would he think? Would it drive a wedge between them? Could he forgive her?

"Sahara?"

She didn't realize that she was crying until Noah wiped away the tears that were flowing down her cheek. Okay, she just had to do this and pray her marriage was strong enough to withstand the truth.

"Noah, I'm not really sure how to say this...."

"Just spit it out. It can't be that bad...."

Spit it out. He wanted it straight, with no chaser. Sahara took a deep breath and exhaled. "Charles Allymer is my father."

Noah's eyes opened wide, and he scooted back on the bed further away from her. Sahara envisioned him spitting imaginary beer across the room, like a cartoon character. The thought almost made her smile. Almost.

"Congresssman Charles Allymer? The man that was at church this morning? He's your father?" he asked.

"Yes, Congressman Charles Allymer, the man that was at church this morning."

Noah stood up. He started rubbing his neck and pacing the room. After a few seconds, he stopped and turned back towards Sahara.

"I thought that your father was dead. That he died on some peacekeeping mission before he and your mother got married." He was staring at her waiting for an answer.

"No, that was a story that he and my mother came up with."

Noah paced the floor again. After a few seconds, he stopped and looked back at Sahara.

"But, I've been with you when people have asked if you were related to Charles Allymer because of your maiden name. You've always said no."

"I know, but I couldn't. I couldn't tell anyone. My mother has always insisted that I tell no one."

The veins in Noah's neck popped out. "But, Sahara...I'M YOUR HUSBAND!!! How do you let two years of dating and seven years of marriage go by and not say, 'Oh, you know how you thought my father was dead...he's not!' I mean the man wasn't even at our wedding! We've always said that the kids knowing their extended family was important to us. How do you not tell Clarissa and Trevor that that they have a grandfather an hour away?

"Do you remember how worried you were about who would give you away at the wedding? Why didn't you pick up the phone and call your father? Hell, we could've seen if he would help pay for the wedding!"

"I know, Noah. I know," said Sahara softly. She had never seen Noah so angry—but she knew that he was justified. She used the back of her hands to wipe away her tears.

Noah paced back and forth. "Okay. Okay. Okay."

She knew that he was trying to calm himself down. "Maybe it will help, if I start from the beginning."

Noah exhaled loudly like he was trying to relieve some of the tension. "Yes, I need to wrap my brain around this." He sat down again at the foot of the bed. "I'm listening."

Sahara took a deep breath. "My mother was young...and naïve. She said that she was hanging out with friends in a DC nightclub when she met him. At the time, he was on the Raleigh City Council. He was in DC for a month working on a task force to which he had been assigned. He told her that he was in town on business. She said that he swept her off her feet, and they spent every minute he wasn't working together. Before she could stop herself, she had fallen in love. "

"Was he married then?"

Sahara put her head down. "Yes, he was married. But, she didn't know that until she told him that she was pregnant...with me."

Noah shook his head. "Wow."

"He tried to get her to have an abortion, but she refused. When I was born, he didn't even want to come to the hospital. But, she insisted that I have his last name. She told him that he owed me that.

"He only agreed when she threatened to go to the tabloids—and on one condition. He made her swear to keep the fact that he was my father a secret. He had a cousin who was in the army and had been killed around that time on a peacekeeping mission in Lebanon. He came up with the story in case someone started snooping and tried to link us to him."

"Did you see him? Was he ever part of your life?"

Sahara thought back to all the school plays, games, graduations...even her wedding. None of those memories included her father. "He sent money. We were definitely provided for, as my mother likes to say." Sahara could feel the tears welling up in her eyes again. "But, no, he was never part of my life." The tears came streaming down. "When I was young, there were a few times that I saw him, but it was always at the dead of night and for a short time. He couldn't get caught with his illegitimate child."

Noah moved next to her on the bed and held her in his arms. "Sahara, I'm so sorry."

She was sobbing. "So many times I wanted to tell you, Noah. So many times...."

They sat there in silence. Noah with his arms around Sahara as she cried.

"We're going to be okay. We can get through this," Noah said after a while.

Sahara slowly breathed a sigh of relief. They were going to be okay. When she opened her eyes to look at Noah, she saw a shadow underneath the door. Someone had been eavesdropping.

....

ELEVEN

EMERY: PROMOTE THE PAWN

*In chess, when a pawn makes it to the other side of the board,
it can be promoted to another piece--most often the Queen.*

She was late. Emery had every intention of being at the airport early. She imagined herself standing by the Starbucks holding a "Welcome Home" sign—the first familiar person Jason saw when he deplaned. That would have made her brother's first trip back to North Carolina in five years special. But, after a night of hanging out with Rozlyn and drinking too much in the name of holiday fun, her body resisted moving at a time that would get her to RDU airport on time to pull that off.

She could hear the *clickety clack* of her heels as she walked quickly through the airport to the baggage claim carousels with the small, homemade sign in her hand. She meandered through the crowd, peeking over shoulders and looking past embraces trying to spot her brother. He was nowhere to be seen.

Emery checked her phone. Yes, she had read it correctly. Twenty minutes ago, her brother sent a text saying that his flight had landed, and he would wait for her at baggage claim. She looked at the time again. The Belles & Beaus Black Santa Brunch would start soon. They needed to head back to Fairchester.

Emery slowly turned in a circle and surveyed the room. Happy people. Grumpy people. People dressed in shorts. Luggage, luggage, and more luggage.

There he was—walking out of the airline office—dressed in a black hoodie and jeans. Two ladies that were waiting for their bags to come off the carousel nudged each other as he walked by. With his piercing black eyes, high cheekbones, and chiseled jaw, her brother always turned heads with his model good looks. Too bad for them, he was gay.

"Jason!" she shouted.

A huge grin spread on his face, as he waved at her. Emery started walking in his direction then broke into a run. Jason opened his arms and scooped her up.

"I missed you, sis." He said while he held her in a long embrace.

"I missed you, too, big brother," said Emery. When her brother put her down, she wiped away the tears that had fallen down her cheek.

"Alright, Jason. I'll be in touch," said a man dressed in a red and black flannel shirt, skinny jeans, and wedge sneakers rolling his luggage behind him. He gave Emery a quick look up and down as he passed her.

Was it? No, it couldn't be. It was one of the guys that had been making out in the car at Honeycutt Park the morning of the Sphinx Mental Health Walk. She only saw the other one for a second because he had quickly ducked down again. But, she got a good look at this guy's face.

Emery turned to her brother. "Is that you?"

Jason laughed. "Nooooo, I'm not Michael's type. He's good friends with a guy I know from high school. Plus, I've been out of the closet way too long. How should I say it?" He tilted his head up for a few seconds and then looked back at Emery. "He likes to help men that aren't aware that that they are gay come to that understanding, if you catch my drift. I believe he gets bonus points if the dude is married.

"But enough about Michael...what's on the agenda? Why did you tell me to wear something nice?"

Emery looked at her brother with raised eyebrows. "That's something nice?"

Jason looked down at his black hoodie and jeans and turned in a circle. "What? You don't like it?"

Emery laughed. Everything about this man, she loved—even the scar on his jaw. "We have to go to this Belles & Beaus thing...so I want you to come with us. Reynard and Riley are already there so we are going to head straight over."

"Belles & Beaus, huh? I see you are still trying to take over the world, one organization at a time," said Jason.

Emery laughed. "No, it's not like that. This is an organization for children. I think it will help Riley take over the world one day."

"I knew there was a taking over the world in there somewhere." They both laughed. "Let me change into my clothes...." Jason pointed at the small garment bag that he was carrying. "...and then we can head out. Let the games begin."

....

Emery turned the dial on the radio so the notes of Donny Hathaway singing *This Christmas* were barely audible and glanced at her brother. "So, how is everything going? You've been doing, okay?"

Jason stared out the window as they took the on-ramp to the freeway. "Yea...I have my good days and my bad days. Mainly good ones though." A small smile came to his lips. "Going to a therapist helps...a lot." He turned to Emery. "Thank you for convincing me to go."

"You know you black folks like to think that talking to someone other than your pastor about your issues is forbidden," said Emery as she pushed the pedal to the metal trying to make up time.

Jason laughed. "Ain't that the truth. But, I think that I have way too many issues to not consult a professional, no offense to the pastors." Suddenly, Jason's face became serious. "Alright, I'll be the first to address the elephant in the room...or car in this case. So, when are we going to see mom?"

Emery stared straight ahead. "Your choice. We can

rip the band-aid off and go after the Belles & Beaus brunch, or we can go tomorrow."

"And, The Major won't know I'm there, right?"

"He won't. If we go this evening, Mom will be at her best."

Jason went back to looking out the window. "Tonight it is"

Emery knew it was hard for her brother being back in North Carolina. She was just glad to have him near her. Glad that he would get a chance to see their mom. Her mother had been in the hospital so many times that the staff understood their situation.

And, Emery knew that seeing their father was not high on Jason's priority list. He and their father had always got along like oil and water. The Major always thought that Jason was too soft, too much of a mama's boy—and, weakness was not something The Major tolerated.

He tried to beat it out of his wife. He tried to beat it out of his son. Emery often wondered why she was spared.

As they entered downtown Fairchester, Emery looked for a parking space near the Pied Piper Tavern, where the Belles & Beaus Black Santa Brunch was being held. The restaurant only had a small parking lot, and all the spaces were taken. People were now parking on the street and walking to the tavern.

"Look, there's Michael's sister."

Emery took her eyes off the road. "Which one?"

He pointed. "Right there."

It was Rashida McLain. She was one of the members of Belles & Beaus.

"You're talking about Michael from the airport, right?"

Jason grinned. "Yes, Michael from the airport. Michael Starks."

Wow. She didn't really know Rashida well, even though she was a Xi. But, she always seemed so prim and proper. Who knew that she had a brother who gave blow jobs in the parking lot? That was pretty scandalous.

After Emery finally found a parking space, she turned to her brother. "Okay, I really need to make a good impression on these women so...."

Jason's eyes twinkled. "Don't worry. I'll be on my best behavior."

Emery locked arms with Jason when they got out of the car. "I'm really happy to have you here."

He kissed her on the forehead. "I'm glad to be here, sis. Now, let's impress the hell out of these Belles & Beaus bitches."

....

The woman in the pink Santa hat bent down so she could hear the little girl more clearly. "Who's your daddy, honey?"

Obviously lost, the little girl looked frantic. "Reynard Edmonds. I'm looking for him."

Emery turned from the registration table and saw a Belles & Beaus mother talking to her daughter. "Riley?"

"Mommy!" Riley, dressed in a red and aqua dress with embroidered winter berries, ran towards Emery but then saw who was standing next to her mother. "Uncle Jason!" Riley's path swerved and she ran into the arms of her uncle.

"How's the best niece in the world?" asked Jason as he twirled Riley around in the air. Emery felt a gust of cold air as the restaurant door opened. "Noah! My man!" Jason put Riley down and walked over to Noah.

"Jason? What are you doing here?" asked Noah as they gave each other dap. He and Jason always really liked each other and got along well.

"I just got into town! I'm here visiting my sister for the holidays." Jason turned and looked at her.

With all eyes now on Emery, it dawned on both Jason and Noah that there was a blemish on their reunion. Not only were Emery and Noah not engaged anymore, but Emery and Sahara were sworn enemies. Emery had told Jason all the things that Sahara said about her.

Everyone was frozen. Was World War III about to erupt?

Emery smiled. It was the holiday season, and she was going to spend it with her brother. She could let bygones-be-bygones for a little while. "You two! Jason, have you met Noah's wife? Sahara, this is my brother, Jason."

Sahara raised her eyebrows like she was surprised that Emery was making the introduction or even speaking to her. After shaking hands and making small talk about everyone's holiday plans, Emery, Riley, and Jason said goodbye and headed inside the main area of the restaurant.

"Well, I'm proud of you," said Jason.

"What?" asked Emery innocently as she waved at one of the Belles & Beaus mothers.

"Look at you being a team player and introducing me to Noah's wife." He paused. "Or, is it more to the story?"

"C'mon, you know I tell you everything. It's all you. You bring out the best in me." Emery laughed. "And, maybe it will throw her off her game. She's also trying to get into Belles & Beaus."

"Riley!" Reynard came running up to her. "Where have you been? I was looking all over for you."

"You were talking to that lady for so long that I got bored." And, unfortunately, Reynard brought out the worst.

For once in his life, Reynard looked embarrassed. Emery knew that he didn't want his daughter to be aware of his shenanigans. The rest of the world be damned. But, she wasn't about to let Reynard steal her joy today.

To make things up to her, Reynard told Riley he would do some of the activities with her. When Emery and Jason walked away, father and daughter were trying to decide where to start—cookie decorating, writing letters to Santa, making candy cane reindeer, or painting ornaments. And, since Riley called him out, Emery knew that Reynard would walk a straight line going forward. She could relax and enjoy the event with her brother.

Adults and children were everywhere—talking, laughing, eating—enjoying the holiday event. Emery walked around and introduced her brother to the Belles & Beaus members. She could see that most of the other prospective members were running around like they were playing a game of tag—introducing themselves to the members, trying to get face time, and moving on to the next target.

But, Emery had been coming to the Black Santa Brunch for years. She knew all the members and they knew her, although that still wasn't a guarantee. She had been sick when she found out that there was only going to be one invitation extended. She knew that the chapter didn't bring in a lot of mothers, but they also hadn't had an intake in a couple of years. She had been prepared to strategize to get one of a few invitations, but she originally hadn't counted on fighting for one slot. When she found out, she knew she had to take her game to a whole other level.

Emery scanned the room. The chapter mothers and

the belles and beaus were wearing pink and blue Santa hats, which helped to distinguish chapter members from other guests. Likewise, it was easy to figure out the prospective members from the other guests. The prospectives were the women doing the complete opposite of what they should.

The buffet tables were filled with food. A waffle bar, French toast, bacon, sausage, fried chicken, and baked macaroni overflowed on one table, while holiday treats, like grape grinches with banana and strawberry Santa hats, reindeer chocolate donuts with jelly bean red noses and pretzel antlers, and candy cane north poles staking claim to white donuts filled the other.

Most people were focused on piling their plates high with food. The prospectives were the ones standing with empty plates holding everyone up because they were too busy trying to have a conversation with the Belles & Beaus member behind them and didn't realize that the line was moving.

Emery looked over where families were taking pictures with Black Santa. The mother whose child was trying to climb on the reindeer balloon decorations while she talked to the chapter president, she was a prospective. At the table in the back of the room, there was a family—mother, daughter, two sons, even the father—dressed in pink and blue from head to toe, and they weren't members of the chapter. Without a shadow of a doubt, she was a prospective.

Last, but not least, there was Eva Ross. Her husband was talking to the Belles & Beaus fathers, some of whom were his fraternity brothers. Her children were having fun taking pictures with some of the belles and beaus at the photo booth. What was Eva doing? Sitting at a table by herself trying her best to not talk to anyone. No, there was not a lot of competition here.

Maybe three people. Raven Cole, Crystal White, and, she hated to admit it, Sahara Kyle. They had been at other Belles & Beaus events, knew a few people in the chapter, and seemed to be reasonably liked. She probably had them beat—but they could give her a run for her money.

"Hello, Emery. It's nice to see you." It was Teri Katz.

"Hi, Teri. I love your outfit," said Emery. She was wearing a black, high neck blouse with a green sateen midi skirt.

"Thank you. I wasn't sure what to wear since this is my first time coming. I can't believe how festive everything is. It's quite a transformation!"

"Yes, it is magical." Emery noticed that Teri's husband was fidgeting by her side.

"Have you met my husband, Jonathan?"

"His reputation as our upstanding city manager precedes him. And, this is my brother, Jason."

Emery saw little beads of sweat on Jonathan Katz's forehead. It was a little warm in the room, but she didn't think that it was that warm. Emery shook the city manager's clammy hand as he held his head down and mumbled, "Nice to meet you." He must be one hell of a city manager because he sure didn't get the job based on personality.

After Teri and Jonathan walked away, Emery saw them talking to one of the county commissioners, who was there with his granddaughter. She could see that the conversation also caught the attention of some of the chapter members. Better make that four—Teri Katz.

Ordinarily, Emery would have discounted anyone that was new to the area. Their ties were not strong enough. But, Teri's game was strong. She was no joke. Emery knew that she was meeting with members, attending events, and, because of her husband, well connected. Yes, she was definitely someone that Emery had to keep her eye on.

....

Emery never liked hospitals. Unfortunately, she had spent enough time in emergency rooms and doctors offices to last a lifetime. Everything was too white, too sterile—until it became marred.

Black eyes. Broken fingers. Ruptured eardrums. Broken arms. Cheek fractures. Broken ribs. Split lips. Cracked teeth. Broken jaw.

Her mother would give a weak reason to explain how it happened. She walked into the door. She tripped and fell down the stairs. Sometimes the army doctor would raise an eyebrow or give her mother a second glance before continuing to scribble on the patient chart. Most of the time, they didn't bother to act like they cared.

"Mom?" Emery poked her head in the hospital room.

"Come in, honey," her mother said softly. Ironically, her mother's round face and rosy cheeks, symptoms of the Cushing syndrome that was the result of years of abuse, made her look like she was in a perpetual state of happiness.

"I brought someone to see you." Emery walked into the room followed by her brother.

"Jason!"

"Hi, Mom." Jason walked over to his mother, who was seated in the guest chair and hugged her like he never wanted to let go. He didn't even glance at his father, who was lying unconscious in the hospital bed in the middle of the room.

Their mother touched Jason's cheek and then went back to her knitting. She learned how to knit after she had moved to the States from South Korea with their father. She was a young wife in a new country, and she had no friends. She told Emery that she found refuge at the small Baptist church down the street, where the little old ladies showed her how to clean chitterlings and collard greens and taught her how to knit. Over the years, knitting had been her mother's source of comfort and solace—and she could still make some mean greens.

Every now and then, Emery's mother would look

over at her husband. Emery motioned for her brother, who was standing against the wall beside her, to sit down next to their mother. "Mom, aren't you happy to see Jason?" asked Emery.

She looked at Jason sitting in the chair next to her and put her hand on top of his. "Of course, I am. I only wish he would come more often. When his father is awake." She smiled at her son.

Jason squirmed in the chair. "Well...you know...I've been busy...." Jason put his head down. "And, I wasn't sure that...that you wanted me to come...." Jason paused and looked over at his father. "I wasn't sure that he would want me to come."

"Of course, we want you to come. You are our son. Don't worry about the silly fight that you and dad had. All is forgiven. That's water under bridge. He'll tell you when he wake up." Although Emery's mother had lived in the United States for decades, her command of the English language wasn't the greatest. She smiled at Jason and returned to knitting. Jason looked at Emery, who shook her head no.

They sat there for thirty minutes like that. Emery's mother knitting, while occasionally looking up at her father as if he said something that she hadn't heard. Jason slumped in the chair and staring into space. Emery standing against the wall taking everything in. All of them held hostage by her father.

Whether awake or in a heart attack induced coma,

The Major was still running the show, and she had been trapped on this square for five years. Do not pass go. Do not collect two hundred dollars.

Emery looked out the window. She remembered everything like it was yesterday.

Jason flew in from San Francisco to visit their parents, and Emery drove down to Fayetteville to see him. They—Jason, Emery, and her mother—were in the living room laughing about a story about Jason's roommate when her father burst into the room. Still dressed in his army fatigues, he walked over to Jason with a furor that generally was only reserved for their mother and picked him up by the throat yelling, "Is it true? Are you gay? Are you gay?"

Jason was trying to get enough air to say something when their father smacked him in the face. Emery and her mother tried to come to Jason's defense, but he easily threw their petite frames off of him. The whole time he kept hitting Jason in the face and shouting "Are you gay?"

Emery was trying to regain her footing to help her brother when it happened. Her father's eyes opened wide, his hand suspended in the air about to deliver another blow to Jason's face, when he collapsed to the floor.

For a minute, Emery thought he had a heart attack and died. For a second, she was relieved. The nightmare that her mother had been trapped in all of these years was over.

But then, Jason started cpr, and her mother called 911. The ambulance came and rushed her father to the hospital. The doctors praised Jason for his heroic actions. The Major had suffered a major heart attack, and without Jason's quick thinking and resuscitation efforts, he would have died. However, the prolonged lack of oxygen led to a coma. The doctors treated the deep cut her father's class ring left on Jason's chin, and he flew back to San Francisco the next day.

Emery had thought that if there was any silver lining to what happened that it was her mother was finally free. She was free from the abuse, free from the lies to cover up what was happening, and free to finally live her life. But, instead of seeing this as a new lease on life, Emery's mother spent every day beside her father's bedside waiting for him to wake up. In the end, her father still won.

Emery sighed. It was time to break up this little party. "Hey, mom. I think we probably need to head back."

"So soon? Maybe your father will be awake soon."

"Maybe." Emery put her purse on her shoulder and walked over to give her mother a kiss goodbye.

Her mother looked up at her. "Forgot to tell you. Alton came by last weekend to say hello."

"Alton?"

"Yes, Alton."

"What did he say?"

"What did he say? Well, he asked about your father and say he saw you in Fairchester. Asked some questions about Riley. He did not know that you had daughter. I always liked Alton." Emery's mother smiled and went back to knitting.

Jason looked at Emery and then gave their mother a kiss on the cheek. "I love you, mom."

"I love you, too, honey." There were tears in her mother's eyes.

Alton came here. Why? And, he asked about Riley. Emery looked back at her mother, who was back to knitting and waiting for her father to wake up. There was no use in asking her.

When they walked out of the room, Jason asked. "Are you okay?"

"Alton? Yes, I just wonder what he wanted."

"Who knows? Although, I'm surprised he didn't know that you had a daughter, although I guess he was in the navy for a few years. What happened between you two? You were such good friends...." Jason paused in front of the car. "How about letting me drive this jag of yours? It's a far cry from Bay Area Rapid Transit."

Relieved to be on a different subject, Emery replied, "That depends. Do you still drive like a little old lady?"

Jason laughed. "If it will get me behind the wheel, then yes."

Emery tossed the keys to Jason and slid into the passenger seat. Jason was telling Emery about this new art exhibit he saw in San Francisco, while Emery checked Facebook.

Joy, Charlotte, and Yancey had tagged her in some photos at the Black Santa Brunch. There was one with Jason, Riley, and her. Emery smiled and continued to scroll down her timeline. She hadn't been on Facebook for a while. Someone had posted pictures of her at The Shield's Holiday Dinner. One of the black boosters from UNC-CH was a member and had invited them. The red sequined gown that she wore that night made her look like a million bucks, and Reynard's Armani tuxedo was tailored perfectly. She had to admit that she and Reynard looked good together.

She yawned and continued to scroll down past the pictures that she'd been tagged in. Paula's birthday party. A business conference in New Jersey. The Sphinx Mental Health Awareness Walk.

Emery paused. Someone had posted a picture of her and Alton as a Throwback Thursday. Alton had decided to enlist in the navy, like his dad, so they went to the fair to hang out one last time, like they used to do when they were younger. She remembered the night vividly.

Her eyelids felt heavy as she put her head back on the headrest. That was another life.

Before long, she drifted off to sleep and dreamed that she was at a party laughing. All of her friends were there. Jason was there, too. It was someone's birthday party. She could tell that she was happy.

A hand grabbed hers and pulled her down the hallway and into a dark room. She giggled at their naughtiness as he pushed her on the bed. Their playfulness turned serious as she reached for the bulge in his pants. She felt herself gasp as he took what he knew was rightfully his.

The passion between them was undeniable. Emery clawed at the sheets on the bed as her body convulsed over and over again. As he continued to drive his desire into her, he locked his lips onto hers. She put her hand on his cheek and as their lips separated, he smiled. It was Alton.

TWELVE

....

SAHARA: OPEN UP YOUR PIECES

*In chess, develop your pieces strategically so
that they can be active and in optimal positions.*

"You're still in your comfort zone, ladies! It's time to take it to another level!" said Antoine, Teri's physical trainer.

The fact that Sahara was covered in sweat, even though she was in a drafty warehouse in the middle of January, seemed to contradict that, but she tried to lift the tire a little higher, just in case. She huffed and puffed her way through the rest of the boot camp workout. God, she was out of shape.

Antoine walked over to Sahara when the workout was over. "Honey, you survived!"

"Barely." Sahara took a sip of water and began to stretch. "But, it was a great workout."

"Well, we have to get Ms. Teri to bring you again!" He tapped Sahara on the butt. "Stick with me, and I'll get those buns in shape for swimsuit season. And, Ms. Teri you need to bring that city manager husband of yours so I can get him right, too."

"I know better than to bring Jon...." Teri paused and

put her water bottle down. "I'll try, Antoine, but this girl is hard to keep up with. I was starting to think she was avoiding me."

"Well, try harder," said Antoine as he looked Sahara up and down before walking over to another group recovering from the workout.

Sahara hadn't been avoiding Teri. She'd just been busy. And, if she was being honest, physically, and emotionally drained. She was trying to come to terms with seeing her father and making sure that her marriage was okay.

"Sahara?"

Both Sahara and Teri turned toward the older white woman who also had been working out at boot camp. It took a few seconds for her face to register with Sahara.

"Mrs. Corbett?" It was Dwight Corbett's wife. "I didn't realize that was you."

Mrs. Corbett smiled. "Yes, I just love Antoine! He is such a character and his workouts definitely keep me in shape." She smoothed her jacket over her size zero frame.

"This is my first time coming, but he is really good. I came with my friend." Sahara turned to Teri. "This is Mrs. Corbett. Her husband is Noah's boss."

"Nice to meet you. Your husband's name is Dwight, right? Dwight Corbett."

"Yes, do you know him?"

"Kind of...He grew up with my mother," replied Teri.

"Oh, are you from White Oak?"

"Yes, I am."

"I have to tell Dwight! I've never been there. Since his family was so small and both his parents died, they didn't have any siblings and neither does he. There's no family there. Did your mother know Dwight well?"

Teri smirked. "Yes. You can say they were like brother and sister when they were growing up." Both Sahara and Mrs. Corbett looked at Teri waiting for her to elaborate, but that was all that she said.

"Well, it is good to see you." Mrs. Corbett lowered her voice and took Sahara's hand into her own. "I really do like Noah. I hope that everything works out." She gave a small wave goodbye and walked away.

That was odd. She hoped what worked out?

"How long have they been married? Do they have any kids?" asked Teri breaking Sahara's train of thought.

"I know they have a daughter." Sahara remembered the granddaughter that Dwight brought to the horse farm the day of Clarissa's party. "I think they also have a son. What's with the sudden interest in the Corbetts?"

"Just curious." It sounded like there was more to the story.

As Sahara did her toe touches, Teri asked. "So, what's been up? I feel like I haven't seen you in forever."

"Nothing much. Just been busy with Noah and the children."

"I thought so, but Natalie asked about you. Just

wanted to check."

"Really? Why did she ask about me?" Natalie Thornton was one of the Belles & Beaus mothers, but Sahara didn't know her well.

"She said that you were sick after the Thanksgiving service. She asked me if you were pregnant." Teri stood up and stretched her back. "I told her that I didn't think so. But, I thought about it later. That could help your chances if you were. Anyway, I told her that you seemed fine to me at the Black Santa Brunch."

The church service on Thanksgiving. Sahara was trying to put the memory of that behind her. "Nooo, I'm not pregnant. I just didn't feel well. That's all." And, she didn't understand why Teri and Natalie were having a discussion about her anyway.

"Are you ready for the Belles & Beaus Tea? You know it's next month."

Sahara did a few side bends. "What do you mean ready? Is there something that I should be doing?"

Teri moved from toe touches to hamstring stretches. "I mean do you have your talking points ready. Why you are interested. How you hope to benefit from being a member. How you think you will be an asset. You know...things like that."

"Well, yes...I mean no. I have answers to the questions. But, I haven't been practicing or anything. And, I thought the purpose of the tea was for them to give us information."

"It is, but Lisa said that they usually ask the prospective members to answer one of those general questions there. It never hurts to be prepared." Lisa Victors was another member of the Belles & Beaus chapter.

"You seem to have a lot of inside info."

"You think so?" Teri took a sip of her water. "It's just stuff that people mentioned in passing while we were hanging out."

"Well, you sure seem to be 'hanging out' with a lot of the mothers in Belles & Beaus."

Teri thought about it for a second. "Now, that you mention it. That is probably true. I guess I would consider some of the members my friends now."

That was an understatement. It seemed like while Sahara had been on the sidelines licking her wounds, Teri had moved up on the prospective member roster.

"Do you want to get breakfast or something?" asked Teri.

Antoine was talking to another client but overheard what Teri said. "Keep your eye on the prize! Do NOT undo all of our hard work!" he yelled.

Teri and Sahara laughed. Sahara grabbed her water bottle. "No, I'm good. If I need to follow anyone's advice—it is definitely Antoine's."

....

The soft sound of jazz streaming from the speakers was drowned out by the chatter and the laughter of the women in the hair salon. *Click.* She was done. Sahara pushed the hood of hair dryer up and waited for her stylist to come get her.

"Girl, did you hear about Mia Johnson?" asked the stylist whose chair was closest to the dryers.

"No...what happened?" asked the client in her chair.

Click, click, click. The stylist opened and closed the barrel of the curling iron before grabbing a section of long hair and sliding it down the curling iron and twirling the ends.

"Apparently...she got fired."

"Get out of here!"

"Yeeesssss...fired. You know she is an accountant. I heard there was an issue with some money missing at her job. They didn't want any of the clients to discover the theft so they kept it hush hush. But, they fired her."

"Scandalous!"

Someone tapped Sahara on the shoulder. "I'm ready for you." Sahara was so busy listening to the other stylist's conversation she hadn't seen Jena walk over.

"Would you like some coffee, tea, or wine?" asked Jena while they walked back to her station.

"I'll take some tea, please," responded Sahara.

After a few minutes, Jena handed Sahara her tea and then fixed the cape around Sahara's neck. "Your hair grew a lot since you were in here last. What made you want to get it straightened?"

"I'm going to the City Gala tonight." Sahara shrugged

her shoulders. "I guess I wanted something different."

"Oh, I know that the gala is going to be nice. I'm glad they are finally honoring The Carolina Times." Jena pulled the flat iron through a section of Sahara's hair, as a familiar voice came from the television. Sahara held her head still while shifting her eyes to it. Senator Barrett was standing with another black senator.

"Hmmpph! Talk about hypocrites," said the stylist with the red hair in the chair next to Jena.

"Ssshh!" Jena said quickly over her shoulder.

"What was all that about?" asked Sahara as Jena turned her toward the mirror so that she could curl the front of her hair.

"You live across the street from the Barretts, right?"

"Yes, I do." Sahara sat a little straighter in the chair.

"Well...." Jena lowered her voice. "There have been some rumors going around about them."

"Rumors? What kind of rumors?"

"There have been rumors for years that Senator Barrett was dirty, but I would think that if he was they would have caught him by now. But lately, people have been talking about Mrs. Barrett and her drinking and the daughter. Lord, I don't know even where to begin with Dara."

Sahara knew that she should leave well enough alone, but she was curious. "C'mon, Jena. You can't clam up now. What are they saying?"

"Dara has always been known as a little flighty, even

when she was growing up. Happy go lucky one day. Debbie Downer the next. But, it seems likes she's come home and is all over the place. Sleeping with this one and that one. A few of them have been married or dating her friends from what I hear."

"Really?"

"Yes, girl. You know when your friends start displaying the same behavior as your enemies, you have somebody in the wrong category."

Sahara took a sip of her tea. She didn't know what to think. She knew Senator Barrett and Meranda pretty well, but she didn't know Dara at all. Clearly, these were just rumors...but was there any truth to them?

Buzz. Buzz.

Jena picked up her cell phone. "Girl, why are you sending me this?" Jena said to the stylist, who just laughed, working in the chair next to hers. "Talk about being a mess. Look at this."

Jena held the phone down for Sahara to see the photo on Instagram. A tall, dark-skinned guy in a long tank top was taking the selfie, and it was clear that someone was asleep in the bed behind him. The caption read *"Have you ever slept with someone else's husband? I just did."*

Something about the guy looked familiar. Those legs.... "I think I know him," said Sahara.

"What?! How can you tell? The red wing chair in the background? Or the gray and black comforter? I don't know anyone who would have that in their bedroom."

Sahara shook her head. "Not the guy in the bed. The one in the tank top." Jena looked at Sahara out the side of her eye. "I mean I don't know him, know him. But, I've seen him. At the park this summer."

The stylist next to Jena put the flat iron down. "Him, I'm not worried about. But, if you know, whose husband that is, you better tell her 'Somebody's sleeping in yo bed!'" She started laughing.

Jena took the cape off of Sahara and handed her a mirror. "Girl, your husband isn't going to know who you are."

Sahara looked at the silky hair that was now well past her shoulders. New look. New attitude. It was now time to take her game to the next level.

....

Dressed in a black velvet long-sleeved blouse and a silver sequined floor-length skirt, Sahara took a deep breath, put her game face on, and opened the door to the convention center. She felt her muscles twinge as she walked to the registration area. The Epsom salt bath that she took before she came did not help ease the pain from Antoine's boot camp this morning.

As she went up the escalator, Sahara could hear the buzz of the crowd outside the ballroom. The City Gala was one of the city's premier events and all of the city's movers and shakers—black and white—came together to celebrate individuals and institutions that had made notable contributions to the city.

But, Sahara was flying solo tonight. Noah had to work late, but he took his tuxedo to work in case he could make it. Sahara wasn't counting on that since working late had become Noah's norm, rather than the exception, lately.

What did Mrs. Corbett say? She hoped that everything worked out. Sahara still had no idea what she meant by that. She had to remember to ask Noah when she got home.

When she stepped off the escalator, it looked like everyone who was anyone was there. In the middle of the room, there was the mayor, a couple of the city council members, and Jonathan Katz, the city manager. Sahara knew that Teri wouldn't be there tonight. Jayla was sick so Teri stayed home with her. Jessica Hanover from the school board was talking to Senator Barrett and Meranda.

Sahara was on her way over to say hello when she spotted Lisa Victors, the Belles & Beaus member that was friends with Teri across the room. That morning, it was clear that Teri was all over this Belles & Beaus membership intake. At first, Sahara thought that Teri was being a little extra with the profile book and everything. However, she was getting to know a lot of the members—and she was new to the area.

Clarissa always asked when they were going to another Belles & Beaus activity. The tea was right around the corner, and only one prospective would receive an invitation for membership. Sahara had to make sure that she got the invitation.

And, Teri wasn't going to be at the gala tonight. Sahara had to leverage this opportunity. She could always bring Teri in once she was a member. She made a detour and headed in Lisa's direction.

"Hello, Lisa. You look beautiful."

Dressed in a cobalt blue floor length gown, Lisa leaned over and gave Sahara an air kiss on each cheek. "So do you, Sahara. Actually, I've been meaning to talk to you. You know that I am the chapter's fundraising chair, and I love, love, love what you did with the Urban League's art auction last year. Are you helping with it again this year?"

"Yes, I am, but the heavy lifting was last year getting everything in place. This year, we are tweaking but not doing any big scale changes."

"That makes sense. If it's not broke, don't fix it."

"Basically." Sahara and Lisa laughed. "We can revamp it again in a few years, but we're going to stick with the current theme for now."

"Well, it was wonderful. You should be proud. I almost didn't attend because I went to the auction the previous year...." Lisa lowered her voice. "It was awful. I'm glad that Faith was able to redeem herself by helping to coordinate last year's."

Sahara knew that Faith Lloyd was the volunteer that

coordinated the art auction the year before she did. She'd heard that the auction was a disaster that year and that Faith had dropped out of the social scene for a while. But, she recently reemerged. Sahara saw her at the Belles & Beaus Black Santa Brunch.

"Faith? No...she wasn't volunteering at the Urban League anymore when I started. That's why I stepped in. The staff was so overwhelmed, and there wasn't a volunteer coordinator."

"Really? That's interesting." Lisa's eyebrow went up. "Faith gave us the impression that she helped behind the scenes with the auction and was heavily involved in turning it around last year." Lisa looked at Sahara as if she was waiting for a response.

Confirm or deny? Faith had nothing to do with last year's auction, but Sahara could soften the blow. Maybe she helped in the front office with something.

"No, that's not true," replied Sahara.

"Well, that's good to know. I'll have to make sure that is clarified to my chapter members." Lisa asked Sahara a few questions about her involvement in other fundraisers and then excused herself.

Afterwards, Sahara made her way over to her friend. "Meranda!"

"Dear, I have missed you!" said Meranda. She handed the passing waiter her empty wine glass and gave Sahara heartfelt hug.

Sahara was a little taken back. Meranda was the

queen of air kisses. Hugging was not part of her normal repertoire. She looked at Meranda, whose eyes looked a little glassy, closely. "Is everything okay? You've been so busy lately. How have you been? How is Dara?"

"Dara is...." Meranda paused as she took a glass of white wine from the tray that one of the waiters was carrying. She took a long sip before continuing. "She's well...." Meranda lowered her voice and leaned closer to Sahara. "...or as well as can be expected. You understand, dear?"

"I'm not sure what that me—" But, before Sahara could finish, Meranda moved on.

"Are you planning to attend the regional conference?"

Sahara was so consumed with all things Belles & Beaus that she forgot that the Lambda Upsilon Alpha regional conference was approaching. "Yes, I'm going to try to make it."

"Wonderful! You know Benetta Jackson plans to run for regional director. She will need your support with campaigning when the time comes."

"Of course." Sahara hadn't even known that Soror Benetta had aspirations to be regional director.

"Oh, dear! There's Winston Smalls. I absolutely must speak with him about Tyrone's...."

Sahara didn't hear what Meranda said as she toddled away. Meranda got a few feet and grabbed the back of some man to steady herself. Meranda looked over her shoulder back at Sahara and smiled. Sahara smiled back. Where was Senator Barrett?

The crowd outside the ballroom was thinning. It was almost time for the gala to start. Sahara chatted with a few more people then made her way through the crowd to find her table. She was looking at the program when someone put his hand on Sahara's shoulder and whispered, "Hello, Gorgeous."

"Noah!" She jumped out of her seat and hugged her husband. "You made it!"

He kissed her on the lips and smiled. "I did, but you are at the wrong table."

Sahara looked at the fifteen printed on the table card. No, this was the table the woman at the registration table told her.

"C'mon." He smiled and grabbed her hand. "Cass asked me to keep him company at his father-in-law's table. Zora is there, too."

Zora. Sahara had been so busy trying to execute her Belles & Beaus strategy that she hadn't talked to Zora in a while. But, Zora didn't have to worry about that. She was guaranteed an invitation because she was a legacy.

As they made their way to the tables in the front of the ballroom, Noah whispered, "By the way, I can't wait to get you home tonight." Sahara grinned.

"Sahara, I would like for you to meet my father," said Zora, as they reached table two. She made an off-hand wave. "And, you already know my mother."

Sahara shook hands with each of Zora's parents. "Hello, Mr. and Mrs. Wilkins. It is a pleasure to finally meet you, Mr. Wilkins." Sahara could see that Zora looked just like her father. He had the same dark complexion and round wide set eyes behind glasses, just like Zora. On the other hand, Mrs. Wilkins had blue eyes and could pass for white, just like Zora's sister.

"The pleasure is all mine," said Mr. Wilkins. "I'm glad that you and Noah are able to join us. Since, my daughter, Nellie, and her husband can't be here, it gives me someone to talk to." Sahara tried to not look at Zora's husband, Cass, who was also sitting at the table. "So Noah, where do you work?"

"I'm a senior vice president at First Southern, Mr. Wilkins."

"Call me Elbert, son." Mr. Elbert Wilkins was listed in the program. Sahara realized that Zora's father was one of tonight's honorees. Mr. Wilkins continued, "You must be the only African American senior vice president there. They don't usually let darkies like us get that high on the totem pole." Sahara wasn't sure who turned more red, Noah or Cass.

Noah let out a nervous laugh. "Yes, I am the only, well the first and only, black senior vp there."

"I'm not surprised. But, that tells me that you have a good head on your shoulders. Is your father in banking, as well?"

Noah looked down for a second. "No, he works in a

restaurant."

Mr. Wilkins slapped him on the shoulder. "So, you're a self-made man. I like that."

Noah and Mr. Wilkins started talking about banking, business, and the economy. Sahara felt a little sorry for Cass, who was just sitting there and not really participating in the conversation. Well, at least there was a conversation in which he could choose to participate. She and Zora were just sitting there like they were strangers. Sahara decided to break the ice.

"Zora, I didn't realize until I saw the program that your father was one of tonight's honorees."

"Yes, I'm glad that Cass and I were able to be here. My sister, Nellie, was so upset that she and her husband couldn't come. But, Daddy told her not to worry. Beautiful people lead busy lives. He would always say that when we were growing up because Nellie would be off with her friends at one event or another, while he, Mother, and I were at home."

Sahara looked at her friend. Her mother taught her that when you don't have anything nice to say to smile...so that is what she did. Thankfully, the mayor walked to the podium to welcome everyone to the gala. After grace was said, the waiters brought out the first course.

Noah bounced his leg under the table, as the video montage of the night's honorees played on the large screens in the room. Once the video was done, a biography was read before each honoree walked onstage to receive his plaque and took a photo with the mayor. Noah kept fidgeting in his chair as if he was nervous. Sahara glanced at him out of the corner of her eye. She had never seen him act like this.

"Mr. Elbert Wilkins was born to...."

Sahara listened intently as they talked about Mr. Wilkins early years growing up in Fairchester and how his grandmother and grandfather were sharecroppers that saved every penny they could to send their children to college. After college, Mr. Wilkins's father started a business. When Zora's father was old enough he took over his father's business. He sold that business and bought a bigger business, and so on and so forth.

As Mr. Wilkins walked to the podium, Sahara looked over at Zora's mother. She was clapping along with the rest of the audience and her lips were curled upward into a smile. Wearing a gold dress and her long brown hair pulled into a bun, she looked a little like a trophy—except for the eyes. Her eyes had no spark, no twinkle, no sign of life. Something about Mrs. Wilkins' eyes reminded Sahara of her mother.

After all the honorees were acknowledged, Sahara looked over at Noah, who was back in deep conversation with Mr. Wilkins. "Like I said, we have been trying to increase our online offerings," said Mr. Wilkins.

"Well, ecommerce and digital marketing are certainly my arena. If you have time, I can certainly come by next week and talk to you further about how I can be asset to your company," replied Noah.

"Excuse me, ma'am," said the waiter before putting a slice of chocolate cake in front of her. Sahara could no longer hear what Noah and Mr. Wilkins were saying over the clink of forks on plates as people ate their dessert.

Sahara took a bite of her chocolate cake. What was going on with Noah? He sounded like he was interviewing for a job. But, she thought that he loved working at the bank. Sure there were the bumps and bruises associated with being a black man in Corporate America, but Noah was performing well there. Why would he look for a new job now?

Sahara thought back to her conversation with Mrs. Corbett after boot camp. What did she say? She hoped that everything worked out. Sahara turned and looked at Noah. Wouldn't he tell her if something was wrong at work?

The program was over, and people started leaving. After saying goodbye to Zora and her parents, Noah and Sahara exited the ballroom. The crowd was moving slowly—people were taking pictures and chatting with old friends—causing bottlenecks, as most of the guests tried to leave the premises.

Noah seemed unfazed. Since his conversation with Mr. Wilkins, he was smiling and seemed to be in a good mood.

When they reached the bottom of the escalator, they walked towards the exit. There was some commotion near the doors that prevented people from moving. Everyone was getting restless and fidgeting as they waited for the crowd to be released.

"Excuse me," said the gentleman in front of Noah when he realized that he stepped on Noah's foot.

"No problem," replied Noah as the man turned to see to whom he was talking.

It was Dwight Corbett.

Both he and and Noah looked shocked to see each other. "Hello, Dwight."

"Hello, Noah."

Mrs. Corbett, who was so friendly when Sahara saw her at boot camp, pretended to be mesmerized by something across the room. Noah looked over Dwight's shoulder to see if the crowd was moving. It wasn't.

"Great program tonight," said Dwight.

"Yes...great," replied Noah.

What was going on? You could cut the tension with a knife.

Finally, the crowd started moving. Dwight seemed relieved. "Well, I guess I'll see you around...." Noah just stared blankly at him.

Sahara and Noah inched their way to the exit behind Dwight and his wife in silence. She knew to wait until they were in a safe place to say something. When they finally reached the car, Sahara turned to Noah. "What is going on with you and Dwight?"

Noah grimaced and held his head down. "I was going to wait until tomorrow to tell you. Dwight fired me today."

THIRTEEN

SAHARA: SACRIFICE THE QUEEN?

In chess, it is sometimes advantageous to
sacrifice the Queen for a strategic advantage.

The cold February sun peeked through the rows of the stark, brown branches lining the sides of the road. Although dormant now, come July, the branches would be filled with fluffy, white Southern cotton. Sahara stared out the window trying to gather her thoughts as they got closer to Mrs. Fannie Winters' home, where the Belles & Beaus Membership Tea was being held.

Every twist of the two lane road made her stomach feel like she was riding a roller coaster. With everything that was going on with Noah and his job, she debated whether she should even bother coming.

The night of the gala, Noah told her that for the past few months Dwight had been finding fault with anything and everything that he did. Yes, Dwight fired him but the bank president, Jeremiah Walters, stepped in and said that Noah should simply be put on probation. According to Noah's performance reviews he went from a star employee to someone who couldn't do anything right in a few months, so human resources wanted to figure out what was going on. They didn't want a lawsuit on their hands. Even though he still had a job for now, Noah wasn't holding his breath. He knew his days at First Southern were numbered.

Teri took the next curve like she was on the Nascar circuit. "Today's the big day!" If Teri was nervous, she sure didn't show it. She was talking a mile a minute. "Aren't you excited?"

"Sure. Can you slow down a little bit?" said Sahara as she grabbed the dashboard in Teri's Maserati.

"Do you think everyone got an invitation? What do you think is on the agenda?" Teri's eyes were wide open as she kept looking at Sahara and then back at the road.

Sahara laughed. "Girl, you need to calm down. And, keep your eyes on THE ROAD."

To be honest, even with everything that was going on at home, Sahara was a little excited and very nervous. She knew this was the last time the chapter members would officially see the prospective members before they voted on who would be invited to become part of the chapter.

"Can you believe that they are having the tea at the Winters Estate? Lisa told me that Mrs. Winters has hosted the tea for years—even before most of the current chapter members were in Belles & Beau," said Teri.

The Winters were one of the oldest African American families, not just in Fairchester, but in the state of

North Carolina. Fannie Winters was in her 70s and was at the top of the totem pole when it came to black society in Fairchester. Her grandfather, a physician, was instrumental in the founding of the area's now defunct black hospital and the establishment of a medical college for black physicians.

Sahara smoothed her hair bun and touched the pearls on her neck. Her final impression to the Belles & Beaus mothers had to be a good one if she was going to be the one invited to join. But, with Noah's job in jeopardy, she wasn't sure that she could afford to be in Belles & Beaus. She pushed those thoughts out of her mind and tried to focus. There was no need in worrying about the money if she didn't get the invitation first.

A large, white antebellum home rose up from the land of cotton, and a sign on the side of the road revealed that it was the Winters' Estate. As Teri drove past the black iron gate, Sahara could see the dormant gardens of the massive property, and all the cars that were already there. Teri swerved a little to miss a gray cat and parked her Maserati behind a blue Range Rover. She and Sahara got out of the car and walked to the white mansion before them.

Sahara rang the door bell and the deep bellow of the chimes seemed to go on for a full minute. She and Teri seemed so small on the house's large wrap-around porch. As they waited at the door, they could hear laughter and conversations drifting out from the other side of the white double doors. Suddenly, one of the doors swung open, and a little girl dressed in a pink frilly dress stood before them.

"Hello. Welcome to the Belles & Beaus Tea. Do come in," the little girl said before curtseying.

"How cute!" said Teri as she returned the curtsey before stepping inside.

"You can give your coats to my brother."

A young man, who looked like he was around thirteen or fourteen, stood in front of a coat rack near the staircase to the second floor. Sahara saw a smile spread across his face when Teri removed her red coat revealing her figure-hugging, cleavage-showing blue dress.

Sahara looked down at her own simple gray dress that was covered by a lavender cardigan sweater. Her big sisters would have killed her when she was pledging if she'd dare to wear the sorority colors as a prospective. Sahara wasn't sure that the same rules applied here, but she opted to be safe rather than sorry. There was only one invitation.

Sahara and Teri passed through the dining room with its striped blue and white wallpaper and crystal chandelier. The twelve person table was set with the finest china and crystal stemware. As they walked into the living room with its ornate double moulding and two large fireplaces on either side of the room, most people were milling about talking, laughing, and nibbling.

The gaiety seemed a little out of place in the room with its antique furniture and moth eaten rugs. Large gilded frames encasing the long line of Winters Family portraits covered the room seemingly passing judgment on the whole situation.

Sahara saw Tania and made a beeline in her direction. When Tania saw them approaching, she shouted, "Teri!"

All of a sudden, everyone started clapping. The room was filled with smiling faces all staring at Teri. What happened? Sahara turned and saw that Teri was bursting with pride.

Tania walked over to Teri and hugged her. "It is absolutely wonderful what you and your husband did."

What did she do? Sahara had no idea what was going on or what they were talking about. However, she didn't want to be the odd man out so she planted a fake "I'm so proud of you" smile on her face and tried to look at Teri the same way that everyone else was. It was only then that Tania turned and realized that Sahara was there.

"Hey, Sahara," she said flatly.

Hey, Sahara. If that was all that she got from her sponsor at the membership tea, it was going to be a long afternoon. Like the paparazzi hounding a celebrity, the Belles & Beaus members circled Teri so Sahara excused herself and wandered over to where some other prospectives were standing.

"Can you believe her luck?"

"Having your face plastered on the news for writing a check to keep the local community center open right before the vote pretty much guarantees that you are getting the invitation."

"Yes, I feel like this tea just turned into a dog and pony show."

"Well, I guess that is the good thing about Crystal White not getting an invitation to the tea. At least she isn't wasting her time."

"I was wondering where she was. What happened?"

Sahara craned her neck to hear, as the woman lowered her voice. "Apparently, she went out with some mothers and had one too many drinks. She started talking about how she didn't love her husband and couldn't stand her son. That was the end of that."

Sahara's mind was racing. Crystal was out? Teri was on the news? She hadn't mentioned anything in the drive over. Were they right? Did this guarantee Teri the membership invitation?

Sahara looked across the room at the Belles & Beaus mothers doting over Teri. Maybe these two were on to something.

But, Sahara wasn't going down without a fight—not by a long shot. She walked over to a couple of members talking in the corner. "Good morning, Violet. How are you doing Yancey?" said Sahara.

"I'm well. I'm glad that you could make it, Sahara. Are

you still volunteering at the Urban League?" said Violet.

"I am. The art auction is next month." Sahara stood a little taller. People did recognize that she would be an asset. "Are you planning to attend?"

"Yes, my husband and I always go. You did a wonderful job last year," said Yancey. Sahara's smile widened as Yancey continued. "You're friends with Teri, right?"

"Yes...." Sahara wasn't sure where this was going, but she kept smiling.

"You should see if she will emcee the art auction this year. She would definitely be a crowd pleaser and incentive for more people to come," said Violet. Apparently, Teri's admirers were far and wide.

"That's a wonderful idea!" Sahara said with her voice dripping with honey.

They continued to make small talk until the president asked everyone to have a seat. Sahara slid onto the edge of one of the couches lining the living room perimeter. Both Teri and Emery were seated near the front, on the same couch as Claudine Lockhart, the president.

Sahara saw that Zora and Ronelle Richards were sitting on the couch with her. Zora looked more uncomfortable to be there than she normally did. They hadn't spoken since the City Gala, and Sahara was surprised to see her. It must be mandatory for legacies to attend the tea. Sahara smiled, and Zora nervously smiled back.

Claudine Lockhart stood up and welcomed everyone to the Belles & Beaus Membership Tea. She thanked Fannie Winters, who was standing in the back of the room dressed in a long black dress with several strands of pearls around her neck like she was judging the proceedings.

"Look at Joy standing there like she owns the world," whispered Ronelle.

"Huh?" Sahara responded.

Joy Perry, the membership chair, introduced herself and started the video. Pictures flashed across the screen as Whitney Houston's rendition of *The Greatest Love of All* played in the background. You could tell from the fashions and the hairstyles which pictures were pulled from the archives and which ones were more recent.

"She doesn't know that I will tell all of the skeletons in her closet. She better quit thinking that I'm playing with her. Like they say, when your friends display the same behavior as your enemies, you got somebody in the wrong category. Well, she does not want me to classify her as an enemy."

What was Ronelle ranting about? Some of the members looked over at them. Sahara scooted over and stared straight ahead at the video. She didn't want them to think she was talking during the presentation.

Preschoolers at a teddy bear tea. Elementary students cooking cultural dishes and reading books highlighting them. Middle schoolers at a hospital dressed in scrubs performing "surgery" on oranges. High schoolers at a nursing home presenting a live exhibit of African American pioneers. A color photo of young children dressed in suits and dresses shaking hands with North Carolina's current governor. A black and white photo of some teens in ball gowns and tuxedos at a formal event. So many activities, and the children were laughing and smiling in all of them. There was even a picture of Zora as a teenager reading to some young children at the library.

Sahara wanted this—this experience, this organization, this life—for Trevor and Clarissa.

When the lights were turned back on after the video, Joy outlined the membership requirements.

Attend chapter meetings. The Belles & Beaus meetings were on a different day from her Lambda Upsilon Alpha meetings so that wouldn't be a problem.

Host activities. From looking at the pictures, it looked like many activities both for the children, the parents, and the entire chapter took place in people's homes. Since they were older, the homes in Sugarberry Grove were not as big as some other houses she'd been in at various events. But, there was definitely enough space to entertain, and Sugarberry Grove was still cache.

Support programs for children in the community. This was one of the things that Sahara loved about Belles & Beaus. So many children could benefit from the mission and tenets of the organization. Sahara was glad that there was a focus on enhancing the lives of all children, not just those in the chapter.

Participate in conferences. All of the conferences included programming for children and the fathers. This wasn't one of Sahara's favorite requirements, but she could make it work.

Pay dues. This was the only requirement that was in question. Would they be able to afford this? What if she did get the invitation, and the financial burden was too much? Meranda said that you had to show that money was not an issue in these circles. But, what if it was?

"Ladies, I've told you a lot of information about us. Now, let's hear from you. Please stand up, and tell us your name and a little known or fun fact about yourself."

Sahara tried to push her concern about the financials out of her mind. Focus. Don't worry about the money right now. You need to get the invitation first.

As Sahara suspected, everybody's fact was pretty basic and a leap to fall in the "little known" or "fun" categories. Emery took the opportunity to share that she was Volunteer of the Year at the women's shelter, which Sahara was sure that everyone knew. However, there were a few surprises. Faith Lloyd said that she was a certified scuba diver and enjoyed swimming with sharks. Eva Ross had been a professional poker player right after college but put away her playing cards for good when she got married.

Then, it was Raven Cole's turn. She stood up and smiled. "I am a member of KNuSigma, Junior League, Gazelles, and The Sphinx. Belles & Beaus is one of the few organizations in which I'm not a member. If I get this, it will complete the set!" Then, she laughed.

No mention of the goals of the organization or her children. Several of the Belles & Beaus member looked at each other. Resume Builder. She should have come up with another fact.

Joy smiled at Sahara, who stood up. "Hi, I'm Sahara Kyle. My favorite singer is Prince. He once pulled me onstage to dance with him at a concert when I was in college. I thought that I was going to faint. My legs were shaking, but I managed to not embarrass myself." Everyone laughed.

When the tea was over, most of the prospectives took advantage of the opportunity to make one last appeal for members' votes. Sahara had just finished talking to Rashida when Teri walked up and grabbed Sahara's hand.

"Come with me," Teri whispered as she pulled Sahara through the living room.

"Where are we going?" asked Sahara as they meandered through the women congregated in the dining room.

"I want to show you something."

They were now back in the foyer so Sahara thought she had changed her mind, and they were about to leave. However, Teri started up the staircase.

Sahara pulled back. "Teri, what are you doing? I don't think we are supposed to be upstairs."

"Sshh! It will only take a minute. I want to get your opinion on something."

Sahara looked around. The foyer was empty. Everyone was still in the dining room and living room talking. Teri had better make this quick.

When they got to the second floor, she and Teri tiptoed down the hall. "Do you know where you are going? Have you been here before?"

"Ssshh!" said Teri as she turned the crystal door knob to one of the rooms. "No, I was just exploring a bit while ya'll were mixing and mingling before the program started." Teri's eyes opened wide. "Isn't this bathroom to die for?"

Sahara looked at the glass shower with the marble walls, the ceiling-to-floor gold mirror behind the clawfoot tub, and the crystal and tea lights chandelier. Teri was right. The bathroom was beautiful.

Teri continued, "This is exactly how I want to remodel my master bath. But, I'm not sure that we have enough room. You really need a spacious bath to pull off all these heavy elements."

Sahara turned around quickly trying to take everything in. "Let's go, before we get caught."

"Okay, but we better go back down using the back staircase. It sounds like people are leaving," said Teri.

Sahara and Teri tiptoed down the hallway. They could hear people chatting in the foyer downstairs as they collected their coats. Sahara and Teri crept down the stairs slowly as to not alert anyone to their transgression. They were halfway down the staircase when there was a loud creak from one of the walnut stained planks. They froze.

"Who's there? Is that you, Tyrone?" said Fannie Winters from behind one of the closed doors upstairs.

Sahara and Teri looked at each other and then flew down the steps like they sprouted wings. As they reached the bottom of the staircase, the little girl that had greeted them at their arrival popped up from behind one of the couches. She had pink frosting smeared all over her face. Sahara and Teri smoothed their dresses, quickly turned into respectable ladies, and innocently walked to the foyer to get their coats like nothing had happened.

They thanked the members that were still there and headed towards the door. As they stepped outside past the old gray cat sitting on the porch, they heard Fannie Winters scolding her grandson for coming upstairs when he was supposed to help with the coats.

"Grandma, I wasn't up here until you called me!" Tyrone replied as the front doors closed.

Sahara and Teri looked at each other and giggled.

....

"Sahara, you only have to stay for a minute. I just

want you to look at the master bathroom quickly to let me know what you think about the space," said Teri.

It had been a long day, and Sahara was ready to go home. She had wanted to get in her car and go home when Teri's Maserati pulled into the driveway of her home after the tea. But, who knew the next time she would be there, so Sahara agreed.

As they stood in the bathroom, Teri asked, "Do you think there's enough room?"

Sahara took her time surveying everything. "I think you can do it."

"Yay! And, I think if I use the same robin egg blue and gray that Ms. Fannie had in her bathroom that it would be a nice complement to the colors in the master bedroom."

Sahara walked out of the bathroom into the master bedroom. The red wing chair contrasted nicely with the gray and black comforter on the bed. Yes, Teri was right. The same colors would work.

Why did Teri's bedroom look so familiar? Sahara looked closely at everything. The wallpaper, the chair, the comforter—she had seen everything before. But, she'd never been in Teri's bedroom. In her head, she heard a voice saying, "Somebody's sleeping in yo bed!"

She had seen Teri's bedroom before—in the picture on Instagram that Jena showed her at the hair salon. The picture with the guy in the tank top and the caption that read, "*Have you ever slept with someone else's husband? I just did."* Teri's husband must have been the married guy in the bed.

"What's wrong?" asked Teri. "You look like you've seen a ghost."

"I...I...I have to go, Teri. I forgot that Noah has a work thing tonight so I have to get home." Sahara tried to get out of there so fast that she bumped into the bedroom door.

"Okay. Call me later!" shouted Teri.

Sahara flew down the stairs and out the front door. She got in her car and drove to the stop sign at the end of Teri's street.

Beep, beep. Jonathan Katz waved at her as he turned onto the street on his way home.

In her rearview mirror, Sahara watched him pull into his driveway and get out of the car. Dressed in a blue three-piece suit, Jonathan Katz was the picture of respectability. There was no way that she could tell her friend that her husband was cheating on her...with another man.

....

FOURTEEN

EMERY: RETREAT AND REINFORCE

In chess, have your piece retreat to evade an attack, and then move into a position to reinforce another vulnerable piece.

"2! 4! 6! 8! Who do we appreciate?" shouted the cheerleaders.

The crowd was going wild. Standing outside the arena by one of the concession stands, Emery said to Rashida, "Well, you may want to tell him to be careful. He could mess with the wrong person...."

"I'll talk to him." Rashida touched Emery's arm. "Thank you for keeping this between us."

"No problem. You know that I have my soror's back." Emery and Rashida embraced. Then, Rashida walked toward the concession stand and Emery headed back into the arena.

"Give me a B!" shouted the eight maroon and blue NCU cheerleaders standing on the arena floor.

The majority of the crowd dressed in NCU's colors followed instructions and shouted, "B!"

"Give me an E!"

"E!"

"Give me an A!"

224

"A!"

"Give me an R!"

Andrew Scott a junior at NCU hit a jumper giving NCU the lead, and the crowd's cheers were almost deafening.

Held annually at the end of February, the CIAA Basketball Tournament was one of the largest black college basketball tournaments in the country. It brought tens of thousands of people to Charlotte and infused the city's coffers with thirty million additional dollars. The stands were filled with older alums of the participating institutions supporting their alma maters and eager to see the athletic talent featured during the tournament. Young alums flocked to the city for the day parties and nightly entertainment associated with the conference.

Emery and Rozlyn still considered themselves "young alums" but wanted to defy the stereotype and attend some of the tournament games this year. Emery waved and gave a thumbs up to Marigold Gwen sitting a few rows down in the stands. Andrew Scott was her grandson.

"I know the holidays are over, and it's not your birthday or anything...." Rozlyn pulled a small box out of her purse and gave it to Emery. "But, I saw this and thought it was cute. I hope you like it."

"How sweet, Rozlyn!" said Emery while she opened the box. Inside was a sterling silver bracelet that read "*Sisters 4 Life*" and had the initials EE and RW.

"I have one, too." Rozlyn stretched out her arm revealing an identical bracelet on her wrist.

"I love it!" Emery put the bracelet on her arm and hugged Rozlyn. "Thank you."

NCU was trying to hang on to the lead they had as Norfolk State tried to make a comeback. Suddenly, there was a commotion behind them. Dara Barrett was stumbling around like she was drunk about six rows back. The people sitting on the row tried to make room for her and get out of her way—but not quick enough. She lost her balance and fell into a man's lap. The skin tight black and gold dress that she was wearing rolled up around her waist. The gentleman seemed to be amused, but his wife didn't and pushed Dara out of her husband's lap in one quick motion. Dara giggled, shimmied her dress down, and continued on her way.

Just then, the crowd went wild, after Andrew Scott hit a three pointer.

"What's wrong with her?" asked Rozlyn.

"Who?" asked Emery.

"Dara Barrett. Since she's been back in town, she is two extremes, spaced out—I don't know that anyone is here—or happy go lucky—I love everyone. Looks like it is happy-go-lucky today."

"Mmmm..." was all Emery said, but Rozlyn was right. Whenever Emery saw Dara she was either all over the place or acting like she was in a coma. She looked behind her. Usually Senator Barrett or Meranda were standing guard over her, monitoring her every move, but they were nowhere to be seen tonight.

However, Emery knew better than to publicly say something about Meranda Barrett's daughter. Listening ears were always around, and Meranda Barrett's reach was wide. It was best to not comment.

Rozlyn's phone buzzed. "I have to get something from someone. I'll be back," she said as she started making her way toward the aisle.

"Do you want me to go with you?" asked Emery.

Rozlyn turned around quickly. "No," she said sharply. "I'll be right back."

Okay. Emery went back to watching the basketball game. As the game went into the final seconds, the NCU crowd counted down.

"10...9...8...7...6...5...4...3...2...1!"

One of the Norfolk State players threw the ball across the floor at the basket just as the buzzer sounded. The ball hit the rim and bounced out. The game was over. NCU won 76 to 73. People flooded out of the stands happy to stretch their legs and get something to eat before the next game started. Rozlyn wasn't back so Emery stayed in her seat.

Five minutes. Ten minutes. People were returning to their seats for the next game. Rozlyn still wasn't back, and Emery started to worry. She got up and walked to the main part of the arena. No Rozlyn. Maybe she was in the bathroom. There was a line coming from the closest one so Emery positioned herself nearby to see if

Rozlyn came out or would pass by.

Whoever was in the bathroom was taking forever. People in line walked away to find another restroom. Maybe it was broken, and there was no one in there.

All of a sudden, the door swung open and Dara stumbled out with her blouse half opened and her skirt hiked up. Of course. Emery shook her head.

Stake-out over, Emery still needed to find Rozlyn. As she was getting ready to leave, she saw the restroom door open again slowly. A man poked his head out, and he and Emery made eye contact. It was Grant Matthews. His wife was an LUA and a member of the Gazelles. Grant quickly looked down and hurried on his way. Scandalous.

Maybe Rozlyn went to the car for some reason. Emery could hear the cheers from the crowd in the arena as she walked down the ramp to the lower level.

As she reached the bottom, a man stepped out of the shadows. It was Alton.

"Hi, Emery."

She tried to do an about face and go back up the ramp, but he grabbed her arm. "We need to talk."

Emery tried to pull away from Alton's grasp but his hold on her was too strong. "Alton, please let me go," Emery said through gritted teeth. "I don't want to make a scene."

"Then don't." He guided her to a dark corner and turned Emery around to face him. "You know me. I don't mean to be so rough, but you won't return my calls."

Emery looked at Alton with his smooth brown skin and brooding eyes. God, how she had loved him. "What do you want, Alton? You of all people know this is not how I like to be treated."

He winced and loosened his grip. But, he didn't let Emery go. "Look, Emery. I know that you have moved on with your life, and I'm trying to move on with mine." Now, it was Emery's turn to cringe. "I have to know. Is she mine?"

Emery had prepared herself for this confrontation when she saw that Alton was back in Fairchester. She looked at him stone-faced. "Is who yours?" Emery wasn't sure what Alton was expecting—how he prepared for this—but answering his question with a question seemed to kill all his resolve. He looked down and let her go.

"I keep thinking about that night and doing the math." Alton rubbed his neck and got a glazed look in his eyes. "Man, how I loved you—always did. Maybe always will. I remember thinking that night was the start of a wonderful life. I had you...I was excited about my commission...." Alton's voice trailed off for a second. "But, I didn't realize that you weren't telling me that we would be together. That night was your way of saying goodbye."

Emery could feel the tears running down her cheeks.

Even then, she knew deep down that all she wanted was to be loved. She went from Noah to Reynard, but she knew that Alton was the one that she loved. However, when he talked about serving the country, he talked with such pride. She had wanted to feel that same sense of excitement, but she had seen what life in the military could do to a man, especially a black man. She knew that she wasn't strong enough to endure that, not even for him.

Alton continued, "I thought that I was over you, but when I saw your daughter...I had to do the math. Sure, she resembles you...but she also looks like pictures of my mother as a child." He lowered his voice. "Emery, please. Is Riley mine? Is she my daughter?"

Emery pulled away from Alton and shook her head. "I can't do this. Not here. Not now." She walked down the ramp.

"Emery...please! Emery!"

She kept walking and didn't look back. She knew if she turned around...She had to get out of there. She needed to find Rozlyn.

Emery got to the lower level of the arena. Where was Rozlyn? Her head started to hurt, and she couldn't breathe. She had to get some air.

Emery pushed the arena door and walked outside. There was Rozlyn, standing in the parking lot with some guy in a leather jacket and Timberland boots.

Rozlyn quickly shoved the duffel bag that was on her

shoulder at the guy. He started unzipping the duffel bag when Rozlyn interrupted him. "Don't worry. It's all there." As Emery walked up, their conversation stopped abruptly, and the guy reached in his jacket. Rozlyn quickly put her hand up. "No, Bodie. She's fine. She's my friend."

Emery saw something black sticking out of his jacket's inside pocket. Was that a gun? She looked at Rozlyn and so did Bodie. He looked at the bag Rozlyn gave him, at Emery, and then back at Rozlyn. Reluctantly, he took the black duffel bag at his feet and handed it to Rozlyn.

"It better be, or you can tell Omar that I'll see him soon." Then, the guy just walked off into the shadows.

"What was that all about, Rozlyn?" asked Emery. "And, what's in the bag?"

"Jesus, Emery!" Rozlyn shouted. "You could have gotten us both killed."

Emery's eyes narrowed. "What do you mean killed? Who was that guy?"

Rozlyn wiped her forehead and her demeanor changed. She let out a nervous laugh. "Who? Bodie? Oh, he's one of Omar's friends."

"He's one of Omar's friends." One of Emery's eyebrows went up. "Well, he didn't look so friendly to me."

Rozlyn laughed again. "Emery, you are so crazy! Well, let me put this bag in the car right quick and I'll be back."

Emery looked back at the arena. She didn't want to

risk seeing Alton again. "Well, I was looking for you be-cause I'm ready to go."

"Okay then. Let's go." Rozlyn put the duffel bag in the back seat of the Escalade and got in the driver's seat. As Rozlyn drove back to Fairchester, Emery's head was still pounding. She looked out the window and thought about Alton. Why couldn't he just leave well enough alone? If only—

Whirrr, whirr, whirr, whirr. Suddenly, red and blue flashing lights were behind them.

"Shit, shit, shit." Rozlyn was saying under her breath, but she kept driving.

Emery looked over her shoulder at the flashing lights and then at Rozlyn. "It's the police, Rozlyn. You need to pull over."

Rozlyn kept driving.

Whirrr, whirr, whirr, whirr. The police car was still be-hind them flashing its red and blue lights.

Emery raised her voice. "Rozlyn, you need to pull over." What was wrong with her? Had she never re-ceived a ticket? She must have been speeding.

Rozlyn had the steering wheel in a death grip and kept looking back and forth between the rearview mir-ror and the side mirror like she could will the police car away. "I can't."

"What do you mean, you can't? Put your foot on the brake and stop."

"I can't. There are drugs in the car."

"You have drugs in the car? What do you mean you have drugs in the car?" Rozlyn didn't answer.

Emery looked over her shoulder. Why would Rozlyn have drugs in the car? She was a suburban mom, for goodness sake. She had a car seat in the backseat to prove it.

Then, Emery saw it. The black duffel bag from Bodie. "Was that a drug deal? Jesus, Rozlyn!" She didn't need this shit. Emery started to panic.

Even though she didn't have anything to do with this, if drugs were found in the car, she would be arrested, too. Emery thought about Reynard...Riley...her job...her reputation. All of that would be in shambles if she was arrested.

By now, they had gone at least a mile with the police car flashing its lights behind them without stopping. Emery knew things could escalate quickly if Rozlyn didn't pull over. "Rozlyn, I don't know what you and your husband are involved in, but you need to pull this fucking car over before you get us both killed!"

Something must have registered with Rozlyn because she started drifting to the shoulder.

Thank you, Lord. Now to get through this in one piece. "Act natural," said Emery as the officer knocked on Rozlyn's window.

Rozlyn slowly let the window down. "Hi, Officer. Is there a problem?" Emery could see beads of sweat on Rozlyn's forehead.

The officer shined the flashlight in the car on Rozlyn and then Emery. "Ma'am, why didn't you pull your car over immediately when you saw my lights?"

"I...I...misjudged the distance. I thought that you were trying to pull over a car behind me."

Good answer. Keep your voice calm and steady.

"License and registration."

Rozlyn turned to the passenger seat. No, her handbag wasn't there because Emery was sitting there. It must be....Rozlyn's eyes opened wide as she realized her purse was in the back, where the duffel bag was.

Don't you dare freak out. "Officer, I moved her purse to the backseat when I got in the car. Do you want me to get it?" asked Emery.

He moved the light to Emery's face and then to the back seat. "Okay, ma'am. But do it slowly, and don't make any sudden movements."

"No problem, Officer." Emery was glad that she had worn her maroon, low v-neck sweater to the tournament. She made sure to lean over far enough so that police officer got a nice, clear view down her sweater as she reached for Rozlyn's purse. When she sat up, the officer was smirking. She put the purse in Rozlyn's lap.

"Here you go," said Rozlyn as she handed the officer her license and registration.

"Fairchester, huh. What brings you to Charlotte?"

"We were here for CIAA, but my husband had to take my son to the emergency room so we are heading back."

The officer looked at Rozlyn, then at the car seat in the back. He handed the license and registration to her. "Slow down, and I hope that your son is okay."

Emery breathed a sigh of relief.

"I will, Officer. Thank you."

Suddenly, the officer shined the light at Emery. "And you...." He reached in his back pocket and then handed something to Emery. "Give me a call." It was a card with his phone number.

Emery looked in the rearview mirror and watched the officer walk back to his car. As Rozlyn pulled the car back into the flow of traffic, Rozlyn said, "I'm sorry, Emery."

Emery didn't answer. She just looked out the window at the black landscape. She couldn't even muster up the energy to go off on Rozlyn. They rode the entire way back to Fairchester in silence.

An hour and a half later, Emery had never been so happy to see the exit for 15-501 and to drive into the city limits. She started stretching her neck and her back in anticipation of hopping out of the car as soon as Rozlyn pulled up to her house when she saw the card on her lap. Paul Murphy. But, why would he give a married woman his number? Didn't he see her wedding ring?

Emery looked at her hand. Her wedding ring was not on her finger.

Where was it? She had put it on this morning. She

remembered twirling it on her finger when they were in the stands watching the tournament. Alton...It must have come off somehow when Alton grabbed her and she jerked her arm away.

Great. Between the confrontation with Alton, being stopped by the police with drugs in the car, and now losing her wedding ring, there was no way that this night could get any worse.

"Don't forget that there are road repairs on Carpenter Road this weekend. You have to take the back way into the subdivision using Spence Road and then Skyline," said Emery. She didn't want to spend an extra minute in this car so they needed to take the most direct route possible.

Rozlyn followed Emery's directions. Instead of going straight on Carpenter Road, she made a right on to Spence Road. "Emery, I'm sorry. I hope...." Rozlyn stopped because there were two police cars in front of them blocking the street. "Maybe I should go back."

As Rozlyn started to back the car up, three police cars with flashing lights pulled up behind her, blocking the car's exit. "What the hell is going on?" asked Emery.

At that moment, the doors of one of the police cars flung open, and two officers ran towards them with their guns drawn.

....

FIFTEEN

SAHARA: HOLD A PIECE HOSTAGE

In chess, if attacked, you can move another piece into position to attack one of your opponent's pieces, thereby holding it hostage and forcing your opponent to figure out if his attack is worth it.

Sahara was sitting on the bed watching an old episode of *The Fresh Prince of Bel Air*, when her cell phone rang. It was Teri. She let it go to voicemail.

She was supposed to go with Teri to CIAA but canceled at the last minute. Ever since she was at Teri's house and realized that Mr. Daisy Dukes' Instagram posting was from Teri's bedroom, Sahara had been avoiding Teri like the plague.

First, Sahara wondered if she was mistaken and it was someone else's bedroom. But, when she looked at the photo again after her hairstylist, Jena, forwarded it...the wallpaper, the chair, the comforter...they were all the same. It was definitely Jonathan and Teri's bedroom.

Then, Sahara tried to reason that although Mr. Daisy Dukes was in their bedroom that didn't really mean that he'd slept with Jonathan. But, why would he be there? And, when you looked at the photo there was clearly someone in the bed asleep. Ultimately, she had come to the conclusion that she'd better face the facts. Mr. Daisy

Dukes was sleeping with Jonathan. And, Sahara did not have the heart to tell Teri.

What was that noise outside? It sounded like trash cans being thrown around. Sahara looked over at Noah, who was sound asleep in bed. He could sleep through an earthquake.

There it was again. Sahara got out of bed and tiptoed to the window. She didn't see anything. The street lamp outside their house was out so their side of the street was thrown into the shadows. But, the rest of the street was brightly lit illuminating the light dusting of snow that was sticking to the grass and the streets.

Ding dong. Ding dong. Someone was at the front door.

Sahara looked at the clock. It was almost ten o'clock. Who could be ringing the doorbell this late at night? Maybe Teri decided to stop by after driving from Charlotte. However, since she and Sahara hadn't spoken to each other that didn't seem plausible. She wouldn't just drop by unannounced.

Sahara looked over at Noah. He burrowed his head deeper under the covers. Should she wake him? She peeked out the window again. No car was parked outside. Maybe she was acting silly. They lived in Sugarberry Grove for goodness sake.

Since the heat was off downstairs, the cold air hit Sahara in the face when she got halfway down the steps. She pulled her robe tighter around her body as she walked to the front door. She could hear singing and feet shuffling. There was definitely someone on the front porch. Sahara looked back towards the top of the stairs. Maybe she should wake Noah.

Ding dong. Ding dong.

Sahara better open the door before whoever it was woke up the whole house. As she got closer to the glass paneled door, the shadowy figure became clearer.

"Sahara! What are you doing at our house so late at night?" said Dara, when Sahara opened the door.

"Dara—" But, before Sahara could finish her statement Dara pushed past her.

"I had such a great time at CIAA!" Dara twirled around the foyer with her arms outstretched. She skipped to the family room, grabbed a throw from the couch, and started dancing with it like it was her dance partner.

"Ssshhh! Dara, Noah and the kids are asleep." Sahara tried to stop Dara from twirling.

"Noah and the kids? Why is your family over here so late? Where's my mother?" Dara came to a standstill. "When did they change everything in here? This doesn't look like my house."

"No, Dara. This isn't your house. This is my house." Sahara walked over to Dara, whose eyes were big as saucers as she stared at the strange surroundings. Was she drunk? "Are your parents home? Do you have your key?"

Dara just stared at Sahara like she didn't understand

a word that she was saying. Then, she started trembling. Was she high? Sahara had to get her out of there. She touched Dara's shoulder." Are you okay?"

Tears streamed down Dara's face. "No. No, I'm not," she whispered. "Please don't tell my parents."

Sahara put her arms around Dara and wiped away her tears. "It's okay. Let's get you home." Sahara grabbed her coat from the front closet and put it over her robe. She pulled the throw tight around Dara's shoulders and quickly ushered her across the street.

There were no lights shining from inside, and the Barrett's house was completely dark. Sahara rang the doorbell and then knocked on the front door. No answer. She could feel Dara shivering beside her.

"Do you have your key?" asked Sahara.

Whatever high Dara was on when she was at Sahara's house was clearly over. Standing before Sahara now was a woman with slumped shoulders and downcast eyes. "I'm going to look in your purse and see if there is a key. Okay?" Sahara looked at Dara but her eyes were blank.

She opened the clutch and found a Gucci key ring. The second key was the charm.

Sahara slowly opened the front door. The Barrett's home always seemed so regal and luxurious when she was there. Now, cloaked in blackness with the only light shining from the street lamps, the furniture created large shadows making the house seem eerie and unnerving.

Dara slowly walked up the stairs to the second floor, and Sahara trailed behind her. She had never been upstairs so she didn't know where they were going.

They walked past the office and another room. Dara walked into the guest room and lay down on the bed. Sahara pulled the down the covers so that Dara could get underneath them and be warm.

"I need my medicine," Dara whispered as Sahara plumped the pillows under Dara's head.

Her medicine? Sahara walked over to the adjoining bathroom and flicked the light switch, flooding the bathroom with light. She shielded her eyes until they adjusted. Medicine. Medicine.

The top of the bathroom vanity was empty so Sahara opened the medicine cabinet on the wall beside the mirror. Lotions. Contact lens solution. Q-tips. Allergy pills. That couldn't be what she was looking for.

Sahara's eyes went down. Maybe there was something in the vanity's bottom cabinet. She squatted down and opened the two doors. There on the floor of the cabinet was a mountain of pill bottles. Sahara glanced toward the bedroom where she could hear Dara softly breathing. Was all this medication hers?

Sahara looked at the first bottle. Dara Barrett was the name on the label on the small yellow bottle. The medication was lithium. She placed it on the vanity's counter. She looked at the next bottle. Dara Barrett. Lithium. She placed it next to the first bottle. The third bottle belonged to Dara, but it was aripiprazole. Sahara put it on the opposite side of the counter. Lithium. Lithium. Aripiprazole. Aripiprazole. Aripiprazole.

When she finished sorting through all the bottles at the bottom of the cabinet, there were still just the two stacks. Given the number of prescription bottles, it seemed like Dara had not taken her medication in months. She just kept getting the prescription refilled like she was.

But, which medication to give her? Sahara looked back to the door. Dara had seemed like she was half out of her mind, but she was alert enough to ask Sahara to not tell her mother. Sahara looked at the little yellow bottles again. Her eyes focused on some numbers that were on the label. It was the phone number to the pharmacy.

Sahara felt her coat pockets. Ugh. Her cell phone was back at the house. She grabbed a bottle from each stack and walked back to the bedroom. Dara's purse was on the nightstand so Sahara opened it. No cell phone.

She would have to use one of the phones in the house. Sahara looked around the guest room, but there was no phone in here. The office. There would be a phone in there.

Although she and Dara were the only ones in the house, Sahara crept down the hall to the office like a thief in the night. When she turned on the light, she saw it—a phone sitting on the desk. She walked around to the other side of the desk and pulled the chair out but then quickly pushed it back. She didn't want to disturb anything.

She looked at the phone number on the bottle and dialed the number. What if no one answered? Just as she thought it was about to go to voicemail, someone picked up.

"Granger Pharmacy."

"Hello. I'm..." Maybe she shouldn't leave her name. "I'm calling for a friend. She asked me to get her medication, but it...it looks like she hasn't been taking it for a while. I found a bunch of bottles. I don't know if I'm supposed to give her one, or the other, or both."

"What type of medication is it?"

"Lithium and aripiprazole."

"Is your friend having a manic episode?"

"A manic episode?"

"Yes, a manic episode. Those medications are generally prescribed together for bipolar disorder."

Bipolar disorder? Dara was bipolar?

Sahara walked back into the guest room. The pharmacist recommended giving Dara a prescribed dose of each medication and contact her doctor.

Sahara gently shook Dara to wake her up and put the medicine in her hand. Dara swallowed the pills and took a sip of the water that was on the nightstand. "Thank you, Sahara." Dara dropped her head back on the pillow and clutched the throw that Sahara had put her shoulders like it was a lifeline.

"You're welcome, sweetie." Sahara whispered back as she pulled the covers up on Dara.

Dara was bipolar. The sullenness when she arrived, the outbursts and behavior that she had exhibited in recent months...everything made sense. Dara asked Sahara to not tell her mother, but Sahara knew that she would need to follow up with Meranda. It was in Dara's best interest.

Sahara slipped out the Barrett's front door as quietly as she slipped in and hurried back across the street. Her house was still quiet when she went inside and hung her coat back in the closet. It sounded like everyone was still asleep, and no one had missed her. Good.

Sahara felt the weight of what just happened on her shoulders as she climbed the stairs. She was exhausted. She would give Meranda a call tomorrow.

The light from the television was flickering in the room. The news was on. Sahara pulled back the covers and slowly climbed into bed trying to not wake Noah who was still fast asleep and snoring in the bed. As she closed her eyes she heard a *ping*. She had a text message. She was too tired to read it now.

Ping.

Another message. She had to remember in the morning to check on Dara.

Ping.

Ping.

Ping.

What in the world was going on? Who was sending her all these texts? Sahara turned over and reached for the cell phone on the night stand. She squinted her eyes to soften the light emanating from the cell phone.

She had ten missed phone calls and twice as many text messages. What was going on? As she sat up in bed and turned on the lamp on her nightstand, her ears perked up at the news report on the television.

"We have been following the current hostage situation unfolding in West Fairchester...."

Sahara recognized the house where the news camera was centered. She shook Noah. Something was terribly wrong.

....

Noah pulled his red BMW to a stop on the side of the road. There were police cars and news trucks everywhere. Red, white, and blue lights were flashing, and the sidewalk was filled with people. If it weren't the dead of night in the middle of winter, Sahara would have thought it was a block party.

Tania saw Noah and Sahara and waved them over to where she was standing. "Have you heard from her?" asked Tania as she hugged Sahara.

Sahara felt numb, but she wasn't sure that it was entirely from the cold. "Yes...no....Well, she called earlier tonight, but I missed the call."

She thought back to when she was watching television and declined Teri's call. She thought that Teri was just calling to catch her up on what she'd missed at CIAA. Had she been calling for another reason? Had she been calling because she knew something was wrong? Sahara may never know.

Suddenly, the area where they were standing was flooded with light. Rowena McGee, the Raleigh news anchor, was standing in the street facing them while her camera man gave her directions. "Five, four, three, two...You're on!" said the camera man as he knelt in front of where Sahara and Tania were standing.

Rowena got a serious look on her face and looked at the camera. "This is Rowena McGee, and I am reporting live from the hostage situation at Magnolia Reserves. As you can see in the background, the police have the house surrounded. We have received word that the police negotiator is here and has made contact, but no demands have been made."

This had been going on for two hours? How did she not know? Dara. She'd been dealing with Dara.

Rowena looked down at the paper that she was holding. "Tax records show that the house is owned by City Manager Jonathan Katz and his wife, Teri, and they've lived in the house for almost two years. Neighbors tell us that they are a kind and generous couple and the parents of one daughter."

Oh my God. Jayla. Was she in the house?

"It has been reported that the daughter is safe with family friends."

Thank you, Jesus. Jayla was safe.

"We know that there are three people inside. The owners of the house and another gentleman. At this time, we do not know who the hostages are and who is holding them at gunpoint. But, everyone is hoping for a peaceful ending. Back to you, Fred." With that, the spotlight went off and they were thrown back into darkness.

Who was the other man that was in there? Why was he there?

"Sahara, are you okay? I know that you and Teri are close."

Sahara looked up. It was Emery. What was she doing here? Probably ready to pick meat off the carcass. Sahara shivered. That was crass, and probably not the best choice of words given the situation.

"I...I don't really know how to feel. I don't know what's going on. We...." Sahara nodded her head at Noah who was standing with Tania's husband, Maxwell. "...came over as soon as we saw it on the news."

"Rozlyn and I were on our way back from CIAA when we drove into all this." Emery pointed to all the emergency vehicles and news trucks. "Rozlyn's car is blocked in by all the police cars. They have a bunch of streets closed off. I guess in case things go bad." Emery looked at Sahara. "But, I'm sure everything will be okay."

Once again, the area was flooded with light. Rowena got a serious look on her face and looked at the camera. "This is Rowena McGee, and I am reporting live from the hostage situation at Magnolia Reserves. It has been confirmed that City Manager Jonathan Katz is holding his wife, Teri Katz, and a Mr. Michael Starks hostage at gunpoint.

"Mr. Starks is not a resident of the home, and it is unclear what his relationship, if any, is to the Katzes. No demands have been made, and the negotiator is trying to bring this to a peaceful resolution. Back to you, Fred."

Sahara felt sick. Jonathan was holding Teri hostage? And, who was Michael Starks?

Rozlyn walked over. "Damn. Ain't this a trip?" She looked Sahara up and down. "I feel bad for your girl. I mean I'd heard that her husband was a little fruity...but damn..."

Sahara cringed. She saw Emery move a couple of steps away from Rozlyn and turn her back. No one said anything.

Getting the message, Rozlyn moved on through the crowd and found someone else with whom to gossip. Sahara, Tania, and Emery remained fixated on the house, not wanting to take their eyes off of it in case something happened. Sahara shifted her feet from side-to-side trying to stay warm when she felt the mood change. The police were moving closer to the house. Something was happening.

The area was bathed in light again. "Five, four, three, two...You're on!" said the camera man.

"This is Rowena McGee, and I am standing here with Lonnell Jenkins, a friend of Mr. Starks." Rowena turned to Lonnell. "Mr. Jenkins, can you add any insight on Mr. Starks's relationship with the Katzes?"

Lonnell Jenkins was dressed in a leather jacket, black turtleneck, and jeans. Their small group stared at Lonnell Jenkins ready for him to shed light on the situation.

"Well..." Lonnell touched the rim of his glasses and blinked a couple of times like he was uncomfortable or the light was shining too brightly in his eyes. "Well, Mr. Starks is currently in a relationship with Jonathan...I mean...Mr. Katz."

People in the crowd started talking amongst themselves at this juicy tidbit. Sahara stared straight ahead.

Rowena turned back to the camera. "Thank you, Mr. Jenkins. Do you have any proof that Michael Starks was in a relationship with City Manager Jonathan Katz?"

Lonnell gulped. He probably hadn't figured on being asked to provide proof. But, Rowena was no dummy. She couldn't set herself up for a lawsuit.

"Yes, ma'am. I've witnessed them kissing and touching each other in public. Once, all of us went to a gay club in Charlotte together. Again, they were very affectionate towards each other," said Lonnell.

Rowena maintained her journalistic composure while

Lonnell Jenkins divulged the salacious details. She turned back to the camera. "The sheriff has also stated that the possible reason for this hostage situation as a lovers' quarrel but he has not—"

Bang!

People screamed and ran trying to seek cover. Sahara didn't move. The police were still outside. The gunshot came from inside the house.

Bang!

Another gunshot, then silence.

Everyone stood frozen. The police. The crowd. Even the news reporters and cameramen waited to see what would happen next.

After what seemed like eternity, the front door flung open. At first, there was nothing. Then, a figure covered in blood crawled out and collapsed on the snow.

Someone in the crowd screamed. Police officers swarmed inside the Katzes' house. Paramedics pulled a gurney out of the ambulance. News reporters giddy to detail the drama that had just unfolded moved into position.

As chaos ensued, Sahara stood there. She knew the lifeless figure bleeding on the ground was Teri. She also knew that this was all her fault.

SIXTEEN

....

SAHARA: WASTED MOVE

*In chess, any move that doesn't strengthen your
position is a wasted move and should be avoided.*

After Teri crawled out the front door, all hell broke
loose. People screamed, cameras clicked, and si-
rens flashed. Sahara tried to ride in the ambulance with Teri, but the officers insisted that she go
home since she wasn't family.

She followed the officer's instructions...but a lot of
good that did. When she and Noah finally got home at
four o'clock in the morning, Sahara tossed and turned
all night. Sometimes she would dream that she saw Jonathan putting the gun to his head and pulling the trig-
ger. Other times, she was the one holding the gun and
pointing it at Teri. Each dream ended with Teri collaps-
ing outside her front door staining the snow covered
ground with blood.

When the sunlight came streaming inside the bedroom windows and woke Sahara up, she had not been
asleep long. Before she opened her eyes, she prayed that
what happened last night was just a bad dream. However, when she turned on the television, it was the head-

line story on every local channel and even in the newspaper.

City Manager's double life ends in tragedy.

City Manager commits murder-suicide.

City Manager kills gay lover, then self in front of wife.

Sahara dragged herself out of bed and to the bathroom to get something for her headache. She popped two caplets in her mouth and swallowed hard. She knew that it would take a lot more than water to help her come to terms with what happened last night.

She needed to go to the hospital to see Teri so she turned on the shower. The hot water felt good against her skin. Maybe it would wash away some of the guilt that she felt.

Sahara stepped out of the shower and wiped the fog off the bathroom mirror. Her puffy eyes, blotchy skin, and dry lips divulged that she had spent too many hours in the cold last night. She slathered some shea butter on her face and looked at herself in the mirror. She might as well skip her usual beauty routine. It was time to pay the piper.

....

The antiseptic smell in Fairchester Memorial Hospital was making Sahara nauseous. Her head was pounding from the lack of sleep, and she had been in such a rush to get to the hospital that she didn't eat breakfast. Plus, her nerves were shot.

"May I help you?" asked a woman in blue scrubs sitting under the *"Nurses Station"* sign.

Sahara tried her best to sound like she belonged there. "Yes, I'm looking for Teri Katz's room."

The nurse continued looking at the computer monitor in front of her. "Sorry. Only family is allowed to—"

"I'm her sister," Sahara said quickly. She had been down this path before.

The nurse looked away from the computer and looked at Sahara over her glasses. "Her mother is on her way from Mississippi. She didn't say anything about a sister visiting."

Sahara shifted her feet. "We're half sisters. We have the same father, but not the same mother. You know how it goes. Papa was a rolling stone." She gave her a small smile hoping that would be the cherry on top.

The nurse just stared at Sahara for a few seconds. "Room M302. We had to move her to the maternity ward where there is more security to stop the news folks from getting inside." The nurse turned back to the computer screen. "Don't stay too long. She needs her rest, *sister*."

"I won't. Thank you." Sahara scurried away before the nurse changed her mind. When Sahara walked into the hospital room labeled M302, Teri was in bed facing the window. "Teri?"

She slowly turned her head and smiled when she saw Sahara standing there. Sahara walked over to the hospital bed and hugged her friend. "Oh, Teri. I'm so sorry." She meant to be strong. But, seeing Teri lying there bandaged and bruised, she couldn't stop the tears from running down her cheeks.

Sahara could feel Teri's chest heaving as she sobbed as well. "Thank you. Thank you for coming," said Teri as she wiped her tears away. "I'm surprised that the nurses let you in."

"Well...." Sahara looked sheepishly. "I told them that I was your sister."

Teri laughed out loud, and then winced. "That's my girl. You always know the right thing to say and when to say it." Sahara looked down at the floor as Teri shifted in the bed. "And, you are my sister."

"Are you feeling okay? Is there anything that I can do?"

"No. They've been treating me pretty good since I got here—like I'm a celebrity. I guess I kind of am...the way everything has been on the news...." Teri went back to looking out the window. "Well, I guess this is one way to get the attention of the members of Belles & Beaus."

Sahara touched her hand. "Don't worry about that." Sahara paused not sure if she should continue. "A lot of members have reached out to me...I guess they know that we are close...to see if there is anything that they can do."

"That's kind of them. Especially since I'm not a member of the chapter." Teri smiled. "This ole Mississippi girl knew they were a classy bunch of ladies. Even if they are from North Cackalackey." Teri and Sahara laughed.

Teri's face got serious. "I just wish...I just wish that I had known...that I had realized...." Sahara wiped away the tears that rolled down Teri's cheek. "You know...I should have known. There were signs." Teri took some tissue from the box beside her bed and blew her nose. "There were rumors about him and a staffer in Mississippi, but he always told me that people were just being messy and gossiping about nothing. And, I had a cousin that told me that she saw him kissing this guy once...but I thought she was making it up. You know to be hateful because she was jealous of our relationship. I didn't know...."

Sahara stood there listening. Part of her wanted to come clean and tell Teri that she had suspected Jonathan was on the down low. But, what good would that do now?

"When I saw them together in bed...everything seemed so surreal. Jonathan didn't know what to do. Michael...the news said his name is...was...Michael Starks...he started laughing and laughing. I remember wondering if he had gone crazy.

"Then, he said this is what happens when you roll up on my sister at CIAA trying to air my dirty laundry. I didn't know what the hell he was talking about or even who his sister is.

I think that is what made Jonathan snap. The fact that he apparently timed their rendezvous hoping that I would catch them. That was when he took the gun from the nightstand...." Tears rolled down Teri's face.

"He held us there for so long. I really think that once his anger subsided and the realization of what he was doing sunk in...he couldn't live with himself. He negotiated to surrender, but then he saw all the news trucks and people outside. He looked at me, said he was sorry, and then....There was so much blood."

Teri lay back on the pillow as her tears kept coming. Sahara went over to her wishing she knew how to heal her pain. They sat in silence, until Teri drifted off to sleep.

Sahara moved to the guest chair and kept watch over her friend while she was asleep. When Teri woke up, Sahara asked, "How long will they keep you here?"

Teri yawned. "Just another day or two. There's nothing physically wrong with me." Teri's voice was really low for a second. "Jonathan didn't hurt me. I think they just want to make sure that I don't do anything to myself." Sahara was concerned about that too. "But, I wouldn't. I have Jayla to think about."

The door swung open, and a nurse walked in and started making notes on Teri's chart. "I'm sorry to cut your visit short, but Ms. Katz needs her rest."

"But, she just got here!" Teri protested.

Sahara patted her on the hand. "It's okay. I should

probably head back home anyway. And, I'll be back to-morrow."

"You promise?"

"I promise, sis." Sahara winked at Teri, who smiled.

....

Sahara walked out of Teri's room and exhaled. She felt like a burden had been lifted. Teri would be okay. She had a long road of emotional healing in front of her, but she would be okay. And, Sahara would be there to help her.

Sahara made a right at the corner and saw a corridor filled with rooms. She should have reached the elevator by now. Was she going the right way?

There was the little picture of the lamb hanging on the wall that she passed when she was going to Teri's room. Maybe the elevator was just a little further. The sounds of cooing and crying babies filled the hallway. Sahara passed a woman in a hospital gown rocking her newborn. Maybe she made a wrong turn somewhere.

She turned around and retraced her steps. There was the lamb picture. She made a left at the corner and ran smack dead into someone.

"Oh! I'm sorry, ma'am!" said Sahara.

"It's quite al—"said the woman before stopping.

As the woman's features came into focus, Sahara's demeanor changed. It was Winnie Allymer. Sahara looked at Winnie, and Winnie looked at Sahara. By the look on each woman's face, neither was sure as to what should happen next—speak or keep walking. Sahara decided to keep walking.

However, she had only taken a few steps, when Winnie's voice rang out. "Sahara, can I speak with you for a moment?"

It had literally been decades since Sahara heard her name on Winnie's lips. The venom and fiery emotion was absent this time, but Sahara could still hear the disdain. She slowly turned around to face Winnie.

Dripping with pearls in a tweed black Chanel suit trimmed in white, Winnie was holding a basket filled with stuffed animals and blankets with a blue *"Welcome Baby!"* balloon tied to the handle. She took a step towards Sahara. "It has been brought to my attention that you are seeking membership in the Fairchester chapter of Belles & Beaus."

Sahara stayed where she was. Why was Winnie so concerned? "Yes...I am," Sahara's voice was barely a whisper.

Winnie took another step closer and smiled. "Dear, you know that can't happen, right?"

"What do you mean?"

"Just as I said. That. Can't. Happen." Winnie was smiling, but there was nothing kind about her words. "I don't think you operated the best judgment in moving down here. The agreement that we had with your mother was that she would receive a nice monthly fee in perpetuity for her silence and to keep you away from North Carolina.

"She did have that one slip up when you were a child...." Winnie let out a sound that was more of a sneer than a laugh. "But, she never made that mistake again. No, it wasn't a wise decision for you to move to North Carolina—but you aren't my daughter so I didn't have a say in that. And, we know that your mother has a history of allowing inappropriate things to occur...."

Sahara's face turned red. She wanted to leave, but her feet were planted to the ground. It was like she was rooted and had to stand there and suffer this abuse.

Winnie took one step closer to Sahara. Her eyes danced, and her smile looked like she was an alley cat about to pounce on a mouse. "Now, I gave you a pass when I saw you at the Darlings luncheon. From listening to her, Meranda Barrett has grown quite fond of you. I can't really control someone selling a ticket to you, so we can certainly agree to not see each other when we see each other. It's done all the time." Winnie's face became serious.

"But, joining Belles & Beaus, THAT cannot happen. My mother was a charter member of the Lake Gaston chapter and Fallon and her brothers grew up in Capital City. Now, Fallon is a rising star in the organization. I think she could be the national president. However, that cannot happen, will not happen, if your connection to her is known." Winnie's voice went up an octave. "And, there is no way...no way...that my grandchildren will ever fraternize with the likes of you and your children."

The likes of you and your children. The likes of you and your children. Your. Children.

Sahara snapped. "Winnie, why do you hate me?"

Sahara took a step towards her. Now, they were standing eye-to-eye.

"I am not my mother, but more importantly, I am not the man who cheated on you with her. While I am a child of that relationship, I am not a second-class citizen. I have let you treat me like that for far too long.

"Even though I got accepted to the Congressional Student Internship program, I couldn't participate because Fallon was an intern. Even though I got accepted to Harvard, I couldn't attend because that's where Fallon was a student."

Sahara's voice got louder. "Now, you are saying that I should not seek membership in Belles & Beaus because Fallon is a rising star in the organization. And, you have the audacity to act like my children...my babies...are not worthy of being around your grandchildren?" Sahara laughed. "Well, you know what? Clarissa and Trevor are also the grandchildren of the great Charles Allymer.

"But, we know that you like picking on little children. I still remember the time my mother brought me to North Carolina to see my father....and you...and you..." Sahara wasn't sure that she could get the words out. "And you called me a mistake and said that my mother should take me back to the gutter where I belonged.

"You're mean. You're cruel. You're an awful person. No wonder your husband seems incapable of loving you."

"Of loving me?" Winnie's mouth turned up cruelly. "Little girl, it is you, whom he is incapable of loving." Winnie threw back her head and laughed for a second.

"You have accused me of these things...not allowing you to be an intern, saying you shouldn't go to Harvard, and my favorite...calling an eight year-old Sahara a mistake...."

"Don't try to deny it Winnie. I remember those words loud and clear that night."

"You heard them alright—but not from me. The great Charles Allymer, as you called him, is the one that did all of those things.

"HE didn't want to run into you on Capitol Hill. HE insisted on telling your mother that you could not go to Harvard. And, HE was the one that told your mother that you were a mistake, always would be a mistake, and belonged in the gutter. Those words came from YOUR father, the great Charles Allymer, not me."

There was a crash behind Sahara, and she saw Winnie's eyes open wide. Sahara looked over her shoulder. Fallon, wearing a bathrobe, was standing the adjacent room's doorway and a tray of food was scattered at her feet.

"We knew that you were coming so I wanted to get

the tray out of the room...and I heard you talking. Mother, is it true? Is Sahara Father's child?"

Winnie ran over to Fallon. "Dear, let's go into your room. You should be resting."

Fallon shook Winnie off. "No, Mother. I want to know if it's true. Is she my sister?"

Sahara just found out that her father was the one that didn't want her anywhere near him. She didn't need to watch as he fell from the pedestal on which Fallon had him.

As she turned to leave, she realized what Fallon meant by "we knew you were coming." Emery Edmonds sidestepped the mother-daughter confrontation that was unfolding in the hallway and slipped out of Fallon's hospital room.

....

SEVENTEEN

EMERY: INVISIBLE ATTACK

In chess, an invisible attack is not seen by the opponent
because the attacking piece is standing still so the
opponent is unaware of the attack until it is too late.

Emery flattened her body against the wall and tried her best to be invisible as she walked quickly down the hospital hall. Fallon went into labor yesterday afternoon and gave birth to a baby boy. With everything that happened last night, Emery did not have a chance to visit Fallon and see the new baby. She came early this morning in hopes of getting in a quick visit before starting her day. She was not expecting this at all.

Congressman Allymer was Sahara's father? Everything happened so fast. She and Fallon were talking while the baby slept in the bassinette. Fallon had mentioned that her mother had been there all night but went home to take a quick shower. Her father was taking a flight from Washington first thing this morning. They'd heard voices in the hallway talking...okay shouting...but really didn't think twice about it. It wasn't until Fallon started tidying up the room in preparation for her father's arrival that they saw...they heard....Emery thought it was best that she got out of there as fast as she could—like she was never there.

Clickety clack. Clickety clack. She switched to walking on her toes so that her shoes would not make so much noise as she walked on the white tile.

"Sir, may I help you? Only family is allowed to see that patient," said a nurse to an older, white gentleman opening the door to one of the hospital rooms.

"I'm Dwight Corbett. Well...I am family...I'm her uncle."

The nurse crossed her arms and raised one eyebrow. "Now, sir...I said only family...."

As Emery slipped past the half-opened door, she saw the reason for the nurse's skepticism. Teri Katz was the patient he was trying to see. Emery quickly put her head down so that Teri didn't see her face. She already had her fill of drama for the day.

....

On Monday morning, Emery's mind ticked through her to-do list as she rode the elevator up to the fifth floor in the BioPharm building. She wanted to follow-up with Dr. Grant as soon as she got to her office. He gave her the phone number to his direct line when she saw him at CIAA this weekend and said to call him first thing Monday morning. He was a little too handsy when Emery saw him on Friday night, but she knew how to use that to her advantage.

"Good morning, Emery! How was your weekend?" asked Jeff Fisher, when he stepped onto the elevator. His eyes lingered a little too long on Emery's breast in the fitted black and gray dress.

"Can't complain, Jeff. How was yours?"

"Great. We took a quick getaway to the mountains."

Jeff used his briefcase to keep the elevator door open when they reached their floor. "Did you hear about the city manager committing that murder-suicide this weekend? Crazy, huh?"

"I did hear about it on the news." Emery stepped off the elevator. "Who would believe that something like that could happen in Fairchester?" She smiled at another colleague as they passed him in the hallway. "So Jeff, how are your numbers? Are you going to beat me this quarter?"

Jeff laughed. "I always try, but I always fail."

"Who knows? Maybe you'll get lucky this time. But, the dinner tonight will help us both."

Jeff stopped at his office door. Emery could feel his eyes watching her walk away. She raised her hand in the air and waved her fingers without looking back. "Have a good day, Jeff. See you tonight."

Emery walked into her office and sank into the leather chair behind the desk. Time to get to work.

She called Dr. Grant and got him to place a huge order from the device side of the business, sweet talked him into giving her the names of a few of his colleagues that were potential prospects, and already set up appointments with two of them when she heard a knock on her office door.

The door swung open before Emery had a chance to say anything. Violet Lowe walked in, closed the door behind her, and slid into the empty chair across from Emery's desk. "Girl, can you believe it?" asked Violet, with her eyes wide open.

"Believe what?" Emery asked without looking up from her computer.

Violet looked around like she was afraid that someone would overhear them, even though they were the only two in Emery's office. "You know...with Teri."

Emery tried her best to not look annoyed, but she liked to keep her personal and professional worlds separate—and she had work to do. "Oh, it's absolutely awful." She hoped that would appease Violet and send her on her way.

"It really is." Violet looked down and shook her head from side-to-side, as if she was trying to physically demonstrate how awful the whole situation was. "I really can't believe that the whole thing happened...in Fairchester...of all places. But, for it to be someone that we know...."

Apparently, this conversation was not ending anytime soon. Violet sat up in her chair and leaned in closer to Emery's desk. "Did you know? Did you suspect that...you know...that her husband was on the down low?"

Emery's mind went back to the morning of The Sphinx Mental Health Awareness Run/Walk. The morning that she had inadvertently parked next to the two lovers, who were now dead, making out in the car beside hers. If she had known then what the future held. "No. I had no idea."

"Well, a few of the Belles & Beaus mothers went to the hospital to visit Teri and ran into Sahara Kyle, who was also there. Teri told them that Sahara had been at the hospital every day and was helping coordinate things with Jayla and Teri's family in Mississippi...."

Now, it made sense. That was why Sahara was at the hospital that day. She wasn't going to see Fallon. She was at the hospital to see Teri. Emery went back to typing on the computer.

"Mmmhmm. That's nice of her." She had to admit that after everything that happened with Winnie Allymer, she was surprised that Sahara had the guts to set foot in the place again so soon.

Violet got a serious look on her face. "And, the mothers seemed to be really impressed with Sahara's concern and support of Teri...." Emery kept looking at the computer but stopped typing. Violet blinked a few times. "I don't know, Emery. With Teri thinking about moving back to Mississippi, given everything that has happened, there seems to be a lot of support for Sahara now." She paused for a second. "Sahara is probably going to get the invitation."

Emery turned in her chair and looked directly at Violet. "What? Are you sure?"

She couldn't believe what she was hearing. Years of networking out the window because Sahara was visiting Teri in the hospital? If only they knew. That's dodging the bullet with one scandal and then standing in the line of fire with another. "Would Fall...I mean Cluster Coordinator Allymer-Tate approve?"

"Oh, you don't know?" Violet raised one eyebrow. "We got an email today stating that there is an Interim Cluster Coordinator now, because Fallon took a temporary leave. The interim is in one of the Eastern Carolina chapters."

Emery's mind was racing. Fallon took a temporary leave? Had this been planned? Was it because of the baby?

It couldn't be. Emery remembered asking if she planned to stay as cluster coordinator, and Fallon said yes. Or, was it because of what happened—

"Well, I better get back to work." Violet stood up. "But, I'll keep you posted."

As Emery watched Violet close the door, she was speechless. Despite all the scenarios for which she had strategized, she was not prepared for this one.

Emery didn't get any work done all day. On every conference call and in every meeting, her mind kept going back to what Violet said. Sahara would probably be the one invited to become a Belles & Beaus member.

She thought about all that she had done. She'd been going to Belles & Beaus fundraisers for years. She knew all of the members of the chapter and invited them to parties and events she hosted. She was even best friends with one of the regional officers. All for nothing. All of her hard work down the drain.

Emery tapped her pen on her desk. She had to think of something. She had to get into Belles & Beaus.

Why were they rallying behind Sahara and not Teri? Sure, the members were going to visit Teri in the hospital. But, why weren't they trying to convince her to stay in Fairchester and bring her into the chapter? The scandal. Her husband killed his gay lover and then himself in front of his wife.

But, Sahara had her own skeletons—if only they knew. If only they knew. Emery repeated the words in her mind again. She turned to her computer and began typing.

....

Emery's cell phone rang. It was Rozlyn. She hit ignore and kept typing on her computer.

It was almost a quarter to six. She started with an email but decided against it. It was probably best for this to be anonymous. Then, she struggled with the words to say. She didn't want to appear gossipy—just factual. She wanted the letter to convey that in an effort to avoid scandal it was in the best interest of the organization for everyone to be aware—

One of the administrative assistants poked her head into Emery's office. "Hey! I thought you and Jeff had that dinner in Raleigh with the doctors from Wake Hospital tonight?"

"Yes, I'm leaving right now. Just had to finish this letter." Emery added one more thing and hit print. She looked up and smile. "Now, I'm ready to seal the deal."

"I know you will, Emery." The administrative assistant smiled back at her. "You always do."

....

The clock in Emery's car read 7:01 *pm*. She was officially late for dinner, but she knew that Jeff would entertain the doctors until she arrived. She had to make one stop before she went to the restaurant. One stop before she mailed this letter.

Emery pulled her car slowly in front of the house and put it in park. The lights in the large house broke through the shadowy haze over the neighborhood created by the rain falling outside. She could see the "*Welcome Home, Baby Charles*" sign planted in the front lawn.

Fallon had told Emery that they were going to name the baby after her father when they were doing a girls' weekend at the spa. They had stayed up to four in the morning laughing and talking. Emery had felt like she was in college again talking to the wee hours of the morning with her roommates.

A light went on in one of the upstairs windows, and Emery craned her neck closer to the windshield to get a better look. Fallon was in the nursery walking back and forth with the baby. Emery could see the large elephant mural on the baby blue walls. She had helped Fallon pick the paint color.

She sat back and rested her head on the headrest. She remembered when Riley was a baby. She would walk back and forth while singing *The Itsy Bitsy Spider* to get Riley to sleep. Emery would think about all the hopes and dreams that she had for her daughter.

Now, one of the things she wanted for Riley was for her to be involved in Belles & Beaus. Being a part of an organization like that could keep Riley on an upward trajectory, put her ahead of where Emery started. She had to keep her eyes on the prize. She knew what she had to do.

Emery put the car in drive and didn't look back. She pulled into the restaurant parking lot twenty minutes later. This was her lucky night. She found a parking space right in front of the restaurant, and two steps away was a mailbox.

Emery grabbed the envelope lying on the passenger seat and got out of the car. She opened the mail box and paused for a second. Then, she quickly dropped the envelope in and hurried inside.

"Hello, gentlemen. Did I miss anything?" Emery smiled and took her seat at the table.

....

EIGHTEEN

SAHARA: FORFEIT?

In any game, a forfeit ends a game prematurely.
The player that forfeits is generally declared the loser.

"The numbers don't lie. It's in black and white. We have reached our goal," said Mr. Johnson the finance director at the Urban League.

"Well, I still think that a more nuanced approach would have also been successful and would have yielded higher donations. But, you are right," said Glynda Clayton, the executive director, as she pointed at the report in front of her. "The Kick Down the Walls marketing campaign resulted in an uptick in members, but the accompanying donations have been more of a trickle, rather than the flood that we had hoped."

"Sometimes, you have to sacrifice quality for quantity. With the membership numbers up, we retain our large corporate donors."

"It is hard to argue with that...unless we don't want to be an organization beholden to Corporate America."

Mr. Johnson groaned. "I'm not going to get into that discussion with you right now, Glynda." He turned to Sahara, who was seated to his right. "Sahara, thank you for putting together the analysis and presentation. I'm sure that Glynda and I can at least agree on that."

"Yes, we do." Glynda stood up and smiled at Sahara. "Thank you for pulling everything together. Keep this level of work up and forget about transitioning to full-time status. In no time at all, you'll be running the place.
"

Sahara laughed. "Thank you."

She gathered her things and walked out of the conference room. Since she and Noah were trying to save up as much as they could to offset the risk of him losing his job, Glynda was kind enough to give her a part-time job as an analyst. It was nowhere near the salary that she made before she became a stay-at-home mom, but it was something. However, with the Urban League's membership numbers up and corporate donors secured, Sahara was scheduled to begin working full-time in a few weeks.

"Thanks for keeping an eye on him," Sahara said to Mia Johnson, the new volunteer coordinator. Mia was a CPA that was in between jobs so she agreed to help out at the Urban League until she found a new job.

"C'mon, Trevor. It's time to pick-up Clarissa." Sahara took her son's hand and led him out of Mia's office. Her part-time schedule enabled Sahara to work around Clarissa's preschool schedule, and for now, they let her bring Trevor to work even though she transitioned from volunteer to staff member. Noah's mother, a teaching assistant in Charlotte, was coming to stay with them this summer so that she could watch Clarissa and Trevor when Sahara switched to working full-time.

"How did the presentation go?" asked Mia before Sahara closed the door.

"Great," replied Sahara as she looked at her watch. They should leave soon. "Thank you so much for your help with the numbers."

Mia smiled broadly. "You're welcome. Enjoy the rest of your day."

Sahara and Trevor hurried out the door. Clarissa's preschool class was holding its Easter Egg Hunt and Picnic after school. Since she worked now and could no longer volunteer in the classroom, she signed up to assist with the picnic. She didn't want to be late so she drove like a woman on a mission and reached the preschool in no time flat. Sahara pulled into a parking space and grabbed Trevor and the cupcakes from the backseat.

"Great! Cupcakes from Harris Teeter. My kids love these." said Missy, Connor Hawkins' mother as Sahara and Trevor walked up. Missy took the cupcakes from Sahara and handed them to Kristen Fitzpatrick's mom. "Barbara, can you put these on the table? Sahara, I'm glad that you were able to make it."

Had there been a question? "So, what do you need me to do?" asked Sahara.

"I think everything is done. The rest of us arrived

earlier and set everything up. I know that you mentioned that you work now so I didn't bother copying you on the emails."

"My job is pretty flexible. I could have come earlier if I had known." Sahara didn't understand why they felt having a job made her unable to contribute, but it seemed like all the decisions had been made.

"Oh, don't worry about that. We had plenty of help, and we figured that since you're coming straight from work that you would want to rest now. Don't worry. There is always clean-up duty."

Sahara laughed. "I'm all over clean up." Maybe she jumped to wrong conclusion about the situation, and they were trying to be considerate. She walked over to the field where the moms had already distributed the plastic Easter eggs and stood on the sidelines. When she caught Clarissa's eye she waved.

Barbara Fitzpatrick, a short red head, stood in front of the line of four and five year-olds eager to swoop down on the field in front of them and claim its bounty. "On your mark. Get set. GO!"

In the blink of an eye, the children scattered looking for the pink, yellow, blue, green, and purple eggs that were scattered throughout the field. Since there were a few siblings participating, they were on the hunt, too.

Most of the preschoolers, like Clarissa, were serious about their egg collection and darted between the grass and other children scooping up eggs as fast as they could. But, some children, including Trevor, moseyed along as if they didn't understand what all the fuss was. They were more concerned about enjoying nature and the experience than gathering a bunch of eggs.

When the field returned to a solid green hue and all the eggs had been found, Barbara stood up. "Now, everyone count your eggs! We have a prize for the child who has the most." All of the children rummaged in their baskets, hoping that they were the lucky winner.

"Anyone have fifteen eggs?" asked Barbara. About twelve children raised their hands. "How about twenty eggs?" Half the hands went down, but six were still up. "Twenty-five?" Three hands came down. "Thirty?" Two hands remained. "Thirty-five?" Only one hand was up, and it belonged to Kristin Fitzgerald.

Her mom looked at the crowd. "What a coincidence! Kristen found the most eggs!"

As Kristen walked over to her mother to get the prize, another mother said, "Barbara insisted that she be the only one to hide the eggs. I bet she dumped a bunch of them somewhere, and told Kristen where they were."

Barbara returned to her emcee duties after Kristen retrieved her prize. "Okay, this year we have a very special golden egg prize—FIFTY DOLLARS!! So, check your baskets! Who has the golden egg?"

You could hear the excitement in the air. Fifty dollars to this age group sounded like a million.

"I have it! I have it!" shouted Timmy Smith holding

up an egg. Everyone froze and looked at the egg that Timmy was waving back and forth in the air.

"Sweetie, that egg is just yellow," said his mother as she quickly pulled his hand down.

With the fifty dollars still up for grabs, the children searched their baskets again. After a few minutes, when no one raised their hands, everyone began to look around.

Kristen's mother got a worried look on her face. "Does anyone have the golden egg?"

Trevor looked up at Sahara and opened his hand. "Mommy...." In his hand was an egg covered in gold glitter.

"We have it!" shouted Sahara as she and Trevor hurried to the front to retrieve the fifty dollar prize. She was all smiles as Trevor took the crisp fifty dollar bill from Barbara. As they walked back to the spot where they were standing, one of the mothers said, "I'm glad they found it. My husband, Roger, works at First Southern, and he told me that Clarissa's father was fired." Sahara felt her face turn red as she slipped the bill that Trevor gave her into her pocket.

With the egg hunt over, everyone pulled out their pretty picnic blankets and spread them on the grass. Everyone except for Sahara. She'd been in such a rush that morning to get to work and get prepared for the presentation that she'd forgotten to put their picnic blanket in the car.

"Mommy, do you want me to get my blanket from the classroom?" asked Clarissa.

Sahara looked at the other families enjoying their neatly packed, healthy lunches while sitting on fashionable blankets like they were part of a Frontgate catalog. "Yes, ladybug. That would be great."

When Clarissa returned with her nap blanket, the three of them squeezed on the small, pink cloth. As they ate their food from Subway, Sahara heard Molly Granger's mother talking to some of her friends that were seated around her.

"She is absolutely devastated. She had no idea her father was...." She lowered her voice to a whisper. "That he was black. I really don't know what she is going to do now.

Another mom chimed in, "I heard he had a wife and child, somewhere in Alabama, that he abandoned and had been living his life as a white man ever since. Even his wife didn't know. Well, his white wife. Can you imagine?"

First of all, Dwight was from Mississippi, not Alabama. Second, he ran away from home when he was in high school and had been passing as white since then. He didn't have a black wife and child back in Alaba...Mississippi.

Why was she even getting defensive? Since Dwight went to the hospital to see Teri and revealed who he was, the bank had been in turmoil. Dwight was fired under the grounds that he lied on his original job application, when he indicated that he was white. Dwight then sued the bank for discrimination. It was one big mess, and Noah was caught in the middle.

Sahara didn't want to hear any more so she walked over to the dessert table to get some sweets for her and the children. The table was loaded with homemade marshmallow treats, brownies, cookies, and cupcakes all stored neatly in now half-empty Tupperware containers. The cupcakes that she brought were still sealed in the cellophane carton. Although they were the only chocolate cupcakes on the table, they had been shoved to the back.

Sahara opened the pack and took three out. She didn't care what anyone else thought. She liked the Harris Teeter cupcakes.

Sahara, Clarissa, and Trevor sat on the small, pink blanket eating their chocolate cupcakes and talking about what they were going to do with the rest of the afternoon. Suddenly, Judy Carrington looked over at them and threw her marshmallow treat on the ground. "I want a chocolate cupcake!" Justin Finnigan, who was sitting on a blanket next to her with his mother and sister, looked over and shouted, "I want a chocolate cupcake, too!" Sahara caught Barbara Fitzgerald's eye and smiled.

When everyone was finished and packing up, Missy Hawkins came over to Sahara. "I hope that you and

Clarissa had a good time. Although you weren't able to help with getting everything set up. I want to make sure that you are okay with cleaning up. I don't want there to be an issue...."

Technically, she arrived at the time they told her too. She wasn't included on the emails to come earlier. But, she said, "Sure. No problem."

Sahara surveyed the field. There were candy wrappers, napkins, empty juice boxes, and other trash strewn on the field. Well, with a few people pitching in, they should get the field cleaned up quickly.

Sahara placed Clarissa's blanket in the car so she could wash it and walked back to the field. Everyone was gone. She turned back to the parking lot and saw a few of the committee members waving and saying goodbye to each other before they drove away.

Was she supposed to clean up by herself? Missy said, "The rest of us came over early and set everything up." Sahara was the only one that wasn't there—so apparently she was the only one tasked with cleaning up. She sighed and began picking up the trash off the field. Thankfully, Clarissa and Trevor thought it was a game and helped her.

When they were almost finished getting everything up, the doors of the preschool flung open. Out walked Molly Granger and her mother. Great. They walked over to where Sahara, Clarissa, and Trevor were standing.

"Um...Hi, Clarissa." Molly's mom turned to Sahara. "I

don't think that we've officially met. I'm Audrey Granger, Molly's mom."

"Hi, I'm Sahara."

Audrey looked around. "Well, I don't want to keep you from what you were doing. I just wanted to make sure that Clarissa got this...." She held out an envelope. "Molly's birthday is in a few weeks, and I want to make sure that Clarissa got her invitation." She paused. "We hope that she can make it."

Clarissa took the envelope. "Thank you."

Molly waved at Clarissa as she and her mother walked away. Clarissa smiled and waved back. Maybe there was hope for them.

....

As Sahara pulled into her driveway, her eyelids felt like lead. Clarissa and Trevor were already asleep in the back of the car. She carried them inside and moved the toys that were strewn over the couch before putting them down. She sighed as she looked at the cluttered family room. There didn't seem to be enough time in the day to get everything done. Sahara looked at the clock. Noah would be home soon. She needed to cook dinner and do the laundry, so cleaning up would have to wait.

Sahara loaded the washing machine and slid the meatloaf in the oven. As she put the bell pepper back in the refrigerator, she eyed the chardonnay that she opened yesterday at dinner. The clock in the kitchen read 3:23 pm. A little early in the afternoon to drink, but it had been a long day. She peeked over at Clarissa and Trevor on the couch. They were still asleep.

She grabbed the bottle out of the refrigerator and took a wine glass out of the cabinet. A little drink wouldn't be bad. Like they said, it was happy hour somewhere in the world.

She was on her second glass when the doorbell rang. Sahara quickly downed the last of the glass' contents and put the bottle away. However, by the time she got to the door, there was no one there.

Although she was in her bare feet, she stepped out on the porch and peered down the street. She could see the mailman in front of the Gipsons' house. Maybe he tried to deliver a package and just left it in the mailbox.

Sahara quickly tiptoed down the outside stairs and towards the street to the mailbox. No package, just a bunch of bills. Mortgage. Gas. Electricity. Water. Car. Student loans. She hadn't realized before just how many bills they had—but she was all too aware now.

As she turned to walk back to the house, a man stepped in front of her. Startled, Sahara took a step back and was about to scream when she recognized him. It was Dwight Corbett—but he looked different.

"I'm...I'm sorry, Sahara. I didn't mean to scare you."

In the past, Dwight always had a shaved head. Sahara tried to not stare at the small wooly afro that had replaced it. "What are you doing here, Dwight?" There was no car in her driveway. That must be his car in front of her neighbor's house.

"I've tried to contact Noah, but he won't return my calls. Or, the bank has instructed him not to talk to me."

"Well, Noah isn't here. He's at work."

Dwight looked down for a second. "Yes, I know. I just want to pass on the information for my attorney. With all the lawsuits flying back and forth, she thought that it would help my case...." Dwight lowered his voice. "....if Noah would testify for me."

Sahara took the business card from Dwight and looked at it for a second. *Yvette Oliver, Esquire. Sheridan, Ellis & Ashton Law Firm.* "Testify for you? Why should he do that?"

"I just thought...."

"You just thought what, Dwight? That the 'brothers' should look out for each other? Well, you stopped being a 'brother' when you left Mississippi, right?"

"I'm sorry. I shouldn't have come." Dwight started walking away.

But, Sahara wasn't done. "And, you know what's sad, Dwight. When you were living your life as a white man, you were a great mentor and boss to Noah. It was only when you realized that your niece was not only living in Fairchester but friends with one of your subordinates, you got scared. You fabricated grounds for Noah to be fired so no one would find out your secret. Now, that everything has been exposed, you want Noah 'to help *a brother* out' and testify. Why should he? White Dwight was much better than the black one."

Dwight stood on the sidewalk speechless as Sahara walked back up to the house and slammed the front door. She took the bottle of wine back out the refrigerator and poured herself another glass. The nerve.

She threw the business card on top of the pile of mail. That's when she saw an envelope sticking out that she hadn't noticed before.

This wasn't a bill. The return address on the envelope read *Fairchester Chapter of Belles & Beaus*. This was it.

Sahara sat down and tapped the thin envelope on the table. She wasn't sure if she was ready to read what was inside. Was this like college admissions? Did a thin envelope mean rejection and a thick envelope indicate acceptance?

Sahara looked at the envelope again. It looked pretty thin.

What was she waiting for? She should just go ahead and open it. Sahara took a deep breath. Her hands were shaking as she slowly tore open the envelope.

Dear Mrs. Kyle, it is our pleasure to invite you....

She received the invitation. She was going to be a member of Belles & Beaus.

Sahara sat down in the chair. She felt like she should call someone. She picked up her cell phone and started dialing Teri's number.

Teri was the one to want the Belles & Beaus membership in the first place. And now, with everything that happened, she had decided that she and Jayla would go back to Mississippi with her mother. Teri said that it was only temporary, but Sahara wasn't sure that she would return. Maybe this wasn't the best time to talk to Teri about this. Sahara hung up the cell phone.

She should call Zora. She knew that Zora got in because she was a legacy so she probably got a letter, too. But, things had been weird with Zora for a while. Sahara didn't really know why things were strained between them. No, she wouldn't call Zora either.

Sahara looked at the letter again and gulped. They wanted how much money in a week for the initiation fee?!

Although Dwight had been fired, the stigma he left on Noah was still there. Noah still had a job—but it seemed that people doubted his skills. Dwight had questioned them but now that the credibility of Dwight, the "other black man" at the bank, was being challenged didn't exonerate Noah. Instead, it seemed to exacerbate the problem.

Noah felt like he couldn't win for losing, so they were still trying to build up their savings just in case. Money was only good for one thing—paying the bills. Noah wanted to make sure that they could pay theirs.

Sahara looked at the initiation fee listed on the paper again. Could they afford to pay it? And, what about after

that? There were annual dues, special events, fundraisers, and conferences. Like Meranda said, it costs a lot to
play in this circle. Sure, she had been invited to be a
member of Belles & Beaus, but could she really afford
it?

Sahara sighed as she put the letter back in the envelope. She got into Belles & Beaus. Funny. She thought
she would be happier.

NINETEEN

SAHARA: CHECKMATE

*In any game, checkmate is when a King is threatened
with capture and there is no hope of escape.*

"A father's love knows no bound, and it is a sad day when the General Assembly cannot protect some of the most vulnerable of our citizens. It is shameful that we could not get enough votes for the passage of Dara's Bill. It would have allowed us to treat mental health more effectively in the state by increasing the number of beds, providing greater access to medications, and funding additional services for people with mental health issues," said Senator Barrett. "But, I will continue the fight...."

"This is Rowena McGee in front of the Legislative Complex on Jones Street. You've just heard from Senator Tyrone Barrett speaking about the mental health bill that the General Assembly failed to pass, even after a tearful and impassioned plea from Senator Barrett on the floor speaking about the challenges his own daughter has...."

Sahara turned off the television and looked in the mirror. The short sleeved, simple white dress was pretty, if not a little dated. She bought it a few years ago for the Lambda Upsilon Alpha Boule. She thought about purchasing a new one for today but decided against it. Given the amount of the Belles & Beaus initiation fee, she thought it was best to not spend any more money and to wear something that she already had in her closet.

"I'm leaving!" she shouted to Noah, who was in the shower.

"Where is it again?" asked Noah.

"At the Marriott. See you at noon!" Sahara gave herself one last look in the mirror and headed downstairs.

"Mommy! You look pretty!" said Clarissa when Sahara walked into the family room.

"You look pretty, too, ladybug."

Clarissa twirled around in her pink and white polka dot dress. "Is it time to go to the Belles & Beaus lunch?" Sahara could see the eagerness in her eyes.

"No, not yet. Mommy has to go first and participate in a ceremony." Dressed in a little baby blue suit, Trevor ran to his mother. "Be careful, Trevor. I don't want you to get Mommy's white dress dirty."

"A ceremony?" asked Clarissa.

"Yes, I have to participate in a ceremony to become a member of Belles & Beaus."

"And, after that we can go to all the Belles & Beaus activities?"

Sahara smiled. "Yes, and after that we can go to all

the Belles & Beaus activities."

"Yay!!" shouted Clarissa, but after a few seconds, her face got serious. "I know that I will see Beckett and Gwendolyn at Belles & Beaus. Can Judy's mom become a member? I think Judy would like to come to the Belles & Beaus activities, too."

Since Molly's birthday party a few weeks ago, Clarissa and her preschool classmate, Judy Carrington, had been inseparable. They played together after school almost every day, and they were so excited when they found out that they would attend the same school for kindergarten. Sahara even had coffee with Judy's mother, Laurie.

"Well, I know that you and Judy are friends, but Belles & Beaus is for children that look like you and Trevor."

Clarissa's eyes opened wide. "Does that mean that now you don't want me to be friends with Judy?"

"Oh, no, ladybug. I am happy that you and Judy are friends. The world is made up of all different types of people. Some people have different skin colors. Some people live in different countries. Some people practice different religions. The list goes on and on. It's always good to know and be friends with people who aren't exactly like you because that helps you to know more about the world, and the people who live here.

"But, groups like Belles & Beaus help us to learn and retain our history and make sure that you and Trevor have the opportunity to create memories not only with your friends at school but also friends like Beckett and Gwendolyn that look like you but you may not have the opportunity to know if it weren't for Belles & Beaus."

"Is there a group like Belles & Beaus for Judy?"

Sahara laughed. "Yes, honey. It's called life. Every day Judy's life is filled with people that look like her. Yours is not."

Clarissa looked like she was thinking about what her mother told her. After a minute, she said, "I think I'm going to like being in Belles & Beaus."

Sahara hugged Clarissa. She hoped she did, too. She said goodbye to Clarissa and Trevor and left for the hotel.

As she drove out of the neighborhood, her cell phone rang. "Hi, Meranda. I'm —"

"Oh, I know that you are on your way to the Marriott for the ceremony. I tried to catch you at home, but Noah said that you had just left."

"Yes, we have to be there early. I'm so excited that you'll be at the luncheon today."

Well, yes, about that...."

"Oh, I forgot to mention that I'm sorry to hear that the bill didn't pass. I saw Senator Barrett's press conference on television this morning. But, I think it is great that he sponsored the bill.

"Hopefully this is a step in changing the stigma associated with mental illness. Dara should be proud. How is she doing by the way?"

"Dara is fine, dear. She is just moody—always has been. I don't know why Tyrone would go and name that bill, of all bills, after his own daughter. I begged him not to...and now...."

Sahara didn't know what to say. She thought that Senator Barrett calling the legislation Dara's Bill meant that....

Meranda continued, "Well, I called to let you know that I won't be able to make it to the luncheon. With the bill and this press conference...I...I...I just think that it will be too much."

Sahara felt her heart sink. The Belles & Beaus letter had stated she could invite family and close friends to the luncheon. She figured that Zora's parents would be there and maybe even her sister, Nellie. Sahara's mother couldn't attend, so she invited Meranda.

When Meranda agreed, she felt relieved. She didn't want to be the only one without additional family. Plus, with Meranda being a former member of the chapter, it would help Sahara to feel more secure...like she belonged.

"I understand, Meranda." Sahara touched the diamond Belles & Beaus pin in her pocket that Meranda gave her as a gift to wear at the luncheon. "And, I have the pin that you gave me. You'll still be with me."

"Yes, dear, I will be there with you in spirit."

They said goodbye as Sahara pulled the car into the

parking lot of the Marriott, which already was filled with many cars with Belles & Beaus license plates and car magnets. The members of the chapter probably had to arrive early to set up.

Sahara walked into the hotel and stopped at the registration desk. "Hi, I'm looking for the Belles & Beaus event."

The gentleman, dressed in a black suit, asked "The ceremony or the luncheon?"

"The ceremony."

He pointed at the hallway. "That's in the Pink Rose Room to the right. The luncheon will be at noon in the Ivy Ballroom, which is to the left."

"Okay, thank you." Sahara checked her watch as she walked down the hallway looking for the Pink Rose Room. She was a little early.

Near the end of the hallway, she could see Joy Perry, the membership chair. That must be where she was supposed to be. As Sahara walked down the hallway she passed Natalie, Yancey, and Lisa walking in the opposite direction. They stopped talking when they saw her, waved, and returned to their whispers after their paths crossed.

Joy smiled when Sahara reached the end of the hallway. "Are you excited, Sahara?"

She could feel the butterflies in her stomach. "Yes, I am!"

"I'm glad to hear it. This is where the ceremony will

be, but we are still setting up. The candidates holding room is down the hall in the White Rose Room. Someone will come down and get you ladies, shortly."

"Thanks, Joy." As Sahara walked down to the holding room, she thought about what Joy said. "You ladies." Zora was also getting inducted today. Was she already there?

When Sahara opened the door, she saw Zora sitting at one of the tables in the room. "Hi, Zo—" Without saying a word, Zora stood up and bolted from the room, brushing Sahara's shoulder in her rush to escape.

Sahara and Zora had not spoken in a while but Sahara didn't expect that reaction. She thought about calling Zora when she received her invitation to join Belles & Beaus, but things had been so different with Zora for so long that she didn't.

As Sahara sat down at the table in the seat that Zora had just vacated, she thought back to the day at the park, when Teri first brought up the three of them trying to get into Belles & Beaus. Now, Teri and Jayla were back in Mississippi. She and Zora were about to be inducted, but they hadn't spoken to each other in months. If only they knew then....

The door opened, and Zora walked back into the room. She glanced at the chair beside Sahara but pulled out a chair across the table. "Hi."

Sahara smiled. "Hi, Zora." They sat there for a few minutes not saying anything to each other. This was ridiculous. Zora was supposed to be one of her closest friends. "How are Cass and Darius? Will they be at the luncheon?"

"Yes, they'll be there. How is your family?"

"They are doing well." There was no need in bringing up Noah's issues at work. "I've started working part-time at the Urban League."

"Really? I didn't know that. Do you like it?"

"So far so good. It's been an adjust—"

Suddenly, the door swung open again. Sahara looked up expecting to see one of the Belles & Beaus members. Instead, it was Emery, dressed in a beautiful, white embroidered organza dress. Her hair, which she normally wore in a bob, was pinned loosely at the nape of her neck showing off a pair of gorgeous, pearl and diamond earrings.

Emery stepped into the room and behind her was Sheree Cotton, the chapter's vice president. Sheree smiled. "Ladies, it's time." As Sahara, Zora, and Emery hurried out the door, Sheree asked, "How are you feeling, Zora? Doing any better with the morning sickness?"

Zora smiled weakly. "A little better. Thank you for asking, Sheree."

"Well, that little one will officially make you the last one standing out of our current members. You'll be in Belles & Beaus forever," said Sheree. Zora let out a small laugh.

Zora was pregnant? Why didn't she mention anything to her? And, why was Emery there?

As they followed Sheree down the hallway, Sahara came to the conclusion that the chapter must have decided to extend two invitations. She should have known that there was no way that Emery would not be accepted.

When they reached the door of the Pink Rose Room, instead of opening the door, Sheree stopped and turned to the three women. "When we get inside, I'm going to lead you to the front of the room...."

All of a sudden Sheree grimaced. She walked over to Emery, who was the last one in line, and moved her in front of Sahara. "That's better...Edmonds, Kyle, and Montgomery.

"Okay, I'm going to take you inside and lead you to the front of the room. Just pay attention during the ceremony and you'll be fine. Claudine will give you the cues when it is your turn to say something." She must have seen the anxiety on their faces. "Smile, ladies. When you walk out of this room, you will officially be members of Belles & Beaus."

The three of them did as they were told. Although she had a smile firmly planted on her face, Sahara still felt butterflies in her stomach as the three of them walked into the softly lit room filled with the glow from the candles that everyone held. Music played in the background as the words of the Belles & Beaus hymn drifted to their ears. The smiling faces of the Belles &

Beaus members also dressed in white greeted them as they entered the room.

Claudine Lockhart, the president, and Joy Perry, the membership chair, stood at the front of the room facing the Belles & Beaus members. There was a table covered with a white tablecloth in front of them, and on it a large gold book, three diamond-encrusted rose pins, a bell, and three tall, white tapered candles burning brightly.

Sheree led the candidates to the front of the room, where they stood across the table facing the officers. She then took her place next to Claudine Lockhart.

Sahara looked at the chapter banner hanging on the wall in the back of the room. This was really about to happen. She was becoming a member of Belles & Beaus.

Claudine picked up the bell and rang it three times. The final verses of the hymn faded away as the mothers formed a large circle around the candidates, and the room became quiet.

"Belles & Beaus was established by our founder Gloria Katey in 1932 to strengthen black families, build self-esteem, facilitate community service, and encourage social development. Although our organization is centered on the child and supported by the father, it is the mother who is the foundation.

"Consequently, it is only through the mother that the family unit is bonded. Likewise, it is through the child that the legacy carries on.

"Dear Mothers of Belles & Beaus, we have assembled on this glorious day ready to enlarge our circle of sisterhood and to increase our family network. Who will speak at this time on behalf of the candidates seeking membership?"

"Madam President, I will," said Joy.

"Madam Membership Chair, do you ascertain that the candidates before us have met the requirements to become members of Belles & Beaus and specifically the Fairfield Chapter?"

"Yes, Madam President, as Membership Chair of the Fairfield Chapter of Belles & Beaus I can affirm that the three candidates before us—Emery Edmonds, Sahara Kyle, and Zora Montgomery—have met all the requirements necessary for membership."

Claudine looked at the three women then continued to read from the ritual book in her hand. "Candidates, having met all of the requirements of membership, are you willing to join this sisterhood of mothers and this network of families devoted to the betterment of not just our children, but all children."

"We are," said the three in unison.

"Candidate Emery Edmonds, please step forward and repeat after me." Claudine paused as Emery moved closer to the table. "I, state your name..."

"I, Emery Edmonds...."

"...promise to uphold the mission and goals of Belles & Beaus as long as I am a member," said Claudine.

"...promise to uphold the mission and goals of Belles & Beaus as long as I am a member," repeated Emery.

"I will work hard for the betterment of Belles & Beaus, at all levels of the organization—nationally, regionally, and in my local chapter." Sahara tried her best to pay attention, but Zora was fidgeting beside her.

"I will work hard for the betterment of Belles & Beaus, at all levels of the organization—nationally, regionally, and in my local chapter."

"I will do my best to help and support all children, not just my own, and help mold them into leaders that are responsible, civic-minded, and knowledgeable about our culture so that they can pass this history and information on to their children in the future."

Emery stumbled a bit over all the words. However, Claudine just waited patiently until she got them all out. Claudine continued, "As long as I am a member of Belles & Beaus, I will do my best to live up to the ideals of the organizations...."

Emery slowly repeated the words, "As long as I am a member of Belles & Beaus, I will do my best to live up to the ideals of the organizations—to develop the children, support my sisters, and make Belles & Beaus a better organization than I found it."

Joy opened the gold book on the table as Claudine said, "Now that you have taken this vow, please affix your signature in the Roll Book of members that have become part of this illustrious organization before you."

After Emery signed her name, she moved back beside Sahara.

"Candidate Sahara Kyle, please step forward and repeat after me." Claudine paused as Sahara moved forward. "I, state your name..."

"I, Sahara Kyle...." Sahara thought about the words that she was saying as she repeated after Claudine. She believed in the value of this organization and knew that being a part of it would have a positive impact on not only Clarissa and Trevor's lives but also Noah's and hers. She wanted to make sure that she took every word and every detail in so that she would remember it.

"As long as I am a member of Belles & Beaus, I will do my best to live up to the ideals of the organization...," said Claudine.

Like Emery, Sahara slowly repeated the words, "As long as I am a member of Belles & Beaus, I will do my best to live up to the ideals of the organizations—to develop the children, support my sisters, and make Belles & Beaus a better organization than I found it."

Sahara's hand shook as she bent down and signed her name in the Roll Book under Emery's name. She could see the names of the members from the previous initiation class on the page beside it. Sahara stood up and went back to her place besides Emery and Zora.

As Zora stepped up and said the vow, Sahara couldn't help but think about their friendship. She and Zora were now Belles & Beaus sisters. What she wasn't sure about was if they were still friends.

And, what about Emery? Sahara looked at Emery out the corner of her eye. They were sisters, too. There seemed to be so much bad blood between them. How would they now interact with each other?

Zora returned to her place beside Sahara, and Claudine continued, "In return for your commitment to your duties as members, you and your family will receive life-long friendships and a network admired by many but duplicated by none."

A voice from behind them said, "Amen." Some of the mothers snickered.

President Claudine looked up from the rituals book and said, "Mothers...." Everyone quickly quieted down. "Will the sponsors or the mentors of the new members please step forward."

Tania, Violet, and Charlotte stepped forward. Tania picked up one of the diamond rose pins on the table and pinned it to Sahara's dress. As Tania and Sahara hugged, Violet pinned Emery and Charlotte did the same to Zora. When Tania, Violet, and Charlotte moved back to their places, Joy handed a white candle to the new members.

"Emery, Sahara, and Zora, you have taken the vows and affixed your signature in the Roll Book. Now, light your candles and join the circle of sisters," said Claudine.

They each walked to the table and lit their candles

from one of the tall candles on the table and then joined the circle with the other members. Sahara looked down at her rose pin and then at everyone's faces as they sang the Belles & Beaus hymn. These were now her sisters.

....

Joy looked like a little kid as she stood on her toes looking through the small glass panel in the top half of the door. "The ballroom is really starting to fill up! I better go see if they need help at the registration table seating people." She looked at the three newly initiated members. "I'm going to cut through this meeting room so that no one knows that you ladies are back here. I'll come get you when it's time for your entrance. I'll be back." She grabbed her purse and walked out through the side door.

Sahara, Emery, and Zora looked at each other. Then, they jumped up and pressed their faces against the glass panel that Joy had just deserted.

The ballroom looked beautiful. The tables were covered in white damask linens and a centerpiece of blue hydrangeas and pink and white roses sat in the middle of each table. Folded white linen napkins tied with blue ribbon were at each place setting, along with little pink mini-cakes with B&B in blue frosting. By the ballroom's entrance, there was a table filled with gifts. Pink, blue, and white wrappings, bows, ribbons, and gift bags were everywhere. Was that all for them?

The ballroom was filled with people. All the Belles & Beaus families were there. Noah, Clarissa, and Trevor were there, too. Noah was talking with Reynard and some of the other fathers. Clarissa and Trevor were laughing and running around with a group of children. Cass, Darius, and Zora's parents were there, too. Sahara saw Zora's sister, Nellie, talking to Violet and Charlotte.

"Oh my goodness! I can't believe they still have it!" said Zora.

"What?" asked Emery.

"The tree! They still have the tree!"

Sahara looked at the front of the room where there was a large Christmas tree that was so tall that it almost touched the ceiling. It was covered with pink and blue ornaments.

"It's not Christmas. Why do they have a tree?" asked Emery.

Zora stepped back from the glass panel and sat down in a chair. "It's the Fairchester Belles & Beaus Christmas tree. The founder of Belles & Beaus wanted every day to be like Christmas for the children—filled with family, friends, joy, and laughter—so that is why she started the original club.

"To commemorate the spirit of the organization's founding, the chapter has a Christmas tree that it sets up for special occasions. They had the tree even when I was growing up in Belles & Beaus." Zora paused. "See the pink and blue ornaments." Sahara and Emery nodded their heads as they looked at all the ornaments on the tree. There had to be over a hundred on the tree. "Each ornament has the name of a family that was part of the chapter."

"Wow," said Sahara. "Even the charter families?"

"Yes, even the charter families."

All of a sudden, there was a *thud* behind them. They turned around but didn't see anything. Then, they heard it again. It was coming from the adjacent meeting room. They could tell by looking at the door between the two rooms that the lights were out. There couldn't be anyone in there. Then, they heard the *thud* again. And again. And again.

Zora's eyes were big as saucers as she looked in the direction of the door. Sahara looked at Emery, who shrugged her shoulders. Somebody had to see what the noise was.

As Sahara tiptoed towards the door, they continued to hear the steady *thud, thud, thud*. When she reached the door, Sahara looked back at Emery and Zora one more time for reassurance.

"Wait...," whispered Emery as she crept behind Sahara. "You may need some backup." Sahara smiled then swung the door open.

"What the—" said a voice in the dark room. Even with the light from the holding room behind her, it took Sahara's eyes a few seconds to adjust to the room's darkness. It wasn't one person in there but two.

"Donna, what are you doing here?" asked Sahara, as Donna yanked down her dress, and Alton quickly zipped his pants.

"We...uh...I...uh...Surprise!" said Donna as she took a step towards the light coming from the opened door.

"We didn't know anyone was back here," said Alton sheepishly. Then, his eyes got wide, and he stopped in his tracks.

"Oh...hi...Emery...Zora." Donna said as she gave a small wave and quickly looked over her shoulder at Alton.

Sahara turned and looked at Emery who was as red as a tomato. Emery seemed more embarrassed than Donna, and Alton and Emery didn't say a word to each other.

"What are you doing here, Donna?" asked Sahara.

"Well, Tania told me that you were being inducted today so Alton and I wanted to come and support you."

"That's so sweet of you!" Sahara hugged Donna while Alton and Emery stood there like statues and avoided making eye contact. Weird. For them to be friends, they both seemed pretty uncomfortable.

"Now that we have totally embarrassed ourselves, we'll go check in at the registration table now." Donna grabbed Alton's hand and pulled him towards the exit. As Sahara stepped away and let the door swing close, she saw Alton turn and look over his shoulder.

"I didn't know they were serious," said Zora when

Sahara and Emery sat down.

"As you can see, they are pretty hot and heavy for each other," replied Sahara. Emery sat there silent, not saying a word.

Sahara and Zora jumped when the door swung open a few minutes later, and Joy glided into the room. "Ladies, it's time." She handed each woman a small box. "Montgomery...Edmonds...Kyle."

Sahara opened the small white box and felt a sense of pride rise up in her chest. Inside was a cotton candy pink Christmas ornament with *The Kyle Family* engraved on it in a blue cursive font. The next line read *Sahara*.

She looked over at Emery and Zora, who had opened their boxes, too. But, Zora's ornament looked a little different. Sahara stepped closer to get a better look.

Zora's ornament was two-toned, blue on top and pink on the bottom. Written in pink cursive font at the top was *The Wilkins Family – Edna* and at the bottom *The Montgomery Family – Zora*. There were tears in Zora's eyes.

Joy went into drill sergeant-mode. "Okay, ladies...I mean...sister moms, everyone is being seated right now. Then, they will close the doors. Claudine will introduce you one at a time. You'll walk in, wave to the audience, and add your family ornament to the tree. They've left a spot right in the front for all three of your ornaments. Just put it there...not on top, not on the bottom...just in the cleared spot.

"Be careful when you are walking out. We've had members to drop their ornaments, then kick it, trip over it, and even step on it. Don't be like them. Get yours to the finish line without any incident. Any questions?"

The three of them shook their heads no.

"Zora, I have your parents' original ornament...." Joy looked down at the small gift bag on her arm. "I'll leave it at your table. You can give it to them or keep it—your choice."

"I think that I will keep it," Zora said softly.

Joy led them out the room's side door, through the meeting room, and into the hallway outside the ballroom. As they stood in the brightly lit lobby awaiting their cue, Sahara could once again feel small butterflies in her stomach. Whatever Claudine was saying in the ballroom must have been funny. Everyone was laughing.

Joy stepped back from peeking through the sliver of space between the closed double doors to the ballroom and her smile faded. "Shoot, you're not in the right order. Legacies first."

Emery, Sahara, and Zora looked at each other. They had automatically lined up like they were during the ceremony. Emery and Sahara moved back, and Zora walked to the front of the line.

"Both legacies need to be up front," said Joy sternly.

Both legacies? Emery and Sahara looked at each other.

Joy rolled her eyes. "You, too, Sahara. The order

should be Kyle, Montgomery, Edmonds. Come to the front. I think the music is about to start."

Sahara's feet remained planted where they were. "I...I...I don't know what you are talking about, Joy."

Oh, God. There had been a mistake. Noah, Clarissa, and Trevor were seated in the ballroom now. What would they think when she didn't come out? Would they be asked to leave?

But, then she remembered. She'd already been initiated. She was a member now. Would they start some sort of proceedings to revoke it? Would they maintain that her membership was approved based upon false pretenses?

Joy, Zora, and Emery were staring at her, waiting for her to move. But, she couldn't.

"Sahara, you belong up here," said Joy as she pointed at the front of the line.

Sahara knew that Joy was irritated, but she didn't move. "I think there has been a mistake. I'm not sure how it happened, but I'm not a legacy. My mother wasn't a member of Belles & Beaus."

Joy crossed her arms. "Okay...but legacy status is also granted to the children of former Belles & Beaus alums. Remember...it is through the child that the legacy carries on. You just heard it in the initiation ceremony."

Sheree stuck her head out the ballroom door. "Get ready. They are about to start the music."

"But, my mother isn't a Belles & Beaus alum!" Sahara felt like she was going to be sick.

"The status is granted to children if either parent is an alum—mother or father." Joy's eyes softened. "Sahara, we know—" The beginning strains of the piano, horns, and drums in Diana Ross' *I'm Coming Out* drifted from the ballroom.

"You know...?"

"We got the letter...."

"What letter...?"

Joy looked at the ballroom door and then back at Sahara. "I'm so sorry. I thought that you knew. Some people even thought you sent the letter...." Joy looked down. "But, clearly, you didn't.

"We received an anonymous letter before the vote stating that you are Congressman Allymer's daughter. HE is an alum of Belles & Beaus. That automatically qualified you for legacy status."

The doors of the ballroom swung open. "Introducing Belles & Beaus member, Mrs. Sahara Kyle," said Claudine Lockhart at the podium.

"Sahara, I'm so sorry. I thought you knew," Joy repeated as she pushed Sahara into the ballroom.

Sahara saw the flash of cameras and cell phones as she entered the ballroom. She felt like a robot as she walked across the floor.

As Diana Ross belted out the words to *I'm Coming Out* in the background, Sahara tried to remember the instructions Joy gave them. Smile. Wave. Don't drop the ornament. Walk to the Christmas tree. Put the ornament in the space. Stand there, and wait for others.

While Sahara listened to Zora being announced and her biography read, her mind was racing. They knew. Everyone knew. She looked at the table where Noah, Clarissa, and Trevor were seated. They looked so happy. Tania and her family were also there. Tania was a true friend and helped her during the process. And, next to Tania were Donna and Alton, who wanted to support her on this special day.

What would her friends think? Sahara looked at the smiling Belles & Beaus members sitting at the next table—Natalie, Violet, Lisa, Charlotte. They all knew.

And, Joy said that some of them thought she wrote the letter. Of course, she didn't, but who did? Who wrote the letter?

"Ladies and Gentlemen, I present to you the newly inducted members of the Fairchester Belles & Beaus Chapter." Everyone stood up and clapped as Sahara, Emery, and Zora stood in front of the Christmas tree smiling.

The photographer ran over and crouched on the floor in front of them. "Get closer together. You're sisters now. Act like you love each other."

The three of them squeezed together. Sahara was in the middle so she put her arm around Zora, who gave her a small smile. She slowly put her other arm around Emery.

"That's it! That's it!" said the photographer. "Now say Belles & Beaus Sisters!"

As they stood there in their white dresses trying hard to give their prettiest smiles, Emery leaned over and whispered in Sahara's ear, "You're welcome, sister."

Then, the three of them said in unison, "Belles & Beaus Sisters!" as the flash went off.

ABOUT THE AUTHOR

Shonette Charles is an active member of Alpha Kappa Alpha Sorority, Incorporated, Jack and Jill of America, Inc., and The Links, Incorporated. Ms. Charles holds degrees from Harvard University and the University of Michigan. A former freelance writer and editor, she resides in Raleigh, North Carolina with her family. Visit her online at www.shonettecharles.com, and check out her blog— Pearls, Poise & Protocol. You can also connect with her on Facebook, Twitter, Instagram, and LinkedIn.

A book club discussion guide for *GAME ON* can be found at **www.shonettecharles.com**.